Lying In

Barbara G. Tucker

Colorful Crow Publishing

Published by Colorful Crow Publishing, 136 W Belmont Drive, Suite 11 #112, Calhoun, GA 30701.

Copyright © 2024 by Barbara G. Tucker

All rights reserved.

Published in the United States of America.

This is a work of fiction. While, as in all fiction, the literary perceptions and insights are based on experience, all names, characters, places and incidents either are products of the author's imagination or are used fictitiously. No reference to any real person is intended or should be inferred.

No portion of this book may be reproduced in any form without written permission from the publisher or author, except as permitted by U.S. copyright law.

ISBN: 978-1-964271-07-1 (HC)

ISBN: 978-1-964271-08-8 (ePub)

ISBN: 978-1-964271-19-4 (PB)

Prologue

June 15, 1939

The spring-green, rolling hills outside Blacksburg appeared to rise and transform slowly before him, as if an unseen hand gently pushed the land up from beneath and shaped it into higher and higher piles of rock and soil. Geology classes at the Virginia Agricultural and Mechanical College had sought to dispel any notions of mysticism about the mountains his professors called Appalachia and his own people called home. His professors had not spent their first eighteen years feeling hemmed in on four sides by these peaks and ridges he now re-entered. Those scientists didn't know the crest of a ridge could make the sun seem closer to the earth, or that daylight could be so short in mid-December. He did.

Arthur Goins had spent over ten months, all of his senior year, in college in Blacksburg, away from his family's home deep in these mountains. His Christmas vacation at home was thwarted by the opportunity to spend the holiday with Ben Farnham's family. And really, with Ben's younger sister Beth Ann. A sophomore at Mary Baldwin in

Staunton, Beth Ann turned out not to be the girl of his dreams after all, just like his older and wiser sister Pansy had warned him.

"She's from money, Arthur. Real money, money way back. She takes for granted what you can't imagine having."

Ben was a good friend who didn't talk about his family's wealth. After Arthur saw the writing on the wall—and the reality of his and Beth Ann's marital prospects—he put romance aside to graduate and secure a good civil engineering job in Richmond with the U.S. government. Anyway, all this talk of war and fighting, again, in Germany had a way of taking a guy's mind off women, even one like Beth Ann.

It had been a long time since he had driven these narrow, potholed, bumpy, winding roads—hardly roads in some places—to the land his parents had owned and farmed in a meager fashion before he was born. A long time since he had taken a trip to see his second mother, Cotella, whom they all called Telly, seeing only her unique soul and not what others did. And so many months of being driven by his studies, dreams of the fair Beth Ann, and finding a lucrative job to remember who he really was, where he really came from, and to whom he really owed his existence.

Had he forgotten so easily?

Arthur had to take that last curve in the road between tiny Clintwood and even tinier McClure, the last bridge, and the last turn onto a dirt and gravel trail before he could fully remember Telly again and all she had done for them.

Part One

Chapter One

October 10, 1918

On the morning of the day she was expected at the Goins' farm, Cotella Barlow awoke when the rooster bossed her into it. It was her last morning of tending to Festa Rose, or really, to Festa's husband Harlan and their five children. During those five weeks, Festa gave all her strength to her newborn girl and recovered from birthing. Normally, Cotella would be up already, baking biscuits. This morning, she lay in her bed, covered with two quilts against the October frost for a few seconds before sitting up quietly and swinging her feet onto the cold floor.

Cotella sat on her bed in the dark to remove her nightgown. She pulled her dress on over her petticoat, dug in her valise for clean undergarments and stockings, and finished her dressing. She worked hard at moving slowly so the bedsprings wouldn't squeak and disturb the three children sleeping in the room with her. They were the youngest of the Rose children she'd been feeding and fussing over for the last month or so. After tying on her worn, sturdy brogans, she crept through the kitchen to the outhouse, choosing not to use the chamber pot this morning despite the autumn cold.

The moon, three-quarters bright, had almost slipped below Foster's Ridge behind the Rose's home, but it supplied her enough light to find the privy and take care of her business. She needed a good cold slap of water on her face and an equally slapping cup of coffee to feel awake. A few steps away from the porch, she pumped the well and rubbed the icy water into her face to wash the sleep from her eyes. The coffee might be longer in coming.

She sat on the porch for a few minutes, surveying the fields, now barren, as the indigo sky lightened to deep gray and then to silverish. Corn had long since been taken to market, along with tobacco and apples. Harlan Rose was one of the few in Dickenson County who could make something close to a prosperous living from farming. Like Tom and Fanny Elkins, who raised her, the Roses owned fertile, flat bottomland.

But Harlan owned a sawmill, too, on his land that butted up against Caney Creek, with a crew of three men who also worked his land. One of them was Terrence Quarles, a colored man, the only one of his kind she knew of. The other two, Eli Daniels and Smith Lee, didn't seem to mind laboring beside a colored man like some would, but they kept their distance. Yes, Harlan was a smart man, a cagey and shrewd one about business, she'd heard people say. But he treated her good when she came every few years to take care of Festa and the young-uns.

Cotella jerked her head up and roused herself, realizing that in her pondering about Harlan and Terrence and sawmills, she'd dropped off to sleep. She detected more light; so had the rooster, who crowed her fully awake again. She stretched, stood, and entered the kitchen. Festa had the coffee on, biscuits in the oven, and ham frying in the iron skillet. The smells wrapped around her head and reminded her stomach to gnaw. Out of habit, Cotella reached for a flipper to turn the ham.

"Telly Barlow, I'm the hired woman this mornin'. You got a long walk ahead of you to get to your next family, so let me fill you up with a good breakfast." Festa had returned to her normal bossy and efficient but kind self this morning. Virginia, her baby, had passed her first month, and seemed strong and hale like all the Rose young-uns. "Sit down, girl. You can get waited on for once in your life."

"Well, thank you kindly," Cotella said, laughing gently and seating herself. Most people she knew here in the mountains called her "Telly," and she'd never run across anyone else with the name her parents gave her. It's pretty strangeness made up for not giving her the extra name in the middle. She figured her momma and daddy were too poor to afford a second Christian name. Festa poured her a big mug of coffee. The steaming dark liquid, with two big spoonfuls of sugar, braced Telly. Soon a plate with two fried eggs, a slab of cured ham, and a biscuit the size of a man's palm appeared before her.

"You want a glass of buttermilk, too? Here's the butter for the biscuit," said Festa, placing a bowl of soft butter on the table.

"Yes, ma'am, that sounds grand," said Telly, and her wish became real before her. It was hard not to envy Festa. She was a handsome woman; not pretty, like girls in magazines advertisements, but strong-featured, with tall, straight bearing. Her thick chestnut hair framed a face of pink skin with only a few smiley lines, no freckles, moles, or pockmarks. Cotella sometimes felt her own eyes searching Festa's face, wanting to touch its smooth softness, and then touching her own, her hands seeking that same smooth skin and finding something else.

But Festa could be a handful, and probably only Harlan, of all the men in the county, could deal with her. Cotella had stayed around for the usual time since Virginia's birth. But Festa had been on her feet a week later, itching to help with the young-uns even though that was Cotella's job and reason for staying with the Roses, not being their kin or anything. "You get back in bed and just take care of feedin' that baby. And rest," Cotella told her. "Pretend like you're a rich lady of leisure during your lyin'-in. Lord knows you'll be harried enough with these six young-uns when I leave!"

Cotella wanted to stretch this breakfast out as long as she could. One, because the food was so good and because she had not had to cook it. Then, the children would be up soon to dress, eat, and walk to the schoolhouse two miles away: Forrest, thirteen; Lawrence, eleven; Althea, nine; Otis, six. Freddie at three would stay home with his momma and baby sister. Cotella wanted to see them all before she left. The children going to school signaled the Roses didn't have to struggle. In a lot of families Forrest and Lawrence would be farming already, and there would be no call for hired men like Eli, Smith, and Terrence, who slept in the barn when they didn't visit family.

"I think I hear Virgie crying," said Festa. Cotella hadn't heard the baby, but she wasn't the momma. Mommas had special ears. "I'm gonna go feed her, Telly, you keep eatin', and help yourself to more if you want." Festa scurried off to nurse her newborn while Cotella sipped the coffee and wished Festa had put some sorghum on the table for the biscuits. She retrieved the Mason jar from the cupboard as if she were in her own kitchen, then sighed. She was a guest this morning; her work at the Rose place was over, unless or until Festa had her seventh baby sometime in the future.

Soon, Harlan came in from his morning chores. "Oh, Miss Telly," he greeted her. "The hired men will be in here after a while. But you know that."

"G' morning, Mr. Harlan. I'm enjoying Festa's mornin' creation here." Cotella liked to use different words sometimes, and Harlan didn't seem to mind. "She's tendin' to little Virginia."

"Oh, yeah. My pretty second girl young-un. I'll be runnin' the boys off from Althea before you know it. I'm better with boy young-uns. Just know what to do with 'em more natural."

"You got some fine boys, there," said Cotella. "They's polite, for one thing. Not always the case."

"They better be." Harlan had poured himself coffee and loaded his plate with ham and biscuits. He sat and slathered butter over the bread and took a big bite. "Oh, sorry, forgot to say the blessin'." He closed his eyes. "Thank you, Lord Jesus, for this food, amen." Harlan took some more bites and cut his ham in big pieces. "I ain't raisin' no hooligans like live in Richmond. Been there one time in my life. Never again. What a crazy mess that place is."

"Sounds like Bristol," said Cotella, drawing on her limited memories from her only journey outside the mountains. For a fleeting second, she thought how sweet it was to sit at the table with a man, watch him eat like he enjoyed it, and just talk about the world. And Harlan seemed to want to talk this morning.

"You know, I was in town two days ago, Clintwood, I mean. Had to do some business with the First Virginia Bank. I'm sellin' some land."

"Oh?"

"Yeah. I got 30 acres I'm sellin' to the Superior Coal Company. They're tryin' to snatch up land. I can't use it for farming—it's all just about straight up—and I already cut all the good wood off it. I can use part of the money to buy another plow and horse. With this war on, coal is king and that ain't gonna change."

Harlan ate several bites before Cotella decided to question him. "Is the war . . . I mean, do you hear anything, um, anything about the soldiers on the American side?"

"Those German bastards," said Harlan, his mouth full of biscuit. He swallowed and gave her a sheepish look. "I apologize, Miss Telly. That's not language I should use around a woman, but this war and the government gets my blood up."

Cotella looked down at her plate. She hoped he couldn't see her slight smile. Harlan was known for his energetic cussing when the mood hit him, even though he was a deacon in their church.

"What I should say is I saw a newspaper in town and the front page said the Germans were withdrawin' back to their land. That's a good sign, I guess. Maybe it will be over soon."

"I don't understand what the killin' and fightin' is about."

"Best I can tell the French and German and limeys and Italians and whoever else just let all their squabbles boil up into one big fight. Anyway, they's all related, way back. Like a big family feud. Then President Wilson decided we needed to send soldiers there."

"Why?"

Harlan shrugged. "No idea. All I know is my boys are too young, and if it's gonna be over soon, they won't be sent off to waste their lives. I wouldn't let 'em go if they were conscripted. I'd hide 'em, or somethin'. I'm not givin' my young-uns up to keep some French or English uppity-up on their throne or in a castle or some such nonsense."

"What is 'conscripted'?" Cotella liked to learn new words, but there was no end to them.

"Called up and put in the army, whether they like it or not. Don't know whose idea that was. That's what Lincoln did to the Yankees in the War Between the States. Damn crazy government." He took a swig of coffee. "Sorry, again, Miss Telly. This all gets me riled up. We got enough problems in this country and this state. Especially with this sickness comin'."

"Sickness?"

"Yeah. They call it 'enfluinzah.' Sounds like a foreign word to me. Makes people real sick. It's in the big cities. And soldiers going to the war are gettin' it bad. In some places they's dying more from the sickness than from the fightin'."

Cotella wanted to ask more questions, but Harlan wiped his mouth and hands like he was finishing his breakfast. Harlan always ate fast; he had places to go. "Did you want me to fry you some eggs?" she said, forgetting she was the guest for a change.

"Nah, I had plenty. Listen, Telly." He looked at her straight on. Few people ever did that. Well, her mommas did, and some of the little children who didn't know any better, but almost no men. Harlan was a good man, even if he did cuss when his church preached against it.

"Telly, you have been helping us since Althea came. That is four children now. Festa tells me you're the best housekeeper and young-un watcher she's seen outside of herself. Even better than her own momma, who could do no wrong." Harlan laughed in a way like he didn't believe that.

"Anyway, she wanted me to give you something extra. I know your pay is usually room and board and five dollars, but here." He fished in his pocket and pressed a shiny piece of round metal into her hand. The coin lay heavy in her palm, but more, the touch of a man's rough fingers in her palm was a strange experience. The last man to shake hands with her was Tom Elkins, so many years before, before people seemed to be afraid to.

"I got this at the bank yesterday, thanks to sellin' that property. I don't know if God will send us another young-un, but you're the only one we'd think about takin' care of ours and we are mighty grateful for you and to you."

Her jaw ached, and she felt the salty water in her eyes coming. She didn't want to cry, but she couldn't hold it back. "Thank you, Mr. Harlan. This is more than I deserve."

"No, it's not. Now, hold on to that. Gold ain't like paper money, no, not at all. It goes up in value, anybody that knows anythin' will tell you that. It might say $20 on it, but that's just today. It will be worth more later, most likely, maybe a lot more."

She couldn't speak, and Harlan had his farm to take care of. "Well, Miss Telly, good luck on your walk today. You have a new family to go to?"

"Yes. Over past McClure. But they aren't new. I've been there some before. The Goins, Leroy and Minnie Goins."

"Oh." Harlan said it like he knew something of the Goins and their reputation. "Like I say, good luck and God bless you. My orchards are callin'."

Eli, Smith, and Terrence appeared at the back door. "Come on in, boys. Plenty to go around. Terrence, you know how to cook up some eggs, so go on and eat up. See you in a half hour or so."

"Mornin', Miss Telly," they greeted her, not in a chorus but one at a time, taking off their caps. Smith and Eli sat down while Terrence cracked eggs into the hot iron skillet. Cotella rose to make way for them at the table and stood in the doorway for a minute. Terrence's skin, deep brown like a hickory nut, always drew her eyes to him in a way that she couldn't help, the same way she wanted to touch his coiled, wiry black hair to see how it felt. She wondered if people stared at his dark prettiness when he wasn't looking, like they stared at her ugliness openly.

Before long, Terrence had scraped the scrambled eggs onto three plates, set two of them before Eli and Smith, and left with his own full plate and glass of buttermilk to eat on the porch. Terrence told her once coloreds couldn't eat at the same table as whites. That didn't make sense to her, but neither did a lot of things folks did to people who were different. Terrence was one of the few colored folks in the county. He said his mother worked as a cook in a restaurant in Pound, over in Wise County, so he knew a kitchen as well as any white woman, maybe better. Eli and Smith dug into their eggs and biscuits with their eyes to their plates and without a thank you to Terrence or to God.

Chapter Two

Within an hour, the strong, round sun crested the ridge behind the Rose farm. Cotella had seen the older children dawdle up the trail to the main road for school. She packed her valise, gave Festa a hug, kissed baby Virgie and Freddie goodbye, and headed in the direction of McClure. The chill, early October, smelling of smoke from the cabins and larger houses she passed, succumbed to the slowly warming sunshine. Ten miles or so meant all the morning and into the afternoon on her feet until she found a boulder to sit on or a fence post to lean against.

Yes, ten miles was a long hike, but about normal for her trips between the mommas she cared for right after their birthings. At least, about ten miles is what Harlan told her it would be. She knew the way to Minnie and Leroy Goins' land pretty well by now, from any direction, after four earlier trips. The town of McClure sat halfway between the Rose farm and her next stay with Minnie and the children. Maybe Minnie's husband Leroy would be there. Maybe not. He didn't stick around much, with his need to find ways, legal or not, to feed the four, and soon five, young-uns. He also tended not to stay around when Minnie was in a birthing way.

A ride all or part of the way from Nora, the closest settlement to the Roses' place, to the Goins' land below Piney Ridge would have been a blessing. But the road seemed strangely empty this morning. Except for that one wagon that appeared one mile or so, she figured, into her walking. When she heard wheels crunching the crushed stones and horses' hooves clopping up behind her, Cotella stopped. She turned to wave and see if it was someone she knew. She recognized Dan Bartley, a second cousin to one of her mommas--who was it? Yes, one of the Ashby clan. She couldn't say she knew Dan really, or had even met him formal-like, only that she knew of him by sight.

She waved more vigorously. Dan slowed his horse as he approached. He squinted at her but did not make signs to stop.

"Could you give me a ride, neighbor?" she called. "I'm on my way past McClure and been walkin' from Harlan Rose's place. I think you're Dan Bartley, right? Kin to Della Ashby?"

The wagon came closer. Dan's squinted eyes opened wide, and he turned his face away. "Ain't goin' that way, ma'am" he mumbled. Instead, he shook the reins sharply and said "Git" to the horse, who resumed her quick trot. The dust from the parched autumn ground rose and enveloped Cotella.

Cotella sighed. Tears formed, as usual. She wiped them away with her nubbied fingers, turned around, and kept walking toward McClure. Maybe Dan had heard about that sickness coming, the one Harlan spoke of that morning. Harlan seemed really worried about it. More than likely, Dan Bartley just couldn't bear to look at her. It wasn't the first time. Or the tenth, or the hundredth. No matter how much it happened, she hadn't gotten used to it yet. Cotella didn't know if the stares, the mouths dropped wide open, or the averted eyes were the worst.

***

Cotella knew that once she reached the crest of Piney Ridge, she would see the Goins' place—less than a house, more than a cabin—nestled in the holler below the Ridge. The west-facing side of Piney Ridge loomed before her, the packed dirt path up and then down, forming the last stretch of her trip. Cotella had begun walking the ten miles from Harlan and Festa Rose's homestead since right after sunrise. Now the sun stood in the middle of the sky, leaning towards the southern horizon. Or as much horizon as she could see in these mountains. The sun and her growling belly told Cotella it was time for dinner. Festa Rose cooked a hearty breakfast now that she was past her lying-in time, but that ham, eggs, and biscuits this morning had long since stopped fending off Cotella's hunger.

Cotella had taken care of Minnie Goins just thirteen months before, and Minnie had gone and gotten with baby in a season instead of trying to keep her husband satisfied without making another young-un. Not that Cotella knew much about what kept men satisfied like that. But Minnie didn't have much sense. Cotella suspected that when she entered Minnie's house, all the order and cleanliness she had left last year would be a long-forgotten memory.

Minnie Goins had already birthed five babies before this one. The first one, Mathis, did not survive but a few minutes, and the remains of his little self lay buried in a tiny pine box under a maple on their land. The next three girls, Pansy, Myrtle, and Mary, came pretty easy and already knew how to keep house, or pretend to, young as they were. Then Minnie stopped baby-making for a while, maybe because her man Leroy was away working for a lumber company most of those years. Arthur then came when Mary was five, a hard birth and a longer lying-in time. And now, another. Another mouth and probably another hard birthing for Minnie.

Cotella heard through gossip that Leroy got himself fired from one lumber company for drinking. He'd gone back to scratch farming, 'sang digging, and keeping a still for a while. Any money that came in stretched thinner than cheesecloth. But the last letter from Minnie said he'd signed up with a building crew that traveled around working for the state, the railroad, or coal mines. For the next month or so, into snowfall time, Cotella would stay with Minnie until her time came and then cook, clean, and chase young-uns while Minnie got her strength back. No, Telly didn't expect to see Leroy much this time.

About 11:00—she knew from the clock on the wall above the counter—she had stopped at Bailey's General Store in McClure. It was empty of customers, and only Old Bailey occupied it this morning.

"G'mornin', Mr. Bailey," she said.

"Who's that?"

"It's Cotella Barlow, Mr. Bailey," she said, at the top of her voice. A lot of folks claimed Jed Bailey was eighty-four and had fought in the Civil War. She believed it. He was the oldest, gruffest, deafest, and blindest person she knew. "Where is everybody? You don't have no business this mornin'!"

"That sickness people are gittin'. People not healthy enough to come to my store. I'm losing money. You don't got it, do you?" He peered through the thick glasses that obscured his watery blue eyes.

"No, sir. I don't have anything like that. Healthy as can be. I want some sugar sticks, though." She handed him a nickel and reached into the candy jar.

"Damn government caused it. Those soldiers bringing it here," mumbled Jed Bailey under his breath as he took the money and handed her a paper sack for the sticks.

"Yes, sir. I need to use your privy out back, too, if you don't mind. And your pump for some water." He didn't respond, lost in his complaints. "I'll be seein' you, Mr. Bailey." She got a grunt in return.

Outside of McClure, her feet aching, Cotella turned east on the unpaved road in the direction of the Goins' house. She really wished now someone had offered her a ride by horse and wagon from Nora. One of those new machines called automobiles would have been ever better. She hadn't even sat in one yet, though she'd seen a few in the county seat of Clintwood and, of course, back in Bristol, even ten years ago. It took a long time for the outside world to reach into Dickenson County. But no one offered, even after her spreading the word of her need. Cotella knew why. Any driver of a wagon or automobile would likely be a man, and most men couldn't look at her, not straight on, or want to be within a few feet.

Cotella's eyes fell on her hand, which clutched the knob of her walking stick. The stick steadied and comforted her. Her right hand and forearm displayed what it always did. Dozens of small balls, like bubbles under her skin. Knots, she called them. Some half an inch, some smaller, some as large as her thumbnail, a few as large as her thumb. That doctor called them tumors. If she just looked at her hand and forearm, she could pretend, for a minute, that they weren't also all over her legs and stomach, breasts and back. And the worst, her face.

That doctor back in Bristol, the only one she ever saw about her knots, told her the one good thing about her disease: at least for now, the tumors were on the outside, not the inside, too. "If they were inside, pushing against your organs—your lungs, stomach, heart—that would kill you. You'd be on your way to an early grave," he said.

"They won't ever go away?" she said.

"Oh, no. Somehow you got this through your family. Do you have Indian in your family? You're not Melungeon, are you? You look like you might be."

"I don't know. Why would that matter?" Cotella wasn't even sure what was said about Melungeons in the mountains was even true. Some people did believe it, and some thought they were a fable. People were people, no matter where their folks came from two hundred years past. So why was this Yankee doctor asking her such a thing?

"Some people who study this disease say Indians and non-whites have it more."

"I don't know much about my kin," she told the doctor quietly. "My folks died when I was thirteen. House fire. My brothers were all older than me. I got taken in by another family, neighbors, until I came here to Bristol."

"I do hope you know how to make a living. You're probably going to have a hard time finding a husband, Miss Barlow. It's going to ruin your looks, and a man would be afraid of how your condition would affect your children."

His words seemed to go straight past her brain to her heart and to her teardrops. She sniffed them back. She didn't want to cry in front of this man. He was too direct and had no manners. Even Doctor Franklin back home knew how to tell patients bad news, and he didn't work in a hospital, have a diploma on his wall, or graduate from some fancy school up north. She sat, wondering what to say next, hoping her voice was strong and plain. The doctor seemed to be losing his interest in her. He had other patients to see.

"What do they call this? Is there a name for it?"

"Yes, but it's a long German one. It wouldn't matter what you call it. You can make something up. People around these hills won't understand it."

And that was it. No one after that ever asked, so she had no call to know its name or use it, other than her knots and bumps. And her curse.

Chapter Three

Cotella's feet now throbbed as much as her stomach complained. At least the path to Goins' place was downhill, although rocky and pitted. As their house came into view and she approached the gate, she heard the barks of Master, Leroy's hunting dog.

"Master, hush. You know me. I fed you when I was here last, plenty. Quit acting like I'm gonna rob the place." Cotella kept dogs at a distance, but she didn't fear them, at least not by habit. Master stopped, gave a low growl, and seemed to dig through his doggy brain to remember this woman's smell and voice. For good measure, she picked up a stick and threw it far into the yard, distracting him.

She pushed at the loose, latchless gate in the ramshackle fence and entered the Goins' yard. Yep, all the order she had put the place to a year ago was gone. It was shameful how sloppy a housekeeper Minnie turned out to be. Cotella reminded herself Minnie had been nursing one baby and growing another most of that time. She stepped onto the small disordered porch, strewn with dirty laundry and smelling of baby wet. She took a deep breath, knocked on the door, and entered without permission. "Anybody home?"

"Miss Telly!" said Pansy Goins when Cotella opened the door. "Momma will be so glad to see you!"

Pansy, now ten, stood only a few inches shorter than Cotella. Her cotton dress looked familiar. Minnie probably had altered it a little and handed it down to her oldest girl. Soon Myrtle, eight, and Mary, six, gathered behind her. Mary hid behind Myrtle and stared oddly at Cotella's face, not in fear, just inquisitive. The girls, blonde, green-eyed, pale, and skinny, resembled each other greatly, like they were the same child in different sizes.

"Miss Telly," said Myrtle, "Momma just said, 'When is that Cotelly Barlow getting here?' She's been nervous as a squirrel all day." Cotella smiled. Myrtle always tried to sound like her momma when she repeated her words.

"Did you bring us any candy?" said Mary in a soft whisper.

"Shush, Mary," said Pansy. "That's nothing to say to a visitor."

"Miss Telly ain't a visitor. She come to take care of Momma and us when that baby comes out of her," said Myrtle.

Cotella reached into the pockets of her woolen jacket remade from a man's coat. "How could I forget to bring you good girls some candy?" She pulled out three sugar sticks and distributed them. "I stopped at Bailey's General Store in McClure just to buy you some."

"Thank you, Miss Telly!" they chorused, immediately taking possession of them and devouring the red and white peppermint.

Cotella quickly surveyed the interior of the shabby four-room house. She knew it well from her earlier visits. Her view of the sitting area, to the right upon entering, revealed a cold fireplace. The kitchen and table, the center of family life, to the left, with an equally cold cast-iron stove. Off the kitchen, a body entered where the children slept, separated by a canvas curtain. Another curtain to the right, off the sitting area, covered the area where Minnie and Leroy and any babies slept.

"Momma's in the bedroom," Pansy said with a full mouth of candy. She chewed it, rather than sucked it, impatient to consume its sweetness. "She's feeling real poorly. But she said it ain't baby pains. It's somethin' else."

Cotella's first task after entering her next home was always to wash her hands thoroughly. She learned the hand washing from her five months in nurses' training in Bristol. Nasty, filthy hands from gardening or tending animals or using the outhouse could cause all kinds of trouble and often did in these mountains. Then she would look in on the momma, usually in bed, who was either about to birth a baby or just had.

When she sometimes helped women in towns, their houses might have three bedrooms; she'd heard of houses with four but had never been in one. Women in those houses sometimes had a servant or cook or even went all the way to the hospital in Abingdon, or further, to birth under a doctor's care. But most of her mommas were poor and gave birth in a small bedroom, lit by oil lamps, helped by a midwife or women kinfolk. If the Goins were not the poorest family she helped after babies came, they were close to it.

But Pansy's words, "She's feeling poorly," stopped Cotella's mind from pondering the state of the house. Harlan's talk and Mr. Bailey's complaints came back to her. She moved to the kitchen to wash her hands.

"How so? What's wrong with her?" Cotella asked while she poured water from the well bucket over her hands in the basin and soaped them up.

"She says she's hot. And thirsty. And she don't want nothin' to eat. She coughs a lot too," said Pansy.

Cotella dried her hands. This was not what she wanted to hear. She had figured the Goinses were so far out of town, and saw so few people, that no kind of sickness could get to them here. Anyway, Harlan had acted like it was mainly in big cities, like Richmond or Bristol. "Has your daddy been anywhere? Like to Abingdon?"

"Yes, ma'am," said Pansy, taking charge of reporting on her parents. "He found himself a good job down there working at the railroad depot they's buildin'. He fetches a ride up to Clintwood on a buggy with some other men and walks home when he has a couple of days free. He was here until two days ago."

"Did he feel sick? Did he say anything about feeling bad, like pain or having a hot head from fever?"

Pansy looked at Myrtle and shrugged. "No. He came and mostly slept. Didn't much get out of the bed, and he didn't talk or eat anything at all. Not like he always does. I guess he was tired from building for the government."

"Listen, girls. Where's Arthur?"

"He's with Momma."

"Girls, I want you to stay out of your momma's room."

"Why?" said Mary.

"There's a real bad sickness goin' on. A lot of people are dying from it in the world outside these mountains. If your daddy laid in bed with your momma, she might have it. I don't want you to fall sick with it, too. Go on, you go outside and play. It's a sunny enough day. I'll tend to your momma. And Arthur."

"Oh, we want to help you, Miss Telly," said Myrtle.

"No, go along, git. I can't afford for you three to be sick if your momma is. Whatever you do, don't go in her room. Stay as far away from it as you can, even if she calls for you. I'm here to take care of her."

They complained a bit and dawdled. "Now, go. And get your coats on," Cotella called. "It's gettin' breezy out there."

The girls gone, Cotella wrapped a dish towel around her face, using a clothespin to secure it behind her head. She stuffed the excess into her shirt collar. That was the closest she could come to the way the nurses in the hospital did it, at least when they were around patients with consumption. Well, not with dish towels that probably needed washing, knowing how Minnie kept house. The nurses and doctors in hospitals wore special coverings on their faces when they did an operation or were around the really sick patients, the "infectious ones," they were called.

Her few months in nursing school seemed like photographs of another person's life now. But some of those lessons stay buried deep in her heart. Cleanliness. Keeping sick people separated from healthy ones. The need for nutritious food to stave off illness. And how disease could seem to come out of nowhere, and from the tiniest little critters, but there was always a reason, if not a cure.

The possibilities ran through her mind, tempting her away from Minnie's room out of fear and uncertainty. Every thought started with "what if." What if Minnie was sick with this thing they were calling the enfluinzah. If the baby came while Minnie was sick, no midwife would come in and Cotella would have to deliver it, without the proper training. She'd brought babies into the world before, but those deliveries were for big strong women like Violet Brown, who'd birthed eight already and didn't need much help. If Minnie's husband Leroy came back sick. Or if he was already lying on his deathbed back in some workman's shack near Abingdon. If they would see anyone for a while, and if there was enough food in the house to get them through this trial.

She heard Minnie's low, guttural voice calling from the room. "Somebody! Who's out there? Pansy? Myrtle? Somebody? Help me." Minnie strained to be heard, as if expending her last breath.

"It's me, Minnie. Cotella Barlow. I'm here. I'm comin'."

Chapter Four

Minnie Goins lay in her bed, still in her nightshirt this late in the day. The room's light was dim, the one curtain drawn. Cotella pulled it back and opened the window slightly for air, filling the room with late afternoon light. It revealed Minnie, her face pale and glossy. Something wet—Cotella knew it was the sweat of fever—coated Minnie's hair and neck, and she had kicked off the quilt. Arthur stood by the bed, grasping at the sheets to steady himself so he could look at his mother, who seemed unaware of him. He bounced on his knees, not quite ready to walk by himself, with an expression of anticipation and perplexity.

"Minnie," said Cotella. "You need to be covered up. It's cold today—there was frost this morning, and the fire's out. I'll take care of that in a minute, but you need that quilt on you. Maybe another."

"No, Telly. I'm so hot. Can you open the window more?"

"That wouldn't be good for you. Do you feel like you have a fever?"

"I guess so. I'm sick. And why are you wearing that towel on your face?"

"There's a bad sickness going around, Minnie. I don't want to get it. I couldn't help you with the children or the house then."

Minnie did not respond. She seemed to have nodded off in a few seconds. She eventually spoke, without opening her eyes, her voice barely above a gasp. "I'm in a bad way, Telly. It hurts. I'm so thirsty, but when I drink, I vomit. I don't care. Get me some water. I didn't want the girls in here. I had to feed Arthur, but he's almost weaned. He still wants the breast, but he's too old for it now. I can't feed two babies. Take him away. He's gonna get sick, too, like me. I know it."

"Yes, Minnie. But you need to cover up. You'll get a chill, even though you're hot." Cotella lifted the quilt with one hand and tried to maneuver Minnie's bare legs and feet back under the sheet.

Minnie kicked at her. She turned her drenched and pallid face to Cotella. "No! No! Don't tell me what to do. Take Arthur and get out of here. Leave me alone. This is my house. You're here to help with the young-uns while I lie in. You're not even a granny woman! When the baby comes, I want Granny Zella. She brings all my babies. You get her for me! Now!"

Cotella stopped. Normally, she would have given Minnie a good shake of her shoulder for smart-mouthing her. But not now. Something bad was wrong with Minnie. For all her faults, Minnie was never mean. Cotella reached down and picked up Arthur, who needed a dry diaper. "Let me feel your head, Minnie."

"No, don't touch me."

Cotella ignored Minnie and laid her knotted hand on Minnie's forehead, then cheek. She pulled it back. Yes, the fever raged.

"I'll make you some ginseng tea. That might help your stomach," said Cotella, not really believing it. She left the tiny room, pulling the curtain across the opening, Arthur on her hip.

Yes, she thought, Minnie had this enfluinzah sickness Harlan and Mr. Bailey talked about, full on. Leroy probably brought it from Abingdon, like Cotella feared. Her mind filled with plans and actions. The girls would have to get busy. The cow needed milking; Pansy was old enough to do it. Minnie kept chickens, and those meant eggs, at least. Was there any other food in the house? She checked the cupboards. Flour, cornmeal, coffee, sugar, but likely to run low before long. Leroy butchered a hog every fall, and it was getting time for that, but where was he? Did he even make it back to Abingdon? How could she get word to him? She would write a letter and give it to the postman when he came. If he came. She did not remember when the mail came through here. The girls would know, yes.

She needed to think, make a plan, and keep her mind off the possibilities that could come. First, make some root tea for Minnie. Make some for the girls, too. Cool some and give it to Arthur. If roots and herbs were all they had for medicine, she would use that until something better came along.

She didn't want to consider the worst. That Leroy was already dead, that Minnie would lose the baby either before or during labor, that her childbirth would sap what strength Minnie had left, and that these four children would end up like her, motherless and fatherless at a young age.

Chapter Five

Spring 1906

Cotella lived like any mountain girl until the age of thirteen. Any mountain girl with a lick of sense, a strong back, and a homely face. Her momma taught her to cook and keep house until that night in 1901, during a drought. Embers escaped the chimney, caught brush near the house on fire, and set their four-room house ablaze while they slept, unaware until flames leapt through the windows. Her momma had already suffocated when Daddy woke them up and got Cotella and her three brothers out of the house. Daddy went in to rescue Momma, and the blazing house fell in on the both of them.

Cotella knew this only because her brothers told her. She did not remember it. Her brothers said she was lying about not remembering, but all her memories of fire and heat, smoke and destruction had vanished. She had no recollections from the time she went to sleep that night until she woke up on a pallet in the home of their closest neighbors, the Elkins. Immediately, she knew something was wrong. She smelled the heavy smoke on herself and saw her nightshirt covered with soot. Her brothers, Homer, John, and Clarence, said Daddy carried her out of the house and put her on her feet. Then she wandered around in the dark until Fanny Elkins took her by the hand and led her to her new home.

Homer, John, and Clarence, being of age, escaped that holler to find work with lumber companies and railroad crews somewhere else. The fire seemed to have freed them from a life of struggling to raise crops and animals in this land where they didn't see the sun until 9 in the morning in mid-summer. That is, after Daddy and Momma were buried in the Primitive Baptist Church cemetery. They sold the family land to Tom Elkins for $500 and split it between the three of them.

Cotella got $20 out of the deal because she was a girl and only thirteen. Some man would marry her one of these days, even if she looked more like Daddy than she did pretty, sweet Momma. Fanny and Tom would see to getting her married off to a good man in the county. The Elkins owned more land, animals, and property than most of the folks around McClure, but they were still poor compared to town folk. So Cotella's brothers consoled themselves that their little sister would be better off without them and fled south with $160 a piece in their pockets.

Once in a while, one of them would send her a letter or a postcard. Once in a while stretched to once a year, or more. Cotella finished grammar school in McClure, an hour's walk to and back every day. High school in Clintwood was too far. She helped Fanny with the garden and housekeeping and tried to earn her keep. No local boys came around to pass time with her.

The Elkins had no children, so Cotella wouldn't take up anyone's space. Fanny was a pretty woman, and a little vain, with olive skin, dark eyes, and lustrous black hair that fell in curls when she let it down of a night. Fanny lived in devotion to Tom and anything he said or did.

Fanny tried to prettify Cotella, like a momma would do, with a few disappointing results.

Tom had the weekly newspaper delivered from Clintwood with the mail, which meant two newspapers each time the mail arrived. Otherwise, a trip to town by horse and wagon happened once every two months or so. The paper assured Cotella that people lived on the other side of the mountains, people who could buy and sell, do and travel. Cotella consumed every bit of the paper: the death notices, the stories about elections and town meetings, crimes and meannesses, even those little boxes of print about foreclosures, debts, and rare divorces.

One day at the age of eighteen, she saw her escape route, her release. Maybe she could follow her brothers to an adventure outside the mountains.

"Look, Fanny. They's a group called the Mountain Ladies of Mercy. They want girls my age to come and learn to be nurses."

"Nurses? What in the world for?"

"It says here they's lookin' for girls who say they'll work for the state of Virginia for five years as a travelin' nurse, ridin' around on a horse or a buggy in one of these counties, helpin' people out. If a girl signs a paper promisin' to do that, they won't charge for the schoolin'."

"You can't ride a horse."

"Yes, I can. Daddy taught me." Horse riding wasn't her strong suit, though, Cotella admitted to herself.

"That sounds too good to be true, Telly. Most girls would want to get married and have a house full of young-uns. I don't see why any young girl would sign up for that. Five years is a long time of schoolin' and workin'."

"Oh, I would. I'd do it right now," Cotella said.

"What are you talkin' about, Telly? You can't be a nurse."

"Why not?"

"Because . . . because . . ." Fanny hesitated. "You've never even been out of this county. You didn't go to the high school. You got no money." She paused, having exhausted her arguments. "Anyway, where would you have to go?"

"It says here Bristol," said Cotella. Bristol sounded as far off and exotic as the ocean, or New York, or Paris, France. "I'm gonna write them a letter. That's what it says to do here in the paper."

Fanny harrumphed. "You're eighteen. You're of age. I guess you have a mind to do this."

Fanny never mentioned it again to Cotella. Maybe she doesn't think I'm smart enough, Cotella wondered. Maybe she just wants me here to help her. Or maybe she's scared I'll get into some mischief or trouble in Bristol. Or maybe she'll just miss me. They don't have any young-uns. Fann will be by herself.

Whatever reason Cotella put to Fanny's indifference, it didn't stop her plans. She found some writing paper and a pencil and wrote a letter in her best hand.

May Second 1906

I am writing this letter because I read about the Mountain Ladies of Mercy in the Clintwood Journal newspaper. I want to attend your nurses training school in Bristol because I would like to be a nurse for the people in these mountains.

I graduated from McClure Grammar School four years ago. I couldn't go to high school as it was too far and there was no money for staying in town. I am writing this letter myself and I did ~~good~~ well in school with my writing and reading and figures. I am an orphan and our neighbors the Elkins took me in. My brothers left to find jobs somewhere else outside these mountains.

I work very hard here for the Elkins and they are good to me. I will work hard at the school and will be a nurse for as long as I need to be. I do not have any bows and will not run off and promise not to get married while I am in the training.

You can write me back care of Tom Elkins, McClure, Virginia, which is in Dickenson County. Thank you for reading this letter.

Signed,

Cotella Barlow

She wanted to send the letter the next day, but the postman only came around every two weeks, two long, dragging weeks before she could hand him the letter, the first she ever wrote to someone not in her family. She knew it might be months before she heard back. She was wrong. Four weeks later, the postman handed her a big, white envelope with a Bristol return address. It was from a hospital in Bristol, not the Mountain Ladies of Mercy.

Chapter Six

Cotella wanted to tear open the envelope, but it looked too clean, official, and important. She handled it carefully and found a thin knife to slice it open at the end. But not before she sat and looked at it for several minutes at the kitchen table. Maybe it said they weren't interested. She didn't know much, she didn't go to high school, and maybe her letter had silly mistakes and made her sound like an ignorant mountain girl. She *was* just a mountain orphan with no background. But why would they send her a thin, short, letter in such a fat envelope? Finally, she took a deep breath and slid the knife through the crease.

She emptied the envelope of its contents: a little book about the history of the Mountain Ladies, a stapled set of papers with rules and regulations for nurses in training—nurses in training! —a clean printed sheet with spaces for filling in, and a letter on hospital writing paper signed by a Sister Berta Rambeau. A typed letter, with a real signature, to her, Cotella Barlow! Her chest exploded in pride and she could barely read the neat black letters on the shiny white paper through her tears.

Dear Miss Barlow,

We are in receipt of your letter of May 2, 1906. We are sending you the formal application to become a student in nursing for the Mountain Ladies of Mercy. If you are accepted, your training will take place at Watkins Hospital of Bristol and you will live in our dormitories under strict regulations.

We will need to receive this application by June 15 for you to be admitted to the September class. You will find complete information about the history of the Mountain Ladies of Mercy and how you will be expected to comport yourself if you become a student nurse.

Yours very truly,

Sister Berta Rambeau

Director, Watkins Hospital Nurses Training School

Cotella looked at the flour company calendar on the wall of the kitchen. Today was May 30. How could she get the application to them in time? Even if she filled it out in the next hour, the postman would not be back for two weeks to pick it up.

Somehow, she would. She would walk by herself to McClure if she had to. It was only five miles, or maybe a little more. Ten miles there and back would tire her out, but it wouldn't kill her. The distance to McClure didn't matter. Only sending this application back in immediately mattered.

"Fanny, look what I got in the mail!" she said when Fanny came in from the garden. "A big letter from the hospital in Bristol. They want me to apply for their nursin' school!"

"They want you to do what?" Fanny set the bucket of dirt-covered potatoes down on the floor. "How do you know?"

"They sent me papers to fill out, and a letter, see?" She handed it to Fanny.

"I don't have my eyeglasses on," said Fanny, her way of reminding Cotella that she had never learned to read well. "You read it out loud."

Cotella did, slowly and emphatically.

"How you gonna get them papers to Bristol in two weeks?"

"If I have to crawl on my knees to the post office in McClure, I will."

"Don't expect Tom to be takin' you into town. He's busy with the plantin'. It's been too wet this spring, and it held up gettin' the crops in."

"I know, I know. This is my doin', I'll take care of it," Cotella insisted.

"And what's this thing about 'Sister' Berta Rambeau? She ain't your sister. Is this like a church group?"

"I don't know."

"I've heard tell about those Catholic women that don't get married and live with each other and cover their heads, having to call themselves 'sister'," said Fanny.

"Yes, but we call each other 'sister' at our church sometimes. You know that. If it's a church group, that's all right. I figure they'd be doing the Lord's work, helping heal people in hospitals and such," Cotella said.

She felt herself growing stronger in the face of Fanny's words. She loved Fanny and Tom, who felt like her real parents now more than Momma and Daddy who died in the fire. She barely remembered her mother and father some days. The one photograph they had of the family back then burned up, like everything else they owned in the house. But Fanny and Tom, kind as they were, and as good at farming as they were, didn't believe in the world past Clintwood to the north and Dante Mountain to the south. No, that was wrong. Tom and Fanny believed the world was there. They just had little use for it.

"Do we have an ink pen in the house?" Cotella said. "I want these papers to look like ... like I know somethin'."

Fanny sighed. "Yes, I do. It's special. I'll let you use it, but only because you're so happy and I don't want to bust open your pride right now." Fanny went to her dresser drawer and brought out a long, low box. "I want to warn you, Telly. You might be gettin' all hopeful and nothin' will come of this. You didn't go to the high school. And they's no money for this."

Cotella hadn't thought about money. "Do you think they charge money to be a student nurse?"

"Other schools charge money, don't they?"

"That advertisement in the paper said me being a nurse for five years would pay for the schoolin'," Cotella countered.

"But how you gonna live? Where you gonna live, and how you gonna eat?"

Cotella felt the squeezing of disappointment in her chest. "I guess I will need some money, after all."

"Right now, I need you to help with the wash. Put those papers up. You can work on it later. We got a pile of real work to do today."

Later that night, by candle, Cotella carefully opened the ink bottle and took Fanny's special pen in hand after she had carefully read all the papers and little book sent in the big white envelope. The rattling concern, the one that kept her heart low all day while she scrubbed clothes and cooked supper for Tom and his field hands, had an answer. In amongst all the regulations, the papers said,

Admission to the Watkins Hospital School of Nursing is free to orphans living in counties in Southern West Virginia, Southwestern Virginia, Southeastern Kentucky, and Northeastern Tennessee. Such young

ladies will work in the hospital and clean the dormitories to pay for their tuition, uniforms, books, and room and board. They will have to provide from private means to pay for personal expenses (toiletries, stationery, postage, etc.).

"Private means" must be talking about any money she had. Well, she never spent that $20 from the sale of the farm. No reason to. It still sat in the bottom drawer of the dresser she was allowed to use. She was used to living without money, so maybe the $20 would stretch long enough to do her as "private means."

The hopelessness from Fanny's talk now lifted, she set about to print in neat letters the answers to the questions on the form. Pens could not be erased, and she didn't want to cross anything out, so it was slow and painstaking work. She thought about the answers a lot before touching pen to paper. After three hours and a full candle, she signed her name to it in a pretty but modest cursive. Now, to get it to the post office in McClure as soon as possible.

Tom announced the next morning that he needed to take the horse and wagon to town, even though it wasn't time for their regular trip. He needed a plow blade carried to and from the blacksmith for repair. "Do you want to go with me and Harley?" he asked. Harley, one of his field hands, had the strongest back and arms for lifting the heavy blade.

Cotella knew Fanny had revealed the news and Cotella's desire to get to McClure no matter what. Tom would never have invited her otherwise, but they would also go out of their way to make Cotella happy.

"Thank you, Tom. That is mighty kind of you to ask me. I want to mail a letter there."

"You must have a beau writing you love letters," Tom teased.

"Oh, my!" She knew she was blushing. "I just have somethin' real important to send off. I want to hand it to the postmaster myself this time."

"So it must be a fella!" Tom laughed. He was such a good man. He loved Fanny so much, even though she never gave him children. He brought Fanny wildflowers he found in the fields, and kissed her in the morning when he left. She knew most men didn't do that.

"No fellas are beatin' your door down to get to me," said Cotella in a soft voice. She knew she brought very little to the unmarried men they knew. She was small, big-eared, flat-nosed, and coarse-haired. Looking in the mirror gave her no pleasure, so it certainly didn't for other people, for the boys in this holler and those settlements around McClure.

No matter. Today she would send the most important letter of her life. The folks at Watkins Hospital would see how much she wanted to be a nurse, to be somebody that mattered.

Chapter Seven

On September 7, 1906, as the sun approached an horizon lower than Cotella had ever seen, she arrived at her new home. She stood, valise in hand, before the rooming house in Bristol that served as the dormitory for young women training as nurses at Watkins Hospital. She paused, staring at the size of the place, daunted by the next step in a long, draining day.

At 5:00 that morning, when the rooster usually roused them, Harley drove her in the wagon to the train stop, nothing more than a platform, at the foot of Cole's Mountain. Her heart and stomach vibrated as the train approached. She'd never stepped into a train, but she'd seen one, a few times, on their trips to and from McClure or Clintwood. Sometimes they rushed by, all power, steel, and smoke. Other times they waited at the station, like a horse ready to pull away from its harness.

She'd have to pay for her ticket on board. Tom had given her the $ 1.00 as a going-away present: seventy-five cents for the ticket to Bristol, and twenty-five cents for a meal that evening in Bristol. She knew that was a sacrifice. She knew she might not see them for months or years. The course of study at Watkins Hospital would take two years, with no holidays or time for trips home.

Cotella hadn't eaten the day before, from nerves. Fanny insisted she eat a biscuit that morning, and packed her some ham and more biscuits for the trip. The train car had a little tap and paper cups for drinks of water to quench her thirst from the briny meat. She should be excited, she reminded herself—and grateful, happy, and proud. This was what she wanted.

But she was terrified.

Harley said very little as he took the reins and drove the wagon to the train platform, and he stood with her, waiting. He was no talker, anyway. Good old Harley. Well, he wasn't old, maybe thirty, and so shy with women. Tom wondered if he'd ever get the courage to court a girl, much less ask to marry her. He did remain on the platform and gave a sad little wave as the engine began to chug and the car moved with a jolt. Was he sad she was leaving, or envious that she was escaping?

Was she escaping? She only knew this county, these itty-bitty towns and settlements, these guarding and imprisoning mountains. This heavily treed world, green for five months a year, orange, yellow, brown and smoky for two, naked, white, and bitter for five. She loved these mountains and hills and hollers and the Elkins because there was no one, nothing else to love and she wanted to love, so much. But she didn't love them so much that the lure of a train out and away from them couldn't seduce her.

It didn't matter now. She'd signed the papers. Watkins Hospital and the Mountain Ladies of Mercy owned her life for eight years. Two for training, one for apprenticeship in the hospital, and five for working as a Mountain Lady of Mercy wherever they sent her. She might be a nurse in a hospital or clinic or by traveling on horseback—or maybe a horse and wagon. She couldn't fully know that future in this moment. Now she had to meet new people, learn, work hard, and prove an orphan from the remotest mountain holler could be respectable.

When she read the booklet she'd received, she learned that yes, the Frontier Ladies of Mercy were religious, something called an "order," all the way from England, connected to some church called "Anglicans." They called nurses at a certain level "sisters" as a respected title. It didn't sound all that respectable to Cotella. She was a sister with three brothers and didn't get respect for that. She had a lot to learn, she guessed.

The train soon sped over the rails. The scenery passed by her windows faster and faster, until the mountains seemed to lower their shields and let her enter an open world, a spacious and flatter one. She had no watch and asked a man who had boarded the train about the time. Less than one hour of traveling and another world appeared outside her window, one a little less green but rolling, with a lower horizon on both sides of the train.

***

Cotella did not have a word for the rush of sights and sounds and senses that met her when she stepped off the train in Bristol, on the Virginia side. She began to walk its streets, burdened with the valise borrowed from Fanny. Later she learned a word in her studies: overwhelmed. She felt like she'd been thrown in Caney Creek in April when the icy mountain waters and spring rains overran the banks and threatened homes. She could barely breathe.

For one, she'd never seen so many people. So many people in such hurries. They must have a lot of responsibilities to be in such a frenzy.

Bristol made Clintwood, with its three streets, one post office, four businesses, and two government buildings, seem like a child's toy village. She had often counted the buildings in the Dickenson County seat, thinking that few was many, checking to see if more had been built. These buildings in Bristol, though—some had four or even six levels. She saw too many shops to count: a bakery, a woman's dress shop, and another, a dry goods store, and men's clothing, and a drug store, and on and on. And to think: Bristol stood in two different states at the same time. She'd be sure to walk to the Tennessee side just to say she had traveled to another state.

She walked what seemed like a mile before she realized she was lost. She had missed her destination, Hawkins Boarding House, which would serve as her home for the next three years, at least. The hectic, bustling, tiring city streets disoriented and confused, fascinated and frightened her. She could ask someone for directions, but no. She didn't want to seem like a stranger, or worse, like a foolish country girl. But she carried a valise, and townspeople would have no reason for doing that. It didn't matter. She would walk back to the train station, and then try again, following the directions in her pocket. She had to do this on her own.

Cotella had walked farther from the station than she thought. The trip back to it fatigued her after the early rising and the long, somewhat terrifying train ride. She sat down on a bench at the rail station and ate the last biscuit from home, and fought the temptation to cry a little out of frustration, exhaustion, and homesickness.

Home. Did she really have a home in Dickenson County? She had a place to stay. Was that the same thing? Tom and Fanny were kind. If she got back on the train and forgot about Bristol, Watkins Hospital, Hawkins Boarding House, and being a nurse and appeared on their porch step, they would take her back, just as before. She believed that.

She would be like that wild boy in the story Jesus told, except that she hadn't spent all her money in sinfulness or lived with pigs.

But having a place to live was not the same thing as a home. As having a man in the bed beside you every night. As a kitchen of your own to cook in, where you could cook your way and no one could say anything about it. As pushing out babies to suckle and love. Little she knew about babies or sleeping with a man, only what she heard from other women's whispers at church meetings or times they gathered to help neighbors butcher hogs or raise a barn. Childless Fanny never spoke of those things, of course.

Surely after two or three years here in Bristol, when she finished and earned her diploma, there would be time to find a husband and have babies, even if she did spend five years as a traveling nurse. That is, if the Mountain Ladies of Mercy held her to the bargain. By then she could have a home of her own. It would not have to be big or grand. Fanny and Tom did better than the neighbors and their kin and they had five rooms; three would suit Cotella.

"You're getting ahead of yourself," she whispered. "The Bible says that about saying 'Lord willing.' Stop figuring out the future. Right now, you need to find the hospital and boarding house." Cotella folded the cotton cloth that wrapped the biscuit, found a water fountain to help swallow the dry bread, picked up Fanny's valise, and followed the directions to her new life.

Chapter Eight

Nursing classes started two days after Cotella arrived at the Hawkins Boarding House. She had one day to accustom herself to all the girls who now surrounded her. She'd never been around so many females; some from Tennessee, some Kentucky, some Virginia, like her. A few were pretty, most were average in looks, and some were homely like she was. Most were poor, like her, and some orphans, too. The girls were as different in temperament as in looks. Some were chattery and friendly, some very quiet; a few proud and uppity and others nosey about her raising. It all made Cotella's head reel.

Over time, she listened and learned why they came to nursing school. Of course, all wanted the skills of a nurse, but for their own reasons. Some as a way to support themselves or to help their families who depended on them. Some came because they loved their church and saw it as a way to serve God. Those girls said they might never marry and would become sisters instead, although the hospital did not expect that of the students. Becoming a sister earned respect, but took much more work and dedication than the few years of training Cotella would get. Some believed that, after fulfilling their commitment, they would earn a steady job in a city hospital and begin a new life outside their mountain worlds.

Cotella tended to hang back from joining in their chatter. Before she made close friends, she wanted to watch from a distance and slowly decide who would fit that role. She had little schooling in friendship, being isolated on the Elkins farm for four years now since leaving grammar school. She wasn't used to meeting so many people, anyway. But the boarding house situation did not allow much privacy or quiet.

She shared a large room with three other girls, who called themselves her "roommates." They all came from far-away families and they seemed used to talking loud so they could be heard over other young-uns. Ruby claimed to have twelve brothers and sisters, but some were not full, only half or step, because her daddy had died three years before and her mother had remarried. Mabel had seven and Opal had six other young-uns at home. They marveled that Cotella was alone. "That would be so quiet!" said Opal. "I wouldn't know what to think!"

After a few weeks, Cotella grew used to the giggles and laughter and sometimes rudeness of four strangers living in a room together without family ties. Opal liked to talk about big cities far away, like Chicago, as if she'd visited there many times. Mabel displayed a photo of a boy, Charlie, on her bed stand. They had kissed, she said, and promised themselves to each other, but Charlie had to earn some money before they could marry. Ruby whispered to Cotella that Mabel probably made Charlie up, and she insisted Cotella go shopping with her on Saturdays. Ruby made sure Cotella enjoyed a Coca-Cola and chocolate bar for the first time.

But most of their serious talk was about being a nurse and the schooling for it. By the second day of classes, Cotella wished with all her heart she had attended high school. Then she wouldn't be out of the practice of reading and learning. The one-room schoolhouse Cotella attended in McClure did not prepare her for the classes at the hospital. The thick books, the starched white uniforms, the stern teachers in their head coverings. The three hours of lectures followed by walks around the hospital to watch and listen and answer questions targeted at them without warning. Then after lunch—sometimes with food she'd never seen before, but liked anyway—five hours of working. All that followed by dinner and study time, with lights out by 10:00.

Lights out should have meant quiet; she certainly needed it because of her exhaustion, but some of the girls wanted to twitter and gossip. As she tried to sleep, she caught some of the chatter, some of it good-natured, some mean, some just plain lies. That Sister Martha Finster came from Boston money and Sister Clotilde, such an odd name, liked pretty young girls more than she did men—a wicked thing to say about one of their teachers. Cotella pushed such ugly talk about one of her betters out of her head.

The work at first was little more than heavy housework. Mopping floors with strong soap that smelled of medicine and fresh pine needles. Changing beds, sometimes with blood or pus or piss, sometimes only because another patient would use it. Operating the big laundry machines, which terrified her at first. Of course, this hospital in a city had electric lights and machines. Of all the things she missed later, the main one was being able to turn on a bright lamp like a magician at any time of day. And of course, the privy in the building and inside running water—that actually came out hot on one side! To think that some lucky people just took this as the usual way to make hot water, without a kettle and stove!

In those late-night whispers, Opal claimed they would be able to touch and talk to patients after their first year of training—that was what she heard from the second-year students. At that point they would also stop having to clean floors—a new set of students would take over—and would actually receive orders from real doctors. Opal made it sound like the second year was easier, without the housecleaning, but Cotella had her doubts.

Doctors were mysteries, too. Such a person did not live in her part of the county. One practiced in Clintwood. She had never met Doctor Franklin, since she'd never been sick enough for Doc Franklin to ride all the way out to her parents' or the Elkins' farms. But she'd heard of him as if he were a legendary figure. She did not know what to expect from these strange, exalted humans. The prospect of speaking to one terrified her almost as much as the laundry machines.

And the cleanliness! Fanny had taught her to keep a house—and probably her momma had, too, although she didn't remember much of that—but nothing like this. Hygiene: that was the subject of the second set of lectures on the first day. That is, after the one about all the rules they had to follow, how they couldn't have any men friends, or "close associates" outside of the training school, how they had to be in the dormitory by 8:00 every evening and in bed by 10:00 for the 5:00 wake up. How they could go to the church of their family's choice on Sunday mornings and visit the downtown section of Bristol for a couple of hours on Saturdays.

Hygiene was the word they used for cleanliness, for getting all the germs away from surfaces and beds and hands. The nursing students learned about germs in the second day's lecture. The teachers showed projected photographs of little animals no bigger than a speck of dust that could kill a person as much as a bullet or a hatchet. Maybe not as fast, but just as dead, with pain and suffering, or leaving them sick for years. Tuberculosis—the new, medical word for consumption. Measles. Pneumonia. Even a cold came from one of them, not really just from getting a chill.

Cotella would have felt that new word she learned—"overwhelmed"—and given up if the other girls seemed smarter and better students than she did. But they didn't. In fact, whenever she was put to the test with a question, the sister only said, "Correct," a musical sound, compared to harsh words of reproof if a student made a mistake or gave a wrong answer. Those beautiful "corrects" made her long and tiring days a little brighter. And they *were* long and tiring. She nodded off over her books sometimes, and often in church, and she enjoyed the naps on Sunday afternoon that refreshed her for the next week.

Most of all, pride filled her heart. The preachers back home called pride a sin, but she couldn't help it. What would her brothers think of their sister living in Bristol, on her own, working, learning, making something of herself, not like any of the silly girls they knew? She had written them but not received a letter in over a year. Perhaps they had moved on and her letters were trying to catch up with them. Tom wrote Cotella for himself and Fanny once a month, but short letters, impatient ones, with brief items of news, mostly about the farm. Too bad Fanny never learned to read and write with ease. She always struggled with it. Her letters would then have been talky and funny and felt like home.

Home. For all her love and thankfulness to the Elkins, and for all that she missed them, Harley, and the neighbors, the boarding house and the halls of the hospital now felt almost like home. In three years, if she obeyed all the rules, pleased the sisters, worked hard, knew the answers to the questions they asked—then she would be called a nurse.

Chapter Nine

In early November 1906, two months into nurses' training, she washed her face one morning and saw two brown spots, big as cherry pits, on her cheeks. How odd. They didn't scrub off. She hadn't been around sunshine to spot up like this all of a sudden. She shrugged and thought nothing more of it. She had more important things to concern her than marks on her face. The next day she saw some on her arms and legs. Over time, she could not ignore them as they raised up as if baking in an oven.

At first, she thought the brown marks on her face were two big freckles. Touching them in the bathroom mirror—how nice to use the toilet inside, where a body slept! —she felt their texture and measured their width. If they were just freckles, they were big and tough. Whenever she had climbed the slopes behind the Elkins house, hunting for blackberries in July, and reached the top and stayed there a while, she came back with a red face and brown sprinkles on her nose. Fanny said rich women didn't like them and thought it meant they were poor. That made no sense to Cotella. In the one mirror in the Elkins house, she would squint at the freckles. "It's because you got that tinge of red in your hair," said Fanny. "Someone back in the old country must have been a real red-head."

Some of the other girls noticed when one raised up on her neck. Then her face. By January Sister Mary Ellen, the kindest of the teachers, noticed.

"Cotella Barlow, please stay to speak to me before you go to supper." No explanation, but Cotella feared what was to come.

"You have a small lesion or tumor on your neck, Cotella," said the sister.

"Yes, ma'am, I know."

"Do you have others?"

Cotella broke eye contact. "Yes, Sister."

"Where?"

"My upper legs. My arms. My stomach. I think my back."

"So, everywhere?"

"Yes. Just about."

"How long have you noticed them?"

"About two months, maybe, Sister."

"I see."

Now that her secret was found out, she decided to ask. "Is this something other girls are gonna catch from me, like one of them germs?"

"No, I don't think so. They would have by now."

Cotella couldn't stop the tears. "Please don't think this is something from sinful living. I've never been—I mean, no boy never paid me any mind back home. Or here."

"I know, Cotella. The signs of venereal disease are different from this."

She didn't know that word, but she figured it was what girls whispered about in the boarding house. "I'm sorry, ma'am. I guess I'll have to see a doctor about it. I've never been seen by a doctor before."

"I suspected you hadn't, Cotella." Sister Mary Ellen stood up. "I will arrange for you to see a doctor who specializes in skin diseases. There is one here, attached to the hospital. Dr. Van Dorren. I'll let you know when that happens, and you'll be excused from your classes or duties when he can see you."

"Thank you, ma'am."

"You may go, Cotella. Do not talk to the other students about this, do you understand?"

"Yes, Sister."

The "lesion" as Sister Mary Ellen called it, stayed. All the others stayed, and more came. Finally, she received a note that Dr. Van Dorren could see her in his office in the hospital on February 2. She would have to miss the lectures that day, about stomach ailments in children and adults.

A nurse who worked for Dr. Van Dorren came into the examining room first and asked her to take off her uniform and wear only her petticoat.

"He's going to see me with no clothes on?"

"Of course he is, silly girl. What do you think doctors do? He can't see your skin through your clothes, and you're here for him to see those raised up places on your skin, ain't you?"

"Yes, ma'am." Cotella felt like a scolded child. Didn't this woman know she would be a nurse like her some day? Was she really even a nurse, or just wearing the clothes? No matter; the woman had exited with a scowl, leaving Cotella to unbutton her uniform's blouse and skirt. She rolled off her stockings and lay all the outer clothes across a chair.

Down to her petticoat and drawers, she climbed up on the table and waited. The cold room goose fleshed her skin around the bumps and lesions, and her legs trembled in fearful anticipation. A man would see her without her outer clothes on, in just her petticoat. It didn't matter to her if he was a doctor. She felt naked and exposed.

She carried no watch, and no clock hung on the walls. She waited, wishing she could be in the lectures. Finally the door opened, and a man entered. She could not tell his age. His brown hair showed only a few gray wisps, and his short and stocky body moved quickly. He looked at Cotella. "Miss Barlow? I am Dr. Van Dorren. Sister Mary Ellen sent you to me to examine your skin tumors, correct?"

Cotella could only nod.

"You're in nurses' training, she said?"

Cotella nodded again.

"You can speak, can't you?"

"Yes," she said, barely a whisper.

"Very good. You're from the mountains, right? I imagine you have never seen a doctor before?" This man spoke English, but not like any one she knew. It was quick and sharp, with no expression.

"No, sir."

"Let me look at your—raised places on your skin." He took a large looking glass out of his pocket and examined those on her upper left arm, on her neck, on the back of her right hand. "Pull up your petticoat, Miss Barlow."

She slowly complied, so that he could see above her knee. He raised it further himself. "Stand up and turn around." He examined her back.

"Thank you, Miss Barlow. You may get dressed and come to my office across the hall immediately."

He left as quickly as he had entered and as he had examined her. She sat stunned. Perhaps it was best he came and went so quickly. Being undressed in front of a man unnerved her, and his brusque manner put her in a pique.

***

Cotella found her way to Dr. Van Dorren's office. The open door revealed a large, well-furnished room, but no doctor. She entered and slowly, carefully, sat in a leather chair, the finest piece of furniture she had ever used. An ornate clock with large golden Roman numbers adorned his office wall. She watched the minute hand jump, then again, then ten times. Then more. His bookcases strained with heavy volumes, and his desk seemed disordered. She could read "University of New Hampshire" on one of the official-looking papers in a gold frame. She tried to create the map of the United States in her head. New Hampshire was up north, above New York. So far away. Why was he here, in Bristol? Did that mean he was a good doctor, or a bad one? Did he come to Bristol because he had to, or because he chose it?

Dr. Van Dorren entered, in a hurry, and slumped into the chair behind his desk. "Miss Barlow, you will have to give up nurses' training and go home."

If he had slapped her face, he couldn't have hurt her more. She said nothing, so the doctor kept talking.

"Your disease will get worse. You will have more and more tumors, of different sizes, all over your body. Probably covering your face, in time, too. It is not cancer—they are not malignant. But they are permanent. It would not do for you to care for patients. It would be too hard on them, and they would be unkind to you, as well. I am sorry to tell you this."

"What? I don't understand."

He talked some more, and asked many questions she couldn't answer clearly. Very little of what he said passed beyond her ears. The disease was complicated, something about nerves. Not very many people had it. She would not die from it, not soon at least. There was no way of knowing what would happen to her later in life. She wouldn't get better. The lumps wouldn't go away. There was no treatment. Some doctors thought it had to do with where your people came from, way back. A German doctor had attached his name to it, but it didn't matter.

"I will tell Sister Mary Ellen and Sister Berta that you should be dismissed, but with a letter of commendation. They have told me you are one of the better students. That makes this even harder, as we always need good nurses."

She could not speak, not with any sense. "I—I—want to be a nurse," she managed to get out.

"Yes, I know. But it can't be. You should go home and find a way to help your people and community in other ways, if you can."

Chapter Ten

October 10, 1918

Cotella carried Arthur into the kitchen, hoping to heaven that somehow his mother's illness had not jumped to him. She found the kitchen in disarray. No fire burned in the stove; it was stone cold, and she wondered how long it had been since the children had eaten any decent food. Before she boiled water, and gallons of it, she'd have to get a fire going.

One of the children, probably Mary, had left an old corn husk doll on the floor. She put Arthur down, "Arthur, darlin', here's a play pretty for you. I'll change your hippens soon as I can." She laughed to herself despite the situation. "Sister Berta Rambeau would tan my hide. Stop using the country word, Telly. 'Diaper' is the proper word for baby britches."

Arthur had turned into a quiet, placid child, she decided, since he seemed for the moment happy to sit on the floor and try to pull the little dress off the doll and rub it on the floor. He'd been fussy as a newborn, and Cotella had stayed an extra month last time to help

Minnie. No one seemed to mind, especially Leroy, who liked Cotella's cooking and housekeeping and even tried to find her a husband from among the men he knew, or so he said. Leroy was known to talk big and promise even bigger, saying things that weren't completely true, so Cotella just laughed lightly and told him to stop his foolishness.

With a fire started in the stove and Arthur distracted, she surveyed the crowded four-room house and sighed. She had her work before her. For now, the girls should stay outside. She peeked out the window. Pansy and Myrtle had etched a hopscotch form in the dirt. Mary fed dried grass to a rabbit her father had trapped and let her keep for a pet. Young-uns like them could play and not feel the need to understand how their lives were going to change before they knew it, Cotella thought, a little envious. "They don't even know how poor they are. Or how sick their momma is," she said out loud to no one.

The water boiled soon after she changed Arthur and had managed to straighten up some of the disorder in the small house. She made ginger tea with ginseng she found stored tight in a mason jar. 'Sang root was plentiful on the Goins' land, and Leroy had been known to hunt and sell it to supplement income when crops were otherwise thin. Sick as Minnie was, she needed as much tea and food as she could get. Cotella used the biggest kettle she could find, let the root-filled water boil hard, then dipped out some for Minnie and added a bit of sugar.

"Minnie, you awake?" Cotella poked her head into the room through the curtain. The room was darkening in the afternoon, as it faced a slope and the other side of the house faced away from the setting sun.

"Yeah. What is it? Leave me alone," Minnie said, weakly and irritated.

"I've got you some 'sang and ginger tea," Cotella said as she entered.

"I'd rather have some moonshine. It would take the pain away," came the weak voice. "Leroy has some Mason jars of whiskey stashed behind the bags of salt in the smokehouse. Or somewhere. I don't know exactly where. But I know he does."

"Don't say fool things. Moonshine wouldn't help you feel any better, and it's bad for the baby." And no telling, Cotella thought, how strong the whiskey was and if it was fit for a strong man to drink, much less a sick, weak woman. Things could go wrong in stills and make the spirits poison. "Can you sit up?"

"No."

"Let me help." She set the tea down on the chest of drawers and came to prop Minnie up. She felt hot, like a blanket that had been hung by a fireplace, her face slimy with sweat. Two large blue blotches stained her cheeks.

"Minnie, did somebody hit you?" Cotella said before she realized what she was asking. The marks were not like bruises from punches, but like the blood in her body had turned colors. "I mean, you look . . ." She stopped herself. "You'll need to stay in bed, for yourself and the baby and the young-uns. Sit up, here."

Minnie's ragdoll arms and legs made her hard to move, her inertia made worse by the extra weight of the baby inside her. She slumped on the pillows.

"Here, take this tea," said Cotella. "You need something in you. Can you eat a biscuit? Drink some milk?"

"That cow needs milked," said Minnie, not responding to the question. "Leroy was supposed to do it when he left. He didn't. It'll go dry."

"I'll do it, tonight."

"I don't want no food. I don't want no tea."

"Yes, you do. Come on, darlin'. You got to keep up the strength for the young-un in you."

"My baby is dead."

"Now, now, Minnie, honey, you can't say that."

"Yes, I can. Up until yesterday, he was kicking me right and left. Worse than any of the others. It stopped yesterday. I can't feel him. A momma knows. Mathis did like that."

Minnie slumped again, then turned over on her side. "Oh, God. My baby's dead! My baby's gone. How is it gonna get out of me?" Sobs convulsed her limp body.

"Minnie, Minnie. We don't know that. Do you feel the pains comin'? Should I send for Granny Zella?"

"Leave me alone. Go away."

"Drink some more tea. You need liquid in you."

"Get your damn tea away from me. And get your damn ugly self out of here, too!"

Cotella caught her breath. "Minnie, I--"

"Go on!" Minnie let out a cry that shook Cotella's bones. Maybe the baby *was* coming. Maybe with the fever and whatever else, Minnie wasn't thinking straight.

No matter, Granny Zella had to be called. The midwife would know better than Cotella would, if for no other reason than Zella's forty years of bringing babies and tending to mommas in all kinds of pain and conditions.

It would be dark in two hours or less. She would have to send Pansy to the nearest neighbors, the Stanleys, who had a boy who could drive their wagon to Granny Zella's cabin and bring her back. Even if this wasn't Minnie's time, Cotella had to do something to get help from somewhere, somebody.

In times like this, Cotella remembered the hospital in Bristol, its cleanness, order, white beds, and big laundry machines. The hot and cold running water and the electricity. The bright lights at any time of day. Minnie's cabin was not in a foreign country. Bristol was a train ride of four hours away, and none of those things were here. Or anywhere near here. Just having a pump in the house would help.

She sighed. None of that mattered now, so there was no call to think of it. She left Minnie's room, pulling the curtain closed, her thoughts running. She filled three cups with the ginger ginseng tea and sprinkled some sugar in them.

"Pansy! Myrtle! Mary!" she called out the front door. "Come up here on the porch."

The three little girls minded her quickly. "Can we come in the house?"

"No, you stay outside. But here, drink these. They are like medicine, but I put some sweet in it. I'll give Arthur some, too." Each girl took a cup, smelled it first, and made a face before putting it to their lips. "It tastes like . . ." Myrtle struggled for a comparison.

"Never mind what it tastes like, Myrtle. Pansy, after you get yours down, I have an errand for you to do for me. For your momma, I mean." The girls sat down on the porch steps and sipped their tea. Cotella retrieved Arthur, who had pulled himself up by a kitchen chair and laughed at his accomplishment.

"Arthur, you can't see your momma for a while. I guess you're hungry. I'll make you some oatmeal. You'll have to learn to drink out of a cup now. Your momma can't feed you . . . no more." She set about to boil some oats.

"Miss Telly, I'm ready for my errand," Pansy said, coming in. "And we're hungry."

"What did you eat for dinner today?"

"Some old biscuits and cornbread and milk from yesterday's milking. That's all there is. We don't know how to make a fire in the stove, and Momma won't let us anyway, and I'm afraid of the cow. She kicked me once and . . ."

"All right, all right, Pansy. I'll milk the cow. Let's go back outside for now. Here, take Arthur. You all don't need to be anywhere near your momma. She's bad sick."

"Why are you wearing that towel on your face?"

"Never you mind. Go on, outside." She pushed Pansy out the door and joined the girls on the porch.

"Girls, come here," Myrtle and Mary jumped up at her command, almost excited. "Pansy, I want you to go to the Stanley place down the road. Tell Beryl Stanley to send one of the boys in the wagon for Granny Zella. I know it's close to a half a mile to their house, but you can do it." She stopped herself. "No, no, not her, not the granny woman. Mizz Stanley needs to send one of the boys for Doc Franklin. We need a real doctor, not the midwife right now. Then you come back as soon as you can. Mary and Myrtle, you will have to get Arthur to drink this tea. Give him little sips, real slow. Or use one of the spoons. I need to milk the cow and cook you all something to eat."

"I want to see Momma," whispered Mary.

"I know, darlin'. But you got to help Miss Telly right now. You're a big girl."

"No, I'm not a big girl."

"Let's play pretend big girl, then, for now."

Pansy was already out of the dilapidated fence and on the main road, half running, toward the Stanley farm. Cotella watched her for a few minutes, until she was out of sight, knowing Pansy felt an urgency she couldn't understand at ten years old. She only knew her momma, big with baby, was so sick she couldn't see her children.

Cotella grabbed the milk bucket and headed toward the barn. Four children, a sick momma, a daddy missing, most likely a stillborn baby. How much the world could change in one day.

Chapter Eleven

February 4, 1907

    Cotella sat on a wooden chair outside of Sister Berta Rambeau's office at Watkins Hospital Nurses Training School. She wore the one winter dress she brought in her valise from the mountains. Her only other dress hung in her small closet in the boarding house room she shared with Opal, Ruby, and Mabel. Beside it hung her uniforms she'd been ordered not to wear for now, and her one dress of a summery, light cotton, not suitable for icy February. Her winter dress, homemade from dark wool two years before, itched.

  The seat was hard on her bottom, the hallway drafty and empty. She wiggled like a young-un because of the prickly dress. She looked at her hand. No change from yesterday that she could see. Maybe that doctor was wrong. Maybe the knots would stop growing. She didn't have that many. Not yet. Not really many that somebody could see if she wore a high collar and long sleeves. She had to make her plea to Sister Berta to let her stay. But they had already told her she could not attend classes anymore, she could not wear one of her student uniforms, until the sisters held an official meeting about her and decided her future. That meeting had happened at 10:00 that morning.

She had learned so much in the last five months or more. She had worked so hard. She had seen what life was like outside of her county, her small mountain community, and the holler that held the Elkins Farm. What life was like beyond those encircling walls of green and gold, or now in winter, those barren guardians. Or had they been just guards, keeping her in a prison?

If Sister Berta demanded she must leave, if that was the final decision, she had nowhere to go but back. Back to home, to the Elkins, to farm work. To cycles of planting and harvesting, canning and cleaning, and sewing and . . . good work, needed work, but not what she wanted. She saw how skilled, how wise, how revered Sister Berta, Sister Margaret, Sister Mary Ellen, and all the others were. Even the doctors talked to them with a measure of respect. And she, homely, unimportant Cotella Barlow was learning to be like them, was earning their occasional nods of approval.

How could she go back? Why must she, just because of how she would look? Surely Sister Rambeau must understand. She was a plain, large woman who had given up the prospect of husband and family and even her country, Canada, to fulfill her calling. The sisters talked a lot about calling, as if God spoke to them from heaven across many miles and said, "You must go to nursing school!" Cotella never heard God speak that way. She just knew she wanted more than what she had lived with until last August. She didn't even know what more meant. Only that she wanted it.

Which was strange, because standing out, being seen, never fit well into Cotella's life. Even in grammar school. Once in a spelling bee, she spelled a word wrong once just so she wouldn't have to keep standing in front of everybody, seen by what seemed like a big crowd. Now she stood out to the other girls in nursing school because she was missing from class and all her fellow students knew something was dreadfully wrong with her.

Opal, the nosiest of her roommates, finally asked her about her knots. Well, how could Opal, or anybody, miss them? Cotella's face bore only a few but very visible tumors, as the doctor called them; two on her forehead, one on each of her cheeks, and the largest, the size of a thumb, on the side of her nose. But the girls with whom she lived so closely saw her bare arms and legs as well. "Cotella, what's wrong? Have you seen a doctor?" Opal asked, kindly enough, but Cotella knew Opal would gossip to all the other students. Cotella just turned away, unable to explain what she didn't understand.

A clock ticked on the wall, slightly off time with her heart, which she could feel in her chest and her temple because of her nerves. The clock said 1:35, and that meant Sister Berta was late. Sister Berta had asked Cotella to meet her in the supervising sisters' offices at 1:25. Sister Berta was never late.

She would have finished lunch and begun supervision of the second-year nursing students on their floors in the hospital by now, usually. How much Cotella wanted to be in the second year of training, to wear the special cap and move down the halls with authority. To actually talk to patients and ask them questions. And it couldn't, wouldn't, happen.

Cotella heard the quiet but rapid padding of soft-soled shoes coming down the hallway, growing louder. She looked up. It was Sister Berta, who waddled just a bit when she walked, even though her steps were brisk and intentional. Sister Berta always had something important to do, Cotella knew. She did not have time to waste.

"I am here, now, Miss Barlow. Please enter." Sister Berta unlocked the office door and switched on the light. Cotella had not yet fully accustomed herself to a lighted room coming from the movement of a finger. She doubted many people in Dickenson or Wise County could imagine such a thing.

"Please have a seat, my dear." Sister Berta pointed to a chair opposite the enormous oak desk. Cotella stopped. Sister Berta had said "my dear." She didn't think the Sister would ever say something like that to her, or that she was capable of it. But Cotella followed orders. Sister Berta, even with sweet words, was not to be disobeyed.

"I have spoken to Dr. Van Dorren," the Sister began. "He confirmed what we thought. Your ... condition is rare, Miss Barlow. I have only seen one other case in my thirty-five years of practicing as a nurse. It is deep in your nervous system, and there is no way a surgeon could even begin to remove the tumors. They will only grow elsewhere. And it is, I'm afraid, only at the beginning."

Cotella just hung her head, breathing hard, in gulps to keep the sobs away.

"I am sorry, Miss Barlow. What I mean is, it will get worse."

"What was it like for that person—the other one who had it? Did it ... hurt?" She wanted to ask if she would die; she hoped Sister Berta would sense that.

"Some. Not extremely painful, but there will be some pain at times. But it will not lead to your death. At least, not in your youth. That is what the doctor believes."

"Sister Berta, I don't want to stop learning to be a nurse," Cotella whispered.

"I understand. But you need to know that this is not a disease of your skin. It is a disease of your nervous system, and I know you have worked hard to understand the anatomy of your patients. So it is not something there is a medicine for, or that can be treated."

Cotella let the sobs come. Sister Berta waited. Cotella wiped her eyes with the handkerchief she'd been taught always to have ready. She tried and failed to tame her breathing.

"I know it is not a consolation, but we believe you would have been a good nurse, and we know you work hard. You're a farm girl and know what hard work is. But you might be in some pain, and develop more . . . tumors. You will be distracted from your training. It would not be the best for you to stay."

Cotella wanted to say something wise and religious, but only anger came out. "And I will be ugly and scare the patients. That is what that doctor said."

"I am sure he didn't say it that way, Miss Barlow."

Cotella couldn't respond. The only thing she ever really wanted was being snatched from her.

"The sisters and I will send a letter to your family at the address we have on file for you. You should write to them as well to let them know you are coming home."

"I don't have family. I stayed with the Elkins before I came here."

"Will they have a place for you still?"

"Yes. They don't have any young-uns. They took me in when I was thirteen."

"Very well. We will write to them. I know it takes some time for mail to get to, um, the mountain towns. We will ask them to come fetch you on the train so that you don't arrive without their knowledge. Until then, you may continue your duties and attend classes. The other students do not need to know until you leave. They may not understand. I suggest—no, I insist—you not discuss it with them."

"I don't understand," Cotella thought. "I don't know what is happening to me." But she only said, "Tom Elkins will come fetch me. He's a kind man."

"That is good to know." Sister Berta paused. "Cotella, I'm going to call you that here, it's a name I think is so unusual and pretty. We sisters will miss you. You will be able to help your neighbors and the people in your town in some ways. You have learned a lot. You have learned about science, about the practice of medicine. You have learned how important it is to be clean, and that sickness doesn't come from evil spirits, but from cells, viruses, and bacteria.

"You've learned to look for the physical and scientific reasons for illness, and to use practical and scientifically proven ways to deal with it, not folk methods and superstitions. I know you feel hopeless now. Your calling will be something else. God will use you in another way. I hope if you take nothing else from your training, it will be that we are nurses because we serve God's people that way."

"Yes, Sister." Cotella could not look at the kind, plain, round face. She could not move. Now that her future and dream had dissolved before her, like snow covered with boiling water, she believed she could feel the knots growing and taking over her life, her body, her will.

"You may sit here until you can collect yourself," said Sister Berta. "When you feel ready, please change into your uniform and attend to your duties. The sisters and I will post our letter to your guardian, Mr. Elkins, asking him to come. Good day, Cotella. God bless you."

Sister Berta placed her hand on Cotella's head, lightly. Cotella felt the warmth and care; she knew it meant more to the sister than just a parting gesture. Just as Sister Berta spoke of a calling Cotella did not understand, she laid hands on Cotella in a kind of blessing like the Bible talked about.

For the first time since she arrived in Bristol, Cotella did not feel that she had to fear Sister Berta or even follow her orders, at least not immediately. She needed to cry some more, or perhaps just ponder what the sister had said. And ponder something more, something else.

Why? Why was this happening?

The sisters talked about God a lot, like some people back home did, as if God stood in front of them, unseen and unseeable yet real, and pointed out the next step in their path. They spoke like God talked to them, even though no one else heard it. That God had a map for them. She had never really thought about that until now.

And that was fine for the sisters, for the people in the Methodist church she went to with Fanny and Tom and that she attended on Sundays in Bristol because she was expected to as a nursing student. And maybe she, Cotella, was an oddity. She must be, if very few people had this sickness she had.

But unlike those other folks, Cotella just didn't believe that God was standing right in front of her, pointing to the next place to walk. Well, maybe it wasn't a matter of not believing, since not believing was a sin and she didn't want to sin. It just . . . wasn't for her. She did not feel it. She did not see it, even in her mind's eye, even when she felt happy listening to the church choir sing familiar, comforting songs.

So why did she not feel and live all they said about the leading of God? And why did she come to Bristol in the first place? Honestly, she didn't know, not now. Did she really want to travel on horseback from homestead to homestead in the mountains, tending the sick? Or did she just want to see the world outside of McClure, Nora, and Clintwood, and this was a respectable way to do it? Did she just want folks back home to see her as somebody other than the little girl whose brothers left her when her parents died? As the quiet, struggling young woman who lived with the Elkins? Maybe she did really want to take care of patients and sick people and bring babies and tend to the dying. Maybe she didn't.

None of this answered the most immediate why. Why was she now among the sick? Why would she get more and more knots and . . .

tumors, to the point people wouldn't look at her, if what the doctor said was true? Sister Berta said that nurses taught the mountain people about science, that diseases come from dirt and germs and cells and little critters like that, not from spirits and haints and spells. Cotella knew most of that before she came here. Only some of the old granny women and people with Indian kin really held on to the superstitions now. Most mountain people, since they didn't know better or have money to pay for city medicine, used herbs and plants to help with the worst of sicknesses. Sometimes those worked and sometimes they didn't.

If her knots and tumors came from some scientific reason, some cells or germs on—what was it Sister Berta said? Her nervous system?—what did God have to do with it? That was her biggest why. Why did God do this to her, or did he? Why did God want her to have an ugly face, to frighten people, and not be a nurse, and go home, and why did God let her parents die so young? If God directed Sister Berta and the others like a ghost walking ahead of them, why didn't God stop that fire or get her momma out of there so her daddy wouldn't die, too?

She looked up at the clock. It said 2:15. Sister Berta had been gone... Cotella didn't know how long before the sister had left her office. She was expected at the laundry now. She blew her nose to finish her cry. Knots and lesions and tumors or not, she would earn her keep until somebody could come and take her home.

Chapter Twelve

October 10, 1918

It had been a few months since Cotella milked a cow. Most of the families she stayed with had a child or a hired man who could do that. Fanny had taught her and that had been one of her chores with the Elkins. She hoped when she went to nursing school that meant the end of cows and squirting their tits on a stool. She never got used to the smell of a cow, and warm raw milk right out of the udders set her stomach off. No matter about that now. The children needed it, especially Arthur, and the cow's udders were full and tight.

The cow, named by the girls something Telly forgot at that moment, complained at this first milking after two days of being left alone and now being approached by a stranger. She shifted her rump and pushed Cotella off her stool. Cotella fussed and let a swear word escape. She asked God to forgive her mouth out of habit, but not because she felt bad about cursing the beast. She righted the stool, gave the cow a talking to, and went at it again. This time the cow acted like it understood Cotella would deliver her from the painful, overfilled udders.

Cotella entered with two full pails, put the milk through cheesecloth to strain it, and sat Arthur on her lap. He dug at her dress first, like she was his momma, but she coaxed him to drink little sips out of the mug. He liked it better than the ginseng and ginger tea. The hungry baby soon drank the whole mug.

The sun was nearing the horizon. Myrtle and Mary still played outside. She could hear them fussing over something. They needed fed, too, and their momma needed tending. They couldn't come in the house, no matter what. Cotella had not removed the dish towel from her face, but she had soaked it through with sweat and breathing. She changed it before scrambling the girls a dozen eggs, cooking some oats, and patting together some dough for biscuits.

"Here, young-uns. Here's your dinner, or the first part of it." Myrtle and Mary took their plates of eggs. "I'll bring you some biscuits and sorghum when they finish bakin'. You'll have to eat out here. You can't go in the house while your momma's sick."

"We have to go in to sleep," said Myrtle, already digging into the eggs.

"We're going to play a game," said Cotella. "You all like fairy stories, don't you? And adventure tales? What's one where people take a trip and don't sleep in their own beds?"

Mary cocked her head. "Jack and the Bean Tree."

"Oh, but that's a scary one," said Myrtle. "And he didn't sleep, he just stole from the giant."

"The Three Little Pigs. They lived in a stick house."

"Not all of them. You're getting it wrong, Mary."

"Now, hush, Myrtle," said Cotella. "There you go, you'll be the little pigs and sleep in the barn."

"But will the wolf blow it down?" Mary's eyes showed real fear at the prospect of a wolf with that much breath, not knowing what a wolf could really do.

"Now, we'll let Master sleep in there with you, and he'll keep the wolves away." Cotella was glad Leroy kept the old coonhound around the place, although some of the time Master was on his own when it came to finding meals.

"That's scary," said Myrtle. "And it's cold, too. I don't see why we can't sleep in our beds."

"I know who slept in the barn!" said Mary. "Baby Jesus."

Myrtle couldn't argue with church doctrine, so she tried another tack.

"Pansy won't like it," said Myrtle, determined to argue.

"Pansy will be fine, and her opinion don't matter right now anyway. Your momma's just too sick. She coughs and sneezes, and that puts germs in the air in the house. I don't want three sick little girls. We'll put all the quilts we can around you. You'll be like cowboys or pioneers."

Myrtle folded her arms, defiant but beaten. She was the fighter in the family. In Myrtle, Cotella saw strength and stubbornness. Right now, Cotella needed her strength, and later in life Myrtle could find her own use for the stubborn streak.

"Let me check the biscuits. I'll bring some fresh milk out to you. Here, take Arthur," she handed him to Myrtle. "Give him some of your eggs to eat. I'll give him some oatmeal in a little while."

The biscuits were on the verge of burning, so she snatched them out and dumped them on a cloth. She could hear Minnie let out a long train of coughs that didn't seem to stop. When would Pansy get back from the Stanleys, and when would the doctor arrive? Yet even as she asked, she wondered if the doctor would know what to do. She dipped a cup of the tea, now cold, for Minnie.

Minnie's frail body with its bulging belly lay spent from the coughing fit. Her arms and legs splayed out like a rag doll. The blue of her cheekbones had spread down her neck and grown to a deeper purple, and she was still wet from fever.

"Minnie, honey, let me help you." Cotella pulled her up and set the cup to her lips. Minnie summoned strength to grasp it and pour the liquid down her throat, eager for something to coat her dry mouth. "More."

"In a minute." Minnie's fever had not broken. "Lie down here."

"My baby's dead."

"I am sorry, honey. This fever is just too much for the little-un." She searched for words, "Arthur and the girls are fine, I sent Pansy off to the Stanleys down the road, and I just got some food into Myrtle and--"

"Who are they?" Minnie said. Was Minnie starting to talk out of her head? "What girls?"

"They are your other young-uns, honey. Pansy and Myrtle and Mary and Arthur, you know them."

"Mathis died. This one is dead. We were going to name him Leroy, Jr., if it was a boy."

"That's good, Minnie, honey. A boy does good to have his daddy's name."

"I'm dead, too," said Minnie. "I saw Granny Mullins. She came to me and said get ready." She started to heave, gasping for air, her chest rising and falling like waves of water, quicker and quicker.

"No, no, you just need to rest. You were just dreaming about Granny Mullins. You miss her." Cotella remembered that Lena

Mullins, well known for her advanced years and decades of living with blindness, had died fifteen years before at ninety.

Minnie summoned her few ounces of strength to raise her hand to point. "No, she stood there by the chifferobe, told me Jesus was coming to get me soon. I know it. I can't breathe." The heaving and struggling began again.

Cotella decided talking only made it worse, and smoothed Minnie's matted, soaked dark hair.

After several minutes, she stopped struggling to breathe and Cotella thought she might be asleep, until Minnie said, "You need to find it, Cotella."

"Find what, darlin'?"

"The treasure."

"What?"

"The treasure. It's under the boards."

Now Cotella knew that what she feared had come to pass. Minnie had truly lost her mind to this sickness. Fevers could drive people to see and say anything. Somewhere in the hinterlands of her life, Minnie had heard about treasure or pirates or some such. How awful. What a thing to think of now, facing her own death, leaving four hungry children in a stranger's hands with no knowledge of her husband's whereabouts.

"You have to find it. Get it."

"Yes, yes, I will. I promise. You rest, honey. I'll be back. I have to see to the young-uns."

Chapter Thirteen

After attending, without any result, to Minnie's needs, Cotella washed her hands carefully with strong soap and some of the hot water she kept on the stove. She placed biscuits on a plate, grabbed the jar of sorghum, and joined the children on the porch to grab some bites of food. She saw Pansy running into the yard leaving the gate open, breathing hard, tears barely visible in the deepening dusk.

"What's the matter, Pansy? Is the doctor coming?"

"The Stanleys wouldn't let me in!"

"What? Did you tell them about your momma? How she needs the doctor real bad?"

"They said no, they couldn't be around me. They said daddy is dead! He got the flunza and died on the side of the road going back to the work camp. Somebody found him. They said Momma has it and we do too and we have to stay away from them!"

It was true, Cotella thought. Leroy had brought it home. The symptoms must not have been bad enough to keep him home. Or maybe they had, but he figured he had mouths to fill, so he'd set out, weak and determined. He'd infected his wife, so thin and overworked that she had no defenses to draw on. Cotella's thoughts and feelings gyrated inside her. What could she do? What was happening? Both parents dead—yet so far the children seemed all right, no fever or vomiting or coughs.

But for how long?

"Pansy, did you tell them to go get the doctor?"

"They wouldn't listen. I stood in the yard and yelled at them. They said I had to git. They weren't gonna come out of the house. They's gonna stay away from people. People are dying in Abingdon and Clintwood and all over, they said. The doctor can't help nobody no ways, so they's no reason to go for him and risk gettin' the flunza."

The germs must have spread from farm to farm faster than she thought. In the space of a day. Even Harlan this morning didn't know its extent, and now…

"Cotella, what are we gonna do?" Pansy said, breath still coming hard.

"I want to see my momma," Mary started to cry in deep wails.

"Daddy is dead? Why is daddy dead?" asked Myrtle, shock and disbelief showing on her face more than grief or fear.

Arthur seemed to sense his sisters' terror and reached up to the only grown-up available.

It was almost dark now. Cotella picked up Arthur and swayed her body to soothe him. She didn't know what to say to the girls, but she could comfort a one-year-old with rocking. He put his head on her shoulders. Fatigue defeated hunger and his eyes closed.

"Girls, let me walk around a little. I need to think and rock Arthur. Pansy, drink some milk and eat the biscuits and eggs. I know the eggs are cold, but it's food. Don't go in the house, whatever you do. Nobody goes in there but me till I say so."

She heard Myrtle whisper to her sister that they had to sleep in the barn tonight. Pansy, too upset to care about sleeping arrangements, nibbled on a biscuit but sat motionless otherwise. She seemed to be reliving the horrifying moments at the Stanleys, being run off by the neighbors and hearing the news her father died alone, collapsed on the side of a road.

Cotella stepped down off the porch. A wind chilled her and she clutched Arthur, who had fallen asleep. She realized at that moment she hadn't taken off her coat since she arrived. She wrapped it around Arthur. At least a baby didn't ask questions. But she had plenty of them for herself to ponder and to ask God. What would tomorrow bring? The next day? Would they all become infected? What could she do if they all ended up as sick as Minnie?

She liked to come to a home, put it in order, rein in the chaos that could happen in a household when a momma was in her last days before a birth or when a baby had just come into the world. That was the one thing she could say she did better than anyone else she knew of. But not today. The disorder only seemed to be spilling out, boiling over, and she had no assurance she could ever tamp it down.

As she rocked Arthur, looking with hopelessness at the three frightened little girls, her mind wandered. It returned to the night of the fire that killed her parents, but she knew they were not real memories. They were only recollections of what she had been told. Or maybe not; maybe she really did remember, and her brothers and other adults just claimed she didn't. Maybe they lied to protect her.

The last time she saw her brothers was the summer before, in 1917. Homer and Clarence found her at a farm outside of Trammel when she was tending to Betsy Loveless. They were on their way up north, out of the mountains, to the northern part of Ohio to work in a factory near a city called Akron. John had joined the army and been killed somewhere in France, they said, after President Wilson declared war. Homer and Clarence said they would write when they got a chance. The chance never came, she guessed. If they had lied to protect her at the time of the fire, they didn't seem too concerned about her since.

Sometimes, after she went to live with Fanny and Tom, she would slip off, saying she wanted to pick blackberries, and find her way to the ruins of their old home. The stone foundation and fireplace and some black metal, maybe the stove, was all that remained. Ivy and weeds began taking over the ruins after two or three years. Some mountain folks believed haints stayed around where their bodies died; she didn't, especially not after nursing school. Those were superstitions, stories, tales told mostly to scare young-uns and to entertain other grownups.

Sitting there on the stump, part of her wished she did believe it. Maybe in her imagination she would see her parents. Would she recognize them now, or their ghosts? Momma was short, like her, pretty but in a quiet way, but with a happy smile, and always working. Daddy was stocky, too, like her brothers, and claimed his grandma was Cherokee. Of course, a lot of people claimed that, to get government land. She hoped her father was not a liar that way. She could understand him wanting some land. There was always just enough—food, clothes, household goods—to go around, no more. But she felt their love, and even sitting on a dried stump after picking berries, she felt a little of it while she peered at the charred wood, iron, and stone.

This sickness wasn't a fire, but it spread like one. Instead of kindling or sparks it was those cells and germs the sisters warned them about so much. Hygiene, cleaning, washing—every day in nursing school that was the lesson. Did this germ come from dirty people? From bad water, or through the air? And like the fire took her parents in their prime, the enfluinzah killed these young-uns' daddy, fast, and would probably take their poor, weak momma just as quickly.

Some young-uns lost their momma, then their daddy, or the other way around, but not many at the same time. She had. Pansy and Mary and Myrtle would, but Arthur would never know the difference, being too little. What about a burial? Where was Leroy laid to rest? How would she know? What would happen to them? Did Minnie or Leroy have family that would take the girls and Arthur in, one by one or together? That was asking a lot of a family in these hills. And she knew there were people who wanted little girls for wicked reasons, as much as she hated to think it of the people in these mountains.

The girls couldn't really do farm work, and a house could only use so many females trying to run it. Arthur was too little. She'd heard of an orphanage in Abingdon for young-uns like them. None of those choices sounded good for these four. She'd known them and cared for them, off and on, for ten years now. She'd watched them grow up, as if in spurts, between visits to take care of their momma. She wanted the best for them and didn't know how to make that happen.

Well, she'd pondered and questioned enough, wandering around in the cluttered yard with Arthur sleeping on her shoulder. Pondering on it would get them nowhere. Four children all alone. Right now, she was the only thing close to a momma or daddy for them, and she had no place to go either.

Chapter Fourteen

By ten o'clock she had wrapped the girls in quilts and found shelves in the barn for them to lie on for the night. She ordered Master to sit and watch out for them; he cocked his head and circled into his own place in the hay. She brought Arthur's small cradle into the kitchen, settled him into it, and placed a rocker for herself between him and the stove. She kept a small fire going in the stove along with the one in the fireplace.

She looked in on Minnie one last time, taking some more cold 'sang tea in case Minnie could sip. Minnie lay with her eyes wide open, staring into the darkness, the oil lamp lighting her enough for the flame to flicker on her glaring eyes and show there was still life there. Cotella looked closer; Minnie's skin, deep purple, could only mean something was wrong with her breathing or lungs. Cotella wished, of all the things from nursing school she learned, she could have studied more about the body and its parts—they called it anatomy. The body was a marvel, with so many bits and pieces all connected, so strong it could sometimes live to a hundred years and yet so weak something the size of a pinprick could kill it.

She moved closer; Minnie's thin, twig-like legs had kicked off the covers again. Dots—red dots, blood red—covered her feet and ankles, up to her thighs. Cotella had never seen such a thing. What could have scratched her or bitten her like that? No, it wasn't anything like bug bites. It seemed like the blood was just coming through the skin. She felt a wave of nausea, and the room stank; there was no other way to say it. Minnie had probably messed her panties—yes, she had. Cotella opened the one window in the room to release the smell and maybe some of the germs, if that was possible.

How had Minnie gotten so skinny? Probably trying to grow a baby and still nurse Arthur, and not getting enough food. No telling how much money Leroy was bringing home. Her thinness probably made her weak and more prone to sickness. Minnie was never much of a housekeeper, but if it came down to her own eating or her young-uns having enough for a meal, Arthur and the girls would have won.

Cotella placed her hand on Minnie's belly. If Minnie were well, the baby would be itching to come out and poking his hands and feet against the womb to show it. Cotella felt no movement. She waited, counted to 100, slowly. Nothing.

At that moment, Cotella finally gave up hope for Minnie. She already, most likely, had a dead baby inside her. If she was turning deep purple, and the blood was oozing through her skin, and she didn't even complain of lying in her own mess, and hadn't eaten for days... and no doctor was coming, and he probably wouldn't know what medicine to give her for this sickness anyway... Cotella knew she would be telling the children soon that Jesus had taken their momma to heaven to be with their daddy, and they were happy and dancing and not sick any more. The children would not understand, but maybe they would believe it.

* * *

Minnie lived through the next day. She regained enough of herself to say, "My sister Viola in West Virginia, a town name of Buckley, I grew up there, can help with the children." That was all. No more about treasure, or boards, no questions about Leroy, no queries about if the children were well, no concern that Cotella might be sick. Perhaps Minnie knew it all, had received a dream revelation that Leroy had contracted something from the depot in Abingdon where he was working. People in the mountains believed the dying received visions and visits.

Later, Cotella would know what the Sheriff told her, that soldiers came through Bristol and Abingdon by train after train on their way from parts unknown out West to Richmond or Washington. They brought the sickness to the mountains unknowingly, and took it on to army camps where many more would die. Leroy, working in Abingdon and maybe even wanting to meet soldiers moving on to the war in Europe, probably contracted the enfluinzah that way.

The day after she arrived, Cotella had to decide between the children and Minnie. Or, between setting the home in order for the children to survive or sitting by Minnie's bed, hoping against reality that her now purple-almost-black flesh would return to pink and she would sit up and ask for some broth. The home was in total disorder, of course. Thanks to the cow and chickens, there would be something to feed the young-uns for a while, but flour and cornmeal would not last forever, and Minnie had only canned two shelves full of beans, corn, beets, and squash.

Cotella felt like she was staying in the only house in the world. She knew there was a wider world, but if neighbors rejected a little girl's pleas for a doctor, what hope was there? How long before the sickness ran through the counties and towns and before people would live, would enter the world again? A month? The winter? And how would she know?

So, that second day, Cotella worked. There was nothing else to do, and it staved off the despair. The pile of dirty clothing diminished a bit. The stove stayed lit all day, and she baked cornbread and biscuits. She killed a chicken and boiled it for broth, in case she was wrong about Minnie. She made soup for the children. She milked the cow again, wishing Pansy could overcome her fear of the stubborn animal. At least the girls could scrub the floors, tend the chickens, and play with Arthur. She knew they were soon to be orphans, and they seemed to know it, too. They did not ask about their mother or their new sister or brother any more. They did not giggle or fuss, not too much for little girls. The best thing for them now was to work, not mourn or mope or ask too many questions.

Of course, they should have been in school. The school was probably closed now, Cotella reckoned. Pansy and Myrtle had not started this fall, for some reason. Maybe their mother needed them at home. More likely, they didn't have clothes or the money for books, paper, and pencils. She did not ask; it would be a source of shame to them. What kindness she could show them she would, even if it meant not mentioning school.

Chapter Fifteen

Minnie died in the night, while Cotella, wrapped in a coarse woolen blanket, nodded off in the rocker by Arthur's cradle in the kitchen.

Cotella awoke to one of the rooster's early calls. She splashed cold water from the pump outside on her face, let herself take in a few seconds of the frosty, quiet morning, and went to Minnie's room.

She had seen death before, twice. First, it was Tom Elkins, dead from stroke and heart failure. The second, Thelma Stamper, one of her mommas, hemorrhaged before going into labor with the eleventh child in fifteen years. They were all the same, but not. Cotella figured Minnie was thirty, thirty-one at most. She would have to find the family Bible for the exact date of Minnie's birth, and to record the date of her death, October 12, 1918.

Cotella didn't know her own official birthday, as all records were burned. Her brothers said she was born in April of 1888, sometime around Easter. Fanny said that sounded about right, because she remembered Cotella's momma bringing her to church for Decoration

Day, and nobody in the hills brought their newborns out among people until they'd lived a while. That made her about the same age as Minnie. Both had seen a lot of living in thirty years, and it showed in their weary bodies.

Minnie had begun to stiffen. Her fingers clutched the sheet in the last minute of pain, revelation, or consciousness. Cotella pried the tight, clenched hand away, fearful she would break a thin bone. Now decisions had to be made, and the worst of all—where, when, and how to bury Minnie's infected body. Mathis, their first, lay under the maple tree in a tiny pine coffin. That tree formed a boundary between the yard and the fields. There would be no coffin, no undertaker, no wake, no preacher, no dinner, and no visitors, for Minnie Goins. The best would be for her children to know where she was, and Cotella would bury her so deep that wolves, foxes, or wildcats would not disturb.

***

After breakfast, Cotella fulfilled another duty: telling the little girls their momma was dead.

"Gather near me here on the porch," she said. She put her arms around them. She was not one to embrace her mommas' young-uns very much, even when she thought they needed more loving and hugging then they got in a big passel of brothers and sisters. But today she would embrace them, maybe even a lot. "Your momma is with your daddy now."

"Where?" said Mary.

"That means she died, Mary," said Pansy. Pansy's abruptness shook Cotella. Since she had run into the yard two nights before, Pansy had changed, barely speaking, only nibbling at food, only following directions from Cotella when she had to, so they could bring some order to the neglected household. And to avoid a scolding from Cotella.

"She did?" said Myrtle. "I want to see her." Did Myrtle not believe her, Cotella thought? Well, why not? Why should Myrtle or Pansy believe her, when she had acted like Minnie would get better if they left her alone?

"I'm sorry, darlin', you can't. Your momma and daddy both died of the disease . . . the enfluinzah . . . that could still be in that room. You can't go in there, and you can't be around her body, even now."

"How are we going to get her in a --- box, a, a coffin, and get her buried?" Pansy struggled to say.

"I—will do it, Pansy." And as soon as possible, Cotella thought, to rid the house of the illness.

"That's a man's job." Yes, Pansy spoke with anger, almost defiance.

"I know. But there is no man here. Other families have sick people, who have died, too, maybe. They can't come here. We have to stay away from them. We have to be alone—for a while."

"How long?" said Myrtle.

"I don't know. Until someone—the law, or a neighbor, or postman, I guess, comes and tells us it's over."

The girls stopped questioning when she mentioned the law. The law was a fearful thing. The law came after their daddy once because he made something way back in the woods he wasn't supposed to, their momma said. Even though some people wanted it and paid good money for it, the law could put him in jail for a week, and the judge had power over them. The girls sat; she felt their trembling through the quilts they had kept around themselves, dragging them in the dirt on their trip from the barn. Pansy started to cry; then Mary began to when she saw her big sister's tears. Myrtle, trying to hold onto her stubborn streak, finally gave in, but hers were quiet tears, not dramatic or forced.

Cotella let them; finally she forgot she had to be strong and began to weep, too.

Arthur needed attending to. "Girls, I need you to be strong and helpful now. That's all I can say. We will have to work hard for . . . a long time."

They did not respond. She waited. Finally, Myrtle asked the most sensible of all questions.

"Are we gonna die, too?"

Part Two

Chapter Sixteen

February 12, 1907

A heart sore, despondent, and exhausted Cotella stepped onto the platform at the foot of Cole's Mountain. Harley stepped out after her, carrying Fanny's valise. It was late in the day, and the stars began twinkling in the clear, cold sky turning to blue black. Harley yawned from fatigue, but Cotella knew today had been one of the high points of his short life. He had made the round trip from Cole's Mountain to Bristol and back on the train, rising early. His first trip to Bristol, his first train trip, his first lunch in a drug store. Harley would celebrate this day and brag on it for months and years to come. He couldn't know it was one of the worst days of her life.

Cotella didn't know when Tom and Fanny received the letter from Sister Rambeau, or what they thought or why they sent Harley instead of coming themselves. She only knew the sister sent a kind but firm letter to Tom and Fanny saying, "Send someone to come collect Miss Barlow immediately, as she is unable to meet her obligations here due to illness." What in heaven's name would they think from such a message? That Cotella was now an invalid, or infected with a dangerous disease from working in the hospital, or worse, from wicked living?

So Cotella did not know about Harley's coming, at least not the exact day. He appeared at the hospital at 11:30 and handed a letter from Tom to the nurse who received visitors at the front door. It asked for Cotella Barlow, stating that the bearer of the letter, Harley Vanover, worked for Tom Elkins and he was sent to escort Cotella home to Dickenson County, Virginia, on the train as soon as possible. The nurse spoke to Sister Alice, who came to Cotella as the students ate lunch. She quietly asked if Cotella knew this man named Harley, and since she did, Cotella should leave now and go with the man who waited for her at the front door.

She wasn't allowed to say goodbye to Ruby, Opal, or Mabel, whose eyes followed, their mouths open, tears glistening to see their friend leave without explanation. Cotella felt like a criminal. She changed from her uniform into the prickly wool dress, hung up the uniform in the small closet as neatly as possible, collected Fanny's valise, donned her warm jacket, and walked out of Watkins Hospital for the last time.

Harley sat in the hospital lobby. As she approached, he squinted, then smiled in recognition, but quickly flinched. His mouth dropped open at the full sight of Cotella's altered face after six months. She knew why and chose to rescue Harley from his speechlessness. He was no more a talker in February than he had been in September.

"Good mornin', Harley. Tom and Fanny sent you." It was half question, half acceptance.

"Yes, ma'am. Uh, Tom's been feelin' poorly. He thinks it's nothin', but Fanny thinks it's his heart."

"Oh. I'm sorry to hear that." Harley, kind but clumsy, took her valise without asking and followed her out the door into the damp and heavy February cold.

"Smells like snow," Cotella said, trying to act and sound normal. "Have you had somethin' to eat? Your dinner, Harley?"

"No. I was hopin', you know, I've heard all my life you can go into a store and sit down and get somethin' . . ."

"Yes, you can. That drug store over there has a food counter. What time is your return ticket?"

Harley dug in his coat pocket to find his ticket. "Uh, I think it says, 1, no 1:10."

"Then you got time. I'll shop a little while you eat. They've got food here you've never seen before. Try somethin' new. I already had my dinner in the hospital dinin' room." She wanted to add "for the last time," but stopped herself.

They entered the drugstore and Harley was introduced to the foreign concepts of a menu, a roast beef sandwich, French fried potatoes, and a cold soda pop. As hopeless as Cotella felt for herself, she couldn't help but smile that Harley was having the adventure of his life. He finished with hot coffee and a piece of apple pie, which he said tasted like it sat out too long, but he enjoyed it anyway.

Meanwhile, she wandered through the store, realizing it would be a long time before she could choose from such well-stocked shelves. She spent one of her dollars on a bag full of Ivory soap, some writing paper and ribbons, and a little device for cutting nails for Fanny. Her twenty dollars from the sale of the land had dwindled to ten since she'd come to nurses' school. But what would she need money for back home? Not much, as long as she went back to live with the Elkins.

On the train ride home, Harley reverted to his quiet self. They did not talk about Bristol, nurses, hospitals, Cotella's health, not even the weather. With a heavy meal on his stomach, Harley succumbed to nodding off and then to a full nap with his head against the cold window, his coat bunched up for a lumpy pillow. Cotella could only stare out the window, sigh, wipe tears away, and look into a bleak future.

When they stepped off the train, no one met them. They faced the long walk on the dirt road home, in the dark, with only the feeble light from homesteads they passed and a half moon to keep them from falling into the ditch. They had to walk slowly, since ice and snow crunched under their feet. Harley, a hefty fellow over six feet tall, kept her from slipping a couple of times, protective in his own way. He carried her valise. The hike on the rough road was difficult, even for a strong man. She herself was a woman weakened by dashed dreams and worse, the prospect of a future with a face and body most people found hard to even glance at.

Fanny waited up for them; Tom had fallen asleep at the table and she put him to bed. At eight o'clock, Cotella re-entered her old home. Fanny Elkins enfolded the younger woman into her care and gave Cotella back her old room. If Fanny considered Cotella the prodigal returned, she didn't say; if Cotella's facial tumors disturbed her, she didn't show it. Fanny could be a little vain herself, but she was not one of those women to gossip about the plainness or flaws of other women's looks.

If Cotella had expected the Elkins' farm to be unchanged, she soon learned how wrong she was. If her own appearance was now something for her second momma Fanny to get used to, Cotella had to adapt to how gray Fanny's hair had grown and how Tom's strength and vigor, which had always seemed twice that of most men, had diminished.

She realized she didn't even know their ages; the subject had never come up before. Soon after she returned, Fanny let it slip that Tom was sixty, and she knew, from past comments she wasn't supposed to hear, that Fanny was two years older than Tom. Sixty and sixty-two;

they were *old*, Cotella concluded. And childless. No son would take over their land and farm. Cotella saw the future: this would not be her permanent home, and she could not hide here for the rest of her life, no matter how she looked, no matter how much she wanted to isolate herself forever.

***

Tom finally saw Dr. Franklin in Clintwood about his heart. He was told he had dropsy and that rest was the only cure. Cotella knew what that meant, that there was too much fluid around his heart and the fluid kept his heart from beating right. The doctors and nurses in Bristol called it "edema." Tom grew more tired and weak, and unlike his normal good-natured self, angry and impatient because he couldn't work.

In reality, Fanny needed Cotella back to keep the house going while she fussed over Tom. Tom could only wander to the edge of his property and tell Harley what to do, and he had to take on another hand, a boy of fifteen named Eldon, to keep up the farm. Planting would have to start soon, Tom said; he had to be the boss man, if nothing else. Most of the time he sat on the porch wrapped in two quilts and watched over his land. Otherwise, he rocked by the fire if sleet, snow, or dark forbade his sitting outside.

Cotella's life did not return to what it was before because she was not her former self. She had lost her innocence in a way. She had eaten of the tree of knowledge, not of good and evil, but electricity, street lamps, and automobiles, and of anatomy and hygiene. She had proven herself valuable to the outside world for a brief few months. But it did not matter. The disease or sickness or nervous condition or whatever she had didn't affect her brain or even her strength, and so far she felt the pain of the tumors pressing on her muscles only now and then. What mattered was how she looked to other people and how she would intrude on their ideas of how a normal woman should look.

So neither Fanny, Tom, nor she was as before. Especially in July of that year.

***

Fanny had grown used to letting Tom sleep until sunlight that summer. He didn't like it and let her know, every morning. "You fuss like an old biddy hen at me," Fanny responded every morning, "And you can't change that, you old rooster." One morning of a day that promised to be damp and hot, Fanny had risen, and Cotella not long afterward, to make biscuits, tend to chickens, and begin the housekeeping. Cotella was scrubbing laundry on the porch, her hands soothed by the warm water but irritated by the rough clothing, when she heard a scream from Tom and Fanny's room.

She rushed into the room. Tom lay with his mouth opened and drooling, but his eyes glistened and jerked from side to side. Fanny tried to get him to sit up, to rouse him.

"He's had a stroke," Cotella said, unsure of her diagnosis but believing some certain words would calm Fanny. "I'll send Harley to get Doc Franklin in Clintwood."

"What are we gonna do?" Fanny said.

"He's alive now. Not everyone dies from a stroke. It just--" Cotella stopped herself. She didn't know what a stroke really did to the brain and body, only the signs of it. "Don't get above yourself, Telly," she thought.

"I'll go tell Harley to get out a horse and go for Doctor Franklin," she said instead.

She ran to the barn, and then she realized Harley and Eldon were in the fields. Corn was eyeball high on her. How would she find them? But the land sloped enough that she could spy Harley and she called for him to come. At first he just waved her off, but she yelled more and more until he ran up to her.

"Tom's had a stroke. It looks real bad, but I didn't say so to Fanny. You'll need to get a horse and ride to town for the doctor."

"Is he gonna die?" Harley asked.

"There's no way of knowing. Even if he doesn't, he'll be a cripple or laying in bed for the rest of his life. But don't worry about that. You need to get on to town, now. Go."

Harley obeyed and ran, and she returned to the house. Not for the first time in her life, she thought how quickly everything could change.

Chapter Seventeen

Tom Elkins lived three days after his stroke. Doc Franklin did appear a few hours after Cotella dispatched Harley, and he gave them no hope for a recovery of any kind. "Only make him comfortable and see what happens," the old country doctor counseled. Sometimes men Tom's age survived a stroke but lost their speech, memory, or movement, he told Fanny. Tom watched silently from his bed as Fanny and Cotella came and went in the bedroom, helping as they could with Tom's immobile body. Cotella wanted to help when he wet or messed himself, but Fanny wasn't about to let another woman see her man's parts. Cotella wasn't ready to do so herself, despite the grainy photos in the anatomy textbooks and what would have been expected of her as a nurse.

Fanny wore herself to a frazzle, not sleeping, and Cotella couldn't get her to rest. But the struggle was not long. Tom passed peacefully at three one afternoon. Fanny let out a wail and collapsed in the bed with him, and Cotella smoothed her hair and shoulders as thunderclouds formed outside and a heavy storm cooled the suffocating July air.

The doctor came again, only to confirm the death for the county. "His brain probably swelled, or his heart just gave out," he concluded. On Saturday the folks at Caney Fork Methodist put him to rest in the cemetery on the hill behind the church, and Cotella pondered her future.

Fanny Elkins had been a farm wife for forty-three years. Now a childless widow, she owned the farm, and she had no desire to hold onto it. Tom, shrewder than most, had saved enough for her to live on, but he was not shrewd enough to know his wife's real leanings. He believed she would run the farm with the help of Harley and other hired men. Fanny, like many women deprived of a husband, saw herself freed from his expectations, no matter how loving the heart from which they rose. When the harvest was in, Fanny visited the First Virginia National Bank in Clintwood and said she wanted to sell the farm for the best price.

The bankers explained her options; sell to another farmer and let a family continue their traditions, or get a better price by selling to a coal or lumber company. Fanny liked the idea of a better price. No family in the country wanted her farm, or if they did, could afford to pay what a coal company would. So by the end of 1907, Fanny had sold out to the Virginia & Kentucky Coal Company. In the process she had told Harley and Eldon they would need to find work elsewhere, and had packed up the house. Fanny Elkins would live the rest of her days in St. Paul, Virginia, with her sister. Lydia, a widow herself of a country lawyer who had left her a secure legacy.

Fanny decided all this without Cotella's advice but did keep her in confidence. Cotella couldn't expect Fanny to keep the farm when an easier life with her sister in town tempted her away. Cotella felt especially bad for Harley, who had worked for Tom for close to twenty years. As a boy of twelve, he had finished school and began as a hired farm hand to help his family. Harley would have to find work on another farm, starting over, staying wherever they could put him up. Maybe he would leave the mountains and try steel mill work in Pennsylvania or cotton mill work in the Carolinas. Probably not. Harley's good soul and strong clumsy body were made for farming, and he confided to her that one day in Bristol was all the city he'd ever need.

Fanny did not forget Cotella's love and service. She handed her an envelope with one hundred one-dollar bills when the papers were signed and the land changed hands. But Cotella's fear of homelessness had come true much sooner than she could ever have expected. She could no longer see the future as a far-off city. It stood stark before her.

***

Her future began with Festa Rose. Through word of mouth, Festa let it be known she was expecting her second baby. She needed a woman to help with the chores, tend the chickens, feed her husband and the hired men, and keep up with the first young-un, who was almost two and into everything. Festa would pay room and board and a quarter a day for the time the woman stayed, until she felt like she could get back on her feet.

Cotella heard this from Fanny, who heard it from the preacher's wife who heard it from the other Methodist preacher in Nora, who heard it from Festa's sister. Cotella didn't know Festa, and she'd never been to Nora, but Festa's baby was due in December and Fanny had set her sights on living with Lydia by Christmas.

And thus, Cotella met her first momma that she helped through the lying-in. After Festa, came Alta Brown. Then Preacher Miller's wife, whom everyone called Mizz Mayellen. Those went well. She had her own space in the room with the other children because those women had somewhat bigger houses and fewer young-uns. But her next momma was Minnie Goins. After Festa and Alta and the preacher's wife, Minnie Goins made Cotella wonder how long and how much she could handle momma-helping. Minnie couldn't keep house well even when she wasn't with a baby; Minnie's husband drank of a night and let his mouth get wild and ungodly; Minnie sometimes just wasn't very kind herself. She asked rude questions about Cotella's knots and lumps and wanted to see her arms and legs, acting hurt when Cotella refused.

Pansy, Minnie's baby, was the first little girl for Cotella. Cotella fell in love with the tiny bundle; she couldn't believe Pansy felt so much lighter than those little boy babies she'd held. It was hard to leave her and go on to the next family. But Cotella could not afford to turn down an offer, and even the worst job was only six weeks long at the most. The mommas in Dickenson County and across the line into Wise County took their jobs of pushing out babies seriously. Most had a baby every two or three years, sometimes only a year or eighteen months apart, so she returned to the same families and same houses with some regularity, even as her reputation spread. If a momma didn't have female kin who could come stay with the family before the birth and for the month or so after, Cotella Barlow would do just as well as a sister, momma, or mother-in-law.

Life was not easy. She had no home, except a small room in Lula Jones' boarding house in Clintwood during those times when no mommas needed her. Those times were short, usually, and she liked the quiet for a change. She took her meals in her room, though. Lula asked her to, for the sake of the other boarders, traveling men and such who just wouldn't understand Cotella's looks.

Yet the mommas and their families seemed unbothered by her appearance after a while. Children were sometimes curious, and would sneak up and push her tumors to feel them. "Horace, you need to know that hurts Mizz Telly, so stop," their mothers chided. After the first time and the scolding, the children did stop, but many children tried it once. Some little girls would cry after being scolded; their feelings hurt but also sensitive to the lady who took care of them. Generally, Cotella liked girls better. Little boys were too rowdy and loud and wanted to crowd in the bed with the mommas and new weak babies. The little girls seemed to sense in their bones that their mommas had to divide their love between a new baby and any others she'd birthed.

Cotella knew that, if she could ever afford a home of her own—an unlikely event—she could become a granny woman and deliver babies. Not that she had any training about deliveries. If she had stayed in Bristol, she would have learned. But the granny women didn't have any true nurses' learning, not really, not like in a school or hospital. At least Cotella had experience in attending births. As 1907 turned into 1909, then 1912 and 1914, she delivered four babies, then two in 1915, but none in 1916 or 1917. She'd watched and helped Granny Zella or Momma Potts many, many times, but they were suspicious of her, of her disease and of her having studied in a city hospital. Anyway, to be a midwife, she would have to stay in a community, and have a home and horse, and then achieve the other midwives' good graces. That could take years.

Besides, delivering babies set her on edge and wore her out. It made returning to the regular chores that much harder. All six of her deliveries had ended well, with experienced mommas and strong babies who breathed quickly and suckled soon. She hadn't had to deliver a legs-first baby, or one with the cord around its neck. She hadn't attended to a momma who couldn't stop bleeding, or to a first momma. Even the healthy births exhausted her for days and left her feeling as if she had gone through all the agony with the mommas. Being wrung out by a birthing when she was feeding families and hired men, cleaning, and gardening just didn't fit together.

Once she entered a new home and started with another family for five or six weeks, she had no time to think about much. That was a blessing. She didn't have time to read, except when a child in a more well-off family would bring her a book of fairy tales or Bible stories to read out loud. She ordered herself one dress and some underclothes every year and a pair of shoes every two from the Sears Roebuck catalog with the pay she saved, usually four or five dollars per home, if times were good for the family and crops came in well. If not, she took less.

She went to church with the family if they asked or seemed to expect it. She liked the singing and some preachers better than others. With some, she wondered why they thought God ever wanted them to preach in the first place. But she had given up on asking questions of God a long time ago, since she didn't get any answers, and she kept her opinions to herself. Although she considered herself Methodist—if anybody asked—she walked with the children and sometimes the daddy to Presbyterian, Baptist, Holiness, or Episcopal services, too.

Ten years passed. At first, each home was new, a little fearful for her, a bit exciting. After five years, she had her rules and her way of organizing work. She knew not to put things in different places, or to change the routines. She didn't introduce new food to the husbands or young-uns. She learned how to cook bland and tasteless for some men and too salty for others, and the men always got what they wanted. She learned children were all different, and it was best not to spank any of them and just let the mommas or daddies do it. Instead, the best thing to do with misbehaving children was to send them to play outdoors if the weather allowed. Some children attended school, and some didn't. That wasn't her business, although she felt sorry for the ones not allowed to learn and made to stay home.

Home. Home was what she didn't have, could not see in her mind's eye, could not let herself imagine. No more than she could imagine smooth, unblemished skin, or a man gazing deep into her eyes, him holding her in bed, or saying she was the prettiest woman he'd ever seen. Or being called Sister Cotella and respected for her training. Whatever she had dreamed when she saw that advertisement in the Clintwood paper at eighteen years old had melted, had turned to a vapor and blown away. She had no more visions and dreams. She had only her mommas, the children, long walks between them, and empty places in her heart.

Chapter Eighteen

October 12, 1918

Cotella knew that she could waste no time in laying Minnie to rest. She also knew she could not do it in the presence of the children. That meant a very late night, perhaps a night of no sleep at all. It would be worth it not to have the children watching and pulling at her skirts while she made a hole five or so feet long and six feet deep. She owed poor Minnie one night of digging by an oil lamp in the south side of the yard while the girls lay bundled safely in the barn for another night. Minnie's short life had been one of sadness and toil with few moments of joy, like so many women in the mountains. Minnie deserved a decent burial as soon as possible, even if the rest of the world turned its back and closed its doors.

At nine o'clock or thereabouts—she suspected the mantle clock ran late and chimed unreliably—she retrieved the shovel, pickaxe, rake, and spade she had found in the barn earlier and hidden from the children. The ground underneath the maple did not give to the first stab of the shovel. It had not rained in two weeks and the dried ground resisted tools. She resorted to the pickaxe to break up the hard dirt. She took off her jacket. She'd be covered in sweat soon, despite the frost that would cover the ground the next morning and the dense fog from her mouth that came with every breath.

After the first foot, she found moist ground; two feet down, as far as she could tell by the dimming oil lamplight, she found it wetter, looser, and easier to move out of the hole, although heavier. She sat and took a break. She'd like to stop at three feet, but that would not do. A wolf or wild dog might desecrate the grave. She'd have to crawl into the hole and dig until it was a foot over her head. She needed a big, strong cup of coffee first, and then to retrieve a ladder and a bucket to carry the dirt up and out. Once the hole was finished, she foresaw an even harder job. Carrying Minnie from her room, placing her gently into her grave without a proper coffin, and covering her forever.

The big cup of coffee helped. She put three spoons of sugar in it, even though little was left, not enough for the winter months they might be isolated from the world. Not enough for the children when they wanted sweetened milk or a cake. She'd give up sugar for herself after this. Tonight, she needed all the sugar and coffee she could get.

At three in the morning, she entered Minnie's room by the light of the oil lamp. She searched through the chest of drawers. Like the rest of the house, the chaotic drawers defied logic. Cotella wanted to find the best dress Minnie had. She found it, a summer dress, yellow with small blue flowers and pearl-like buttons up the bodice. Pansy would be able to wear it soon. Should she save it for Pansy, or waste it in the ground?

Practicality won. She searched for another dress and found a plain blue housedress. For a shroud she used a sheet, the most worn one in the big chifferobe in Minnie's room. She tore strips to bind the sheet tightly around Minnie's body. She left Minnie's wedding ring on her finger. In that, practicality did not win out. The ring could be saved, sold, given to the first child to marry, to Arthur's bride, she argued to herself for a few seconds. No, Cotella decided. Minnie deserved to be buried as a woman who loved her man and young-uns. It wasn't fair that Cotella, not even kin, a paid servant really, was making these choices for the mother and children. She was the only one there to make them. Fairness or justice had nothing to do with any of this.

Cotella wanted to fall into bed, even if she was covered with dirt and sweat. Her exhaustion didn't matter. Minnie had to be in the ground, fully buried, by the time the children heard the rooster and wandered out of the barn, looking for an adult. A grown man would have found Minnie's light body no burden, but it was almost too much for Cotella. From the porch to the grave by the maple tree, she used a wheelbarrow. "I'm sorry, Miss Minnie. I know you ain't a sack of potatoes. I'm just not strong enough to do this gentle-like."

Filling the hole was a little easier than digging it. The untruthful clock told her it was almost 5:00 when she dragged herself into the house and fell into the girls' bed for as long as the children would let her.

***

"Girls. We need to say good-bye to your momma."

"What do you mean?" said Myrtle.

"Where is momma? I want to see her," said Mary, standing up, ready to run to her mother's room.

"No, she's dead, Mary. Don't you remember?" said Pansy. Her voice boiled with anger.

"I mean we have to have a funeral for her," Cotella said.

They were finishing dinner. It was the first real cooked meal the children had eaten for days. Cornbread, beans, a little of the chicken that remained, boiled eggs, cooked apples, and squash from the few cans their mother had set up. Cotella pretended they were picnicking. She laid out a quilt on the grass and let them carry plates and spoons out to the yard. She still wanted to keep them out of the house until she could clean every corner of Minnie's room. Arthur toddled around the yard, picking up dirt with every fall. He had taken his first steps the day before his mother's death. Cotella had missed it. No one clapped or praised him. He simply had three sisters to imitate. Cotella added to her mental list the need to give the children baths. No way of knowing how long it had been . . .

"We need a preacher," said Pansy. "You can't have no funeral without a preacher. Mary and Myrtle ain't never been to a funeral. I have. They don't know nothin' about funerals."

"In usual times, we would, honey. But the preacher can't come. I want you to think today about your momma's favorite song and Bible story and what you would want to say to her or about her. Each of you can say something or sing a song. Then we'll have a prayer and you can put flowers on her grave. That is what folks do at a funeral."

As they finished their dinner on the quilt, the girls sat quietly. Maybe, Cotella thought, they are thinking of what their momma would like. Arthur wandered around the dried autumn grass, sometimes giving up on steps and crawling, grinding dirt into his little overalls. Cotella wanted to play with him, swing him around. She didn't usually like her boy young-uns, but Arthur was different, somehow a happy little fellow in spite of his mother's fevered indifference, his father's absence, and his sisters' teasing.

She wanted to go to bed and sleep for days, but something drove her. There was so much to do. She told the girls to find the family

Bible and look in it for a Scripture to read. They would have the funeral at 6:00, with the sun setting. In the meantime, Cotella went into Minnie's room. She stripped the bed and pulled the light mattress outside to hang on the clothesline. No, she decided. It needed to be burned; the stains and stench of vomit, urine, and blood would never come out.

She washed the sheets by hand in strong lye and the hottest water she could endure and hung them up. She took a bucket with more lye and more boiling water and scrubbed the floors and walls and kept the window open. The room smelled clean, finally, if not pleasant, as if death and disease had fled, leaving behind a sense of new emptiness. The children could sleep in the house tonight and feel they had returned home. Maybe.

Chapter Nineteen

Cotella had been to many funerals in her thirty years of living, some in houses, some at the cemeteries, some in churches. She'd sat through a Methodist, a Holiness, and three kinds of Baptists. The Primitive Baptist Church held a funeral for her momma and daddy after the fire. Before that, her parents expected her to attend funerals if someone in the family or the farms around them died. There was always sad singing, and Bible reading, and then a sermon when the preacher talked about heaven and sometimes said kind words about the person who died. The dead person lay in the coffin, sometimes with it open and sometimes closed, depending on how they died, what they looked like, or what the family wanted. People died all kinds of ways in the hills. Some got cancers that grew and grew on the skin or inside their bodies. Some just had their hearts give out, like Tom. Some got drunk and fell into wells or off cliffs because they wandered afar. Some died in childbirth. Some got into fights, and shooting or knifing caused their end.

Whatever this sickness was, this enfluinzah thing, it was a new way to die, it seemed like. Minnie turned almost black and bled from her legs without wounds. The coughing was the worst she'd ever heard, like Minnie's thin body was going to rip apart. Minnie didn't have much hope, from the beginning. She was weak and overworked, big with baby, and worn out. She probably never ate well enough and living had exhausted her body even before the enfluinzah. Even without the sickness, having the baby might have set her back a long ways, more than an average woman. If Minnie hadn't died and the baby had been born, Cotella would probably have stayed with the Goins longer than usual, considering Minnie's condition.

Now, with Minnie and Leroy gone and death all around them, she didn't know how long she would have to stay. Soon she would have to start writing some letters, for if and when the postman came around. Maybe he wouldn't. Maybe he had the sickness, too. Maybe a neighbor would come soon. Maybe the postman and the neighbors and the law would forget about them for months. Should she send Pansy to another house in a few days? Should they all set out on foot to walk to town? That would be very hard on Mary, and carrying Arthur . . . but the pioneers did it. The folks who came here journeyed by foot down the mountains from New York or Pennsylvania or from the East, Richmond mostly, to settle deep in these hills. It was not impossible.

She would think about it. Right now, the children needed to hold a funeral for their mother and say good-bye. These were her thoughts the day after she dug the grave for Minnie Goins and put her in the ground. She didn't want to help the children with the funeral. She didn't want to cook their dinner or change Arthur or clean the house or listen to the girls fuss. She wanted to sleep until she woke up of her own accord and not the rooster's. Then pack her bags and walk away.

That was impossible. Without her, the young-uns would die, and she had nowhere to go.

***

They met at the maple tree as the sun lowered behind Piney Ridge.

Cotella held Arthur in her arms. He sensed the need to be still and let her hold him, so he rested his head on her shoulder. Mary sang her song for her mother. She didn't know all the words to the "Sweet Will of God" and her six-year-old voice couldn't reach the high notes, but she remembered the song made her momma happy. In fact, she did little better than hum and whisper some phrases of the ethereal hymn. Cotella wanted to cry, not so much for Minnie's passing as for Mary's effort to honor her mother in her child's way. Myrtle carried the big family Bible out to the tree and Pansy held it while her sister read the Christmas story in Luke. Cotella didn't ask why. Maybe it was Myrtle's favorite story in the Bible. Maybe because it was about a baby and a mother, and maybe it was the only one Myrtle could find in the family Bible on her own.

Pansy said that she would preach the sermon. She imitated their preacher a little bit. "Beloved, we are here to lay Sister Minnie Goins to rest. She was a kind and generous mother. She followed the Bible where it says to work hard and go to church. She didn't fuss at her young-uns and she only whipped them when they sassed her over and over, and that wasn't very much and she used a switch that wasn't very hard or big. She sang when she worked sometimes. She liked "Amazing Grace" and "Barbara Allen" and "Wildwood Flower." Sometimes she was sad, 'cause her husband Leroy had to go far away to work.

"I think Minnie is in heaven. She should have lived longer, but she got sick and died real sudden-like. Miss Telly wouldn't let us see her, but we'll try hard not to be mad about it. Mo—I mean Minnie liked that part of the Bible about 'The Lord is my shepherd I shall not want for nothing even if I walk through the valley of death and I will fear no evil because God comforts me.'"

Pansy stopped. "That's my sermon, Miss Telly."

"That was real good, Pansy. I think you girls put on the best funeral I've ever seen."

"What do we do now?"

"I will say a prayer, and you girls can put flowers on her grave. You can come and do that any time you want."

"It's too cold for flowers, Miss Telly. We looked for some. They all died with the frost. They were ugly and dried up."

"Oh, I forgot about that. We will think of something else, then." The girls looked at her, with empty, forlorn faces. They didn't know what to do next. Cotella didn't either. They seemed not to understand fully that their mother was really gone, her body under all that dirt, and not even protected by a pine coffin. Cotella wasn't sure they could understand it all. And even stranger, they had not asked about their daddy since Pansy came running into the yard, frantic and terrified. She'd seen their faces, unable to look at her, staring into space, unsure what to show or feel. Cotella decided that it was time to pray and end this show they were putting on, and then maybe the little girls could cry their hearts out now that they were orphans.

"Dear Lord Jesus, we thank you that you gave us these young-uns' momma, Minnie, for all these years and that she is not suffering anymore. We pray that someone is doing the same for her husband and these children's father. Please help us to know what to do. Keep us from getting sick with the enfluinzah and help the people who has it. Amen."

Cotella let the girls decide when to leave and what to do. They wandered away, silently and without destination, to mourn in their own ways, until she could fix an evening meal, let them sleep in their own beds that night, and fall asleep herself, more tired than she knew was possible.

Chapter Twenty

With Minnie buried and no sign of how long they would be alone, unvisited by neighbors, Cotella needed to investigate every inch of the house, the barn, the outbuildings, and the Goins' land. There might be food, cured meat, meal, or something she could trade when the time came. She knew that it was not within her rights to act as if their belongings were hers to use, but she alone was responsible for the children for the time being and they needed food. Eggs and milk and biscuits and cornbread would do for a while, but it would not be long before even these children, used to being poor and eating simple food day to day, would start to complain. Worse, Cotella had no real way of knowing how long the world outside would forget about them.

The cupboards' contents did not give her much assurance. The sack of flour, from what she could tell, was down to ten pounds, and cornmeal less. Coffee enough for a week of regular use, but the children didn't drink it and she would just have to ration it for herself. A couple of pounds of sugar, maybe, a half a jar of sorghum, what felt like five pounds of dried white beans, some oats in the bottom of the sack, and plenty of lard, thank the Lord. The hog they killed last year must have been a grand one.

Yes, it was. She found pigs' feet still hanging in the smokehouse. Not her favorite, but now was not the time for choosiness. She could use it in a pot of beans or stew. A full sack of coarse salt sat in the smokehouse for curing meat, along with several sacks of old dried corn that could be ground into meal if she could transport it to a mill—but when? Other than chickens, there was no more meat. The chicken coop housed twenty hens. Yes, eggs would be their staple food, but the hen's laying might go down with cold weather. It usually did, from her memory. And the cow would produce more than enough milk and butter, no worries there.

The Goins did not keep a horse, just an old mule for plowing that looked at this stranger with disinterested suspicion. Cotella decided to leave him to his own business in the pen until the first snow when he needed the barn for shelter. Mules scared her, the way cows scared Pansy. They kicked like the devil and moved on no man's timetable.

The Goins owned a wagon for hauling supplies and farm products to market, but otherwise walked wherever they went. Cotella did not let herself ponder on how Leroy spent his paycheck, or how much he earned and how much of it he gave to the household. He was known for drinking and for moonshining, like so many men. There was only so much you could do with all that corn, the easiest crop to grow. After everyone got their fill of corn on the cob, either it got dried and ground into meal or went to animal feed. That is, if it didn't get mashed and distilled into something the government didn't like you making because they couldn't find the stills and tax it. The preachers didn't like it because they saw what it did to families, and the women didn't like moonshine because it made some men mean and others lazy.

Thinking of Leroy and his stills made her wonder if he kept a gun in the house. Well, maybe not the house, but somewhere on the property. She asked Pansy, who mused on it for a bit. "He carries a pistol with him when he goes walkin' to his work crew. In case he sees a bear or other wild critter." Or a fellow he didn't trust and had a history with, Cotella thought. Cotella noticed Pansy spoke like her daddy was still living.

So, whoever found Leroy, and she didn't know when it would be that the law or a preacher or somebody would come to the house with that news, that person got a gun in the deal. Maybe they would return it sometime. "He has a rifle, too, but we ain't allowed to know where it is," Pansy added, after a thought.

The presence of a gun somewhere on the property reassured Cotella a bit, except she would have to look for it. She could handle a gun if she needed to—Tom Elkins had seen to that. Having a gun in these times, a woman alone with four children a ways out of town, would sure make her feel safer. There was no protection otherwise. Master would howl up a storm, but a shout from an intruder or a growl from a black bear would probably send him running to hide. Cotella made a note to hunt for the gun when she had a free minute. Even so, a gun could not keep the specter of hunger away, or the enfluinzah.

The garden had been picked and now was wilted after the several frosts. Irish potatoes, sweet potatoes, and turnips could be their last hope from the garden. Good potatoes could be fried and boiled, smashed and made into soups. With the limited jars of vegetables, Cotella doubted they would get much past Christmas on the food in the house, and it was now October 13. Two months or more. Maybe by Christmas that war would be over and the cloud of this sickness lifted and blown away. People would get off their sickbeds, go back to neighborliness, and the mail would come. Then she could send for meal and flour and coffee, and she could find Minnie's sister somehow for the young-uns' sake.

But there was no doubt about it. If they were to have enough food, they—she—would have to kill a hog.

Yet . . . it was a three- or four-man job. It was a task for a community party. It was not something she could do alone. She had attended plenty of hog-butchering parties over the years, but the men always took charge while the women cooked and visited and gossiped. How would she do it?

She would have to ponder and plan. She didn't even know where the Goins hogs were now. Like many folks, Minnie let the new piglets, born in spring to the brood sow and then weaned, run over the hills and root for hickory nuts and acorns for the summer and into fall. That is, the ones Leroy wouldn't have sold. Getting the pigs back in the yard was a job she'd leave to Myrtle and Pansy. It would give them something to keep their minds from their grief.

As if she didn't have enough to do, something else bothered her. A lot. The girls should be in school. Probably there was no school now, closed for—what was that word they used in nursing school for making sick people stay in their houses—quanteen, or carnteen? But Pansy and Myrtle hadn't gone to school at all this fall, either from lack of money or from needing to help their momma. School was free, if the children could walk there, but they needed new clothes and shoes.

It wasn't fair or right that the girls missed schooling. The world was changing. It might be different when this enfluinzah and the war were over, whenever that would be. She heard that women in the cities wanted to vote, that they marched in the streets and pulled silly stunts to get the government to pay attention to what they wanted. She heard about it one day when she was traveling through McClure, on the way to another momma. Some old men were arguing loudly in front of the post office, claiming that it would never happen and it was a damn fool idea. Women, they fussed, weren't smart and should be happy that their husbands could vote and that was enough.

Those old men were the fools, in her mind. What about a woman with no husband? What about a woman who earned her own keep and worked hard at it to boot? She worked as hard as just about any old man she knew, in her own way. Not that she really wanted to vote, and she was too busy to chain herself to a gate to try to get it, but she'd take the vote if they gave it to her.

So, things were changing and girls couldn't afford to be without schooling. Cotella herself knew she would have had a better time of nursing school if she had been able to finish high school, or at least go to some of it. Reading was the first thing they needed, but so far she couldn't find any books in the house other than the Bible and some old magazines and newspapers used for kindling. Reading was just a part of what the girls should learn. There were numbers and history and all that. Pansy and Myrtle seemed pretty apt for schooling; Pansy spoke pretty well for her mommas' funeral, and Myrtle read the Bible without stopping much. Yes, they needed schooling before they forgot much more of the little bit they had.

Her long reverie about how to survive ended with Arthur whining for his next meal. At least now the girls could come and go as they pleased in their own house. It was probably as clean as it had been since the end of Cotella's last lying-in visit. Even so, Myrtle and Pansy kept their distance from Cotella. They knew what Cotella had done. She'd dug a hole and thrown their momma's body in it. Mary was too young to understand the difference between momma in heaven and momma in the ground. She clung silently to Cotella's skirts much of the day and played with Arthur, Master, or her rabbit the rest of the time. She spent her day as if her sisters had exiled her from their interests and good graces.

Cotella occupied her mind making mental lists for her and the children. Survive. Keep feeding and cleaning and caring for the young-uns the best she could in the absence of anyone else. Dig up potatoes. Think of a way for the girls to get some schooling, and before that, make sure everyone had a bath; the young-uns were starting to have an odor. Have the two older girls find a hog and bring it into the pen. In a week or two, walk the family in the direction of McClure to find some help, hoping enough time had passed for people to recover from the sickness. Write a letter to the postmaster in Buckley, West Virginia, to find Minnie's sister in case the postman came. Forget about Minnie and Leroy's privacy and secrets and try to find some money or other signs about what she should do about the girls and Arthur. And figure out how to butcher a hog all on her own, if it came to that.

Chapter Twenty-One

In her years of helping mommas with their lying in, Cotella wondered sometimes if she should just leave this life, these mountains. She could pack up her belongings, buy a train ticket out of Dickenson County, and ride to Richmond or Charlotte or back to Bristol and find a job as a maid or housekeeper, an office girl or sales girl in the city. She took pride in her ability to get her work done, to organize a home, to bring order and cleanliness to a house, even one like poor, befuddled Minnie's. Then she would see her reflection in the bucket of water, a piece of metal, or now in the children's searching eyes. She would remember she was as foolish as those old men arguing that women weren't smart enough to vote like a man. No one in the world outside the mountains would hire her or want her around them. Sister Berta and that doctor—she'd forgotten his foreign-sounding name—had sure made that clear. Then Mary or Arthur or some other child in some other house pulled at her skirts and she remembered her place and young-uns who needed her.

Right now, what they needed was food. She gave the potato-digging responsibility to Myrtle and Pansy and wrote them out what she called a "check," when they finished, for ten cents worth of candy the next time they could all go to Bailey's General Store. The unturned south end of the garden yielded a half a barrel full of Irish potatoes, sweet potatoes, and mostly turnips—not her or the children's favorite. With the potatoes collected, the dinner menu expanded a little to potato soup with the meat from the cured pigs' feet and the milk and butter from the cow.

Then, using the biggest wash pot she could find, she started to boil water to fill the washtub and made sure the children were free from the dirt of the last two weeks. Arthur got to play in the tub. After she made sure he had taken care of his business, she submerged him in the warm water. He relished the wetness and the splashing and laughed down to his belly. She breathed a prayer of thanks that he was a content baby after all of this trouble and pain. He had conquered walking since she arrived and was rarely off his feet when he wasn't asleep.

She put the clean children smelling of fresh soap to bed. Once alone, she dumped out the water, filled the tub with the warmest water she could stand, and washed off the grave, the sweat, and the body odor from herself. She took as long as the water stayed warm. She slept like a baby after the warmth and the release from the filth.

The next day Cotella devoted three pieces of her special writing paper she carried from home to home to write a letter in her best hand. She addressed it to the postmaster in Buckley. She said she was taking care of four children near McClure, Virginia, and their mother and father were dead from the enfluinzah. The mother, Minnie Goins, said she had a sister in Buckley, named Viola, but she died before giving a last name or address. Minnie's family name was Wilson, but that was common and if the sister was married it would be something else.

Could the postmaster help her find this woman? Cotella tried to explain in the letter that she didn't know of any other kin, the family was poor, and the children were little and too young to be sent out to strangers or an orphanage. She decided that until she was able to post the letter, prayer would help it along and move the postmaster to ask some questions in the town for her. Cotella had no idea where or how big Buckley, West Virginia, was or how kind the postmaster. If she didn't hear by the time the sickness was over, she would have to go to the Sheriff for help.

***

Pansy, of course, balked at being sent to find the hogs. "I'm scared of 'em," she said. "They's mean as snakes. Anyway, the one we had last year was so big, I don't think he could get through the front door."

Cotella reasoned with her. "That's fine because no hog is comin' in through that door and into this house. That's not what we need him for. A hogs' for killin' and eatin'. All we got to eat is eggs. I don't want to kill chickens unless I have to—then we get less eggs."

"I hate lookin' for the hog." Pansy wasn't ready to give up her argument, weak as it was. "I don't know where to look."

Cotella changed her tactics. "You'll find him. Just listen good, rather than callin' for him. No hog is gonna come at a call, like a dog. Anyway, wouldn't you like some nice hog's liver with some of those potatoes, once we butcher it? Umm! I can taste it now."

Pansy's eyes did grow wide, and a rare smile flashed across her face. "I love me some fresh meat after a killing." She said it like Minnie would have. "But killin' a hog is man's work. You can't do it."

Cotella wanted to say digging a grave was man's work, but she didn't. And in her deepest heart she hoped that the trial they were in would be over soon. She also figured Pansy's reluctance was as much from sadness as from laziness.

"Maybe by the time we kill the pig, a man will be around and the sickness will be liftin'. We won't do it for another month. It's got to be good and cold outside through the day, or the meat will get spoilt."

"All right," Pansy sighed. "At least Myrtle is goin' with me."

"And I don't hear no whinin' about it from her, so you can't stop yours. Now them hogs, they might be together. Once you find 'em, at least get the smaller one to come home, if the bigger one is ornery and won't follow you. The smaller one won't be as mean, I reckon. Use a switch to nudge him home, and we'll keep him in the pen for a while, and give him some dry corn. They like that."

Pansy looked like she wanted to sass, to say something like "You go hunt the hogs and I'll see to Arthur," but she didn't. "Can I go tomorrow?"

"No, you and Myrtle need to start this afternoon. I'm smelling rain might come tomorrow, or somethin' colder. So, get on with you."

Pansy frowned, but kept her feelings to herself. "Dress warm," said Cotella as Pansy went to fetch her sister, "and be home before the sun goes down."

Cotella felt a pang of conscience sending the little girls off like that to hunt a pig. They might meet up with the wrong kind of person, like a stranger with a hidden still who wanted his secret kept. She sighed. A moonshiner might be sick like anybody right now, or maybe was such a loner that he wouldn't catch any enfluinzah. There were mean, mean people, men mostly, in this world, and the little girls were pretty enough, now that she washed their hair and faces, put clean clothes on them, and tied their hair back with ribbons for once.

She went to the porch to watch them wander in the direction of their daddy's small patch of bottomland and then head up the slope on a narrow trail. They carried oak switches almost as long as they were tall to whip at the young hog, maybe one-hundred pounds or so, if they found it. A three-man-sized hog, one of 200 or even 300 pounds, would be much better for feeding a family of four young-uns for a year, but she couldn't handle that.

As it was, Cotella would have to construct some kind of contraption to hang the hog for gutting, if Leroy hadn't left one in the barn. A pig of one hundred pounds she might be able to pull up; she'd carried Minnie to her grave somehow, after all.

Her conscience continued to bother her all day for forcing the two girls to find the pig, so she bundled up Arthur while he napped and took him and Mary outside to the porch to watch for their return. She prayed and worried all afternoon, until she heard a pig's snort right before sunset. "We got him," Myrtle called, yards behind the animal as he meandered toward the house. Yes, they had, but not without each putting a tear in each of their dresses that would have to be mended. And not without needing another bath.

The mottled black hog, shoulder above Cotella's knee, looked to be a little more than 100 pounds and was none too interested about getting in the five-by-nine pen reserved for the year's candidate for hog butchering. It took Cotella and the girls some running and shooing and whipping to direct him in, where he was rewarded with some dried corn and fresh water, known to help the meat taste better. He'd eaten roots and nuts and whatever else he could find in the woods for five months.

"Did you see the other one?"

"Yes, ma'am," said Myrtle. "He was three times the size of this one, but he didn't pay us no mind."

"Which was fine with me," Pansy said, as if relieved. "This one's smaller, but he was agreeable, at last. Well, sort of. That other one looked mean as a bear."

"You girls did fine. I'll add ten cents to your paycheck." Yes, maybe before Thanksgiving, when they would need to kill the hog, they could all go to Bailey's store, see neighbors, and find out about the world outside this holler below Piney Ridge. And find some help.

Chapter Twenty-Two

Two weeks after Kaiser Wilhelm—what they named the hog—came home, Cotella decided that, if she could get some help to butcher the Kaiser, now was the time to try. The only way to find help was to journey to town. It was November 18, a Monday, according to the calendar hanging on the barn wall next to the cow's stall, which she visited every day. She milked early, before the children rose, to get it over with. Of all the chores, she hated milking the most. The squatting on the stool, the pinching of her fingers on the tits, the odor, the head turned and pressed against the cow's flanks—all put cricks in her body, making her feel as if she were already old.

As she left the barn, the clear sky turned from indigo to purple. Stars gave their last sparkles and disappeared in anticipation of the sun. Today might be the day, she thought, to leave this holler with the children, who had never shown any signs of illness and ate heartily what she was able to give them. She believed they could make the trip of five miles or so out of the holler to McClure, and if the Lord willed, someone would come by on the road and give her and four tired children a ride.

After breakfast, she bundled them up in jackets without a word of why, and said, "Let's go. Maybe you can spend your paychecks, girls, at Bailey's store." She considered hitching the mule and wagon, but she had never hitched an animal like that, and her memories of the mule's obstinacy changed her mind. Instead, she placed Arthur in one of the wheelbarrows—the lighter one. "This will be like a baby buggy I saw in Bristol," she said. Arthur waved his arms and laughed as she struggled to push him through the yard, up the rugged pathway, and out of the holler to the rugged road that would lead to the main road to town.

The sun rose and warmed them. She encouraged them to tell stories, and they did their best. Some of them were simply memories of their earlier years, some were confused versions of something from the Bible, and a few Jack tales were thrown in. She knew the way to McClure on the packed dirt road well enough to detect when they were within two miles. She saw a felled log on the side of the road. "Let's rest."

"We done told all our stories, Miss Telly," Myrtle said. "You tell one."

"Once we get walkin' again."

"I'm thirsty," said Mary.

"Hunt around in this." Cotella handed Pansy a flour sack. "I put some milk in a big mason jar for Arthur in there, and a cup. There's plenty for you each to have a swallow."

After their rest, she rose. "Let's go. If we're lucky, this morning you young-uns will get to see a body other than me, and I'll see a body other than you all, which will be nice for all of us."

They set off again. Houses began to appear near the road. All the farmhouses to this point had sat way off the main road, such that knocking on a door would take up time they needed and only tire the children worse. Some of the houses perched up against a slope, with high steps to the door. She began to wonder about the wisdom of this trek, but the sight of houses—no people yet, only their houses—within yards of each other meant they were getting close to town.

She figured they would be in the center of the town in five minutes. Not that McClure was much of a town. It barely counted as one, especially after her days in Bristol. Bailey's General Store had no electricity, no cold soda pop, no icebox, and not even a water fountain. It was only a little house with a wide front porch, well painted but otherwise ramshackle. Inside, five rows of shelves lined three sides, and the fourth held a counter. Neat barrels and sacks sat on the floor—flour, meal, salt, coffee, and other staples. Cotella's mouth watered at the thought of strong coffee with a teaspoon of sugar. The coffee had given out two weeks before. Bailey tended to charge more than he should since he was the only store around, but he wasn't too crooked about it. He did have to bring in supplies from Clintwood and Pound. She didn't care; she missed her coffee so much, she'd pay him what he wanted for a pound or two.

Beyond Bailey's store were a blacksmith, a post office, and a two-story house with two offices, one for a lawyer who worked for the county and the other for the Sheriff and deputies of the county to use when they needed it. Scattered around these buildings were a few three- and four-room homes. On the other side, a narrow creek flowed southward toward the bigger Caney Creek. Despite its size, the creek flooded in spring and threatened the homes.

She could see Bailey's Store up ahead. Yet something was very strange.

No residents were in their yard or walking the road, even though the day had warmed up. No one was walking to and fro in town, only the five of them. How queer we must look, she thought, a short ugly woman like her pushing a baby in a wheelbarrow, following three little girls, wandering into town. She glanced to her side and saw a flash of a something—a woman's face and a swaying curtain. She had a feeling of being watched, looked at, but not because of her tumors and knots. Not even because they looked like a parade of poor, bedraggled mountain folks.

Soon they stepped up onto the porch of Bailey's store. She tried to turn the doorknob, but it didn't give. She shook it. Her heart felt like a big hand clenched it.

"They's closed," she heard from behind her. She turned; a girl, about fifteen, had emerged partly from the house across the road.

"For how long? When's he gonna open? We come a long ways," Cotella called back.

"They ain't open 'cause people ain't trading right now."

"Why?"

"Why? Don't you know nothin', lady?" The girl stepped out on her porch, slowly, unsure this woman and children were far enough away. "Don't you know what's goin' on?"

"I know somethin'. You don't need to sass me, young-un," Cotella said. "I know there's been a sickness, that enfluinzah. I know all about it."

"Then that's why they's not open. They will be one of these days, though, maybe."

"How do you know?"

"My family owns it. Mr. Bailey is my momma's grandpa."

"Oh, for heaven's sake," said Cotella.

"That girl needs her hiney whipped for her sassy mouth," said Myrtle.

"We walked all this way for nothin'," said Pansy. She sank down on one of the benches on the store's porch, and Mary followed her example.

"Move over, Mary," said Myrtle, and wiggled in next to her, sighing.

Cotella felt all the fatigue of the last month crowd in on her. The rude girl still stood on her porch. "You know anybody that's been sick? That's died?" Cotella called.

"Oh, yes. A bunch of people been sick. It's been awful. Coughin' and blood and all kind of things. Turning black right before they died. My grandpa said fifteen people 'round here he knows died with it, and almost a hundred in the county."

"That number should be two more," thought Cotella. Instead, she called back to the girl. "These children's momma and daddy both died of it. We know all about this sickness. Now we need help. Is there anybody to help us?"

"Are you kin to those young-uns'?"

"Never you mind," said Cotella. "Is there anybody that can open this store, or give us a ride back to our house, or some hired men who could help with a hog killin'?"

"No. They's still a lot of sick people. Doc told us to stay inside, and away from the neighbors, until he told us different."

A woman, probably the girl's momma, came through the door, pulled her back in, and slammed the front door shut. "Well, that's my answer," Cotella said to herself. "No supplies, no help. At least, according to that fool girl. Surely somebody around here... Maybe I just needed to knock on every door." She sighed. As always, the children looked to her for their next move.

"Let's eat the biscuits and fried eggs I brought." She tried to sound happy.

"Look!" said Pansy, pointing to an area beside the door. "They left a crate of Coca-Colas out here."

She was right. Maybe old Bailey had just forgotten about them in all the confusion.

"Can we have one?"

Cotella looked up and down the road. She didn't want to teach the girls they could get away with stealing, but they were all thirsty. She had promised them some candy, and it had been a long walk. She would leave four nickels in the box and hope Bailey found them, and pay the rest later if that wasn't enough. And she wanted one too, real bad.

"Yes, but we ain't stealing it. I'm leaving him twenty cents in the crate."

"Oh, no, Miss Telly, we would never do that," said Myrtle sincerely, but anxious for the soda pop.

Cotella used the bottle opener nailed to the wall and handed each girl a bottle. She downed half of her own. The cold, oversweet liquid tickled her nose but wet her mouth and throat, as always. This made up for the missed coffee. "Ooh, that makes my nose burn," said Mary.

"She ain't never had one," said Pansy. "If you don't like it, Mary, me and Myrtle can share yours."

"No, it's mine," said Mary, clutching it to her chest.

"You know, 'ain't' isn't a proper word," said Cotella.

"It ain't like a swear word," said Pansy.

"No, I don't mean that. It's not proper English."

"That's what the school teacher said," chimed in Myrtle. "But nobody much listened to her."

Cotella held in her laugh. Yes, Myrtle's streak would get her in trouble, or keep her out of it.

Chapter Twenty-Three

The five of them sat on the store's porch, chewing on the biscuits filled with scrambled eggs and sipping the soda pops. Cotella felt revived a bit. She found the spoon and other mason jar with cooked apples and oatmeal she brought for Arthur, who needed his diaper changed. She fed him and helped him drink his milk in little sips. "Here, one of you let him taste your Coca-Cola," she said. "He came on the trip, too."

"He didn't walk a step, though," said Pansy, but she gave him a taste with the spoon. He made a face, then changed his mind about it, and grabbed for the spoon. Cotella gave him some of hers. "That's enough, sweetie."

Her eyes fell on the porch floor and she noticed something new. A newspaper had been left under the crate, half showing. "Pansy, Myrtle, go move that crate and bring me that paper. Maybe we can learn something."

The paper was from October 11. It had no reports about the sickness. It said the American soldiers won some battle in Germany, and it looked bad for the enemies of the "Entente Powers," whoever that was. They seemed to be talking about the British and Americans, so the enemies, Cotella decided, must be the Germans. The war news made her head hurt. Nobody had ever explained it to where she could understand it, just that a lot of soldiers were dead and had to be buried in France, including her own brother John. The newspaper also gave reports about the election for Congress, and picture advertisements for women's clothes, and stories about robbers and a shooting over in Kentucky. The paper was from Norton, in the next county. It didn't help her understand the state of the sickness much, but she folded it up and stuffed it in the flour sack anyway. She could use it for the girls' reading lessons.

They stayed on the porch of Bailey's store for quite a while. She knew they'd have to start out soon so that dark didn't fall on them. Ten miles of walking in one day was too much for young-uns, for anybody. How she wished a wagon would come by, at least for part of the way home. Then she remembered her letter to the postmaster in that West Virginia town. She reached into her heavy jacket's inner pocket and pulled it out. "Myrtle, take this letter and put it in the mailbox. The post office is two buildings down from here."

Myrtle inspected it. "Who's it for?" She peered at the address. "Somebody in West Virginia? Where is that? Who do you know in West Virginia, Mizz Telly?"

"It's the state right next to this one. That school of yours ain't teachin' you much if you don't know your states. And you young-uns need to mind your own business. Go on, put it in the mailbox. We need to get walkin' back."

Cotella pondered their choices while Myrtle posted the letter. Should she send Mary, a pretty little tow-headed girl, to the door of the first house they came to? Would the people inside answer? Or be as skittish as the mother of the sassy girl across the road? She would try once, and hope that Mary was treated right. Better the face of a sweet child than her own, which brought such stares and fear from those she didn't know.

They started on their way, this time with the girls lagging behind Cotella and the wheelbarrow. After a few minutes they reached some houses grouped together on the edge of the settlement, and Cotella picked a small, well-kept home.

"Mary, go up to the door, and knock, hard, like this, with your fist."

Mary's look was part skeptical, part confused, but she mounted the house's porch and pounded on the door. Nothing. "Try again, honey," Cotella called.

The door cracked, but Cotella could only hear a faint, female voice. "What is it, child?"

Mary, frightened, had no answer and ran back to Cotella. An elderly woman eased her head through the crack to see where the child disappeared to.

Cotella called from the road. "Ma'am, we live way out in the country, and walked here to see if anybody can help us. These children lost their momma and daddy already. We have food, but it's gonna give out if we can't buy some or get some help with the farm." She hated how she sounded, desperate, pleading, and weak. The woman tried to understand where the voice was coming from; Cotella wondered if she was near blind or deaf.

"I'm sorry. I'm by myself, with my husband here. He's old, with a weak heart," the voice said, through the crack, behind the door. "I don't want him to get the sickness. I can give you a few cups of flour. We can't get no groceries right now either."

"No, ma'am, we don't want to take from you. God bless you. We'll be moving on." The woman withdrew her head and shut the door. "I won't put Mary through that again," Cotella thought.

Someone with a mule and a wagon did come from behind them a mile out of town. "Please, could you give us a ride?" she called as it approached.

"Are you sick?" the driver, a bearded, stocky man in dirty overalls called back. "No, we are healthy. We haven't been sick at all. But we're real tired. We walked more than five miles already today."

"That's a passel of young-uns," the man said as he stopped the wagon. "Climb in the back. I can take you a piece. But don't ask no questions."

The back of the wagon held a coffin-like pine box. Cotella decided that meant either he was carrying a body, or he was hiding moonshine in the box. He didn't act or talk like a grieving man on an errand to bury some kin. She asked no questions, and he wasn't interested in conversation. It didn't matter. She was thankful for the ride even if he didn't help with loading the children or the wheelbarrow into the back of the wagon. They had to sit on the floor of the wagon with legs crossed, and her foot went to sleep.

Stopping after what seemed like four miles, he called back. "I'm turning off the main road here." Cotella took the clue, and they all climbed down. Her thank you brought no response from the driver, who whipped the mule and slowly moved on to his right, even though there was only a narrow trail. Yep, Cotella thought. Moonshine.

"About half a mile to go, girls," she said.

"Tell us a story, Cotella," Myrtle said. "We told you all ours this morning. We don't know no more."

She told them Cinderella. It was new to them, and they loved it, but peppered her with questions. "What is a godmother?" "Wouldn't a shoe made out of glass break and hurt her feet?" "The mean stepsisters cut off their toes to wear a shoe?" "That prince shouldn't have let her run off like that. Couldn't he run as fast as a girl?" "I think she was beautiful and those other girls were just jealous as could be." "Are all stepmothers mean?"

Sometimes these children just wore her out. "Tell us another one. Tell us one about you."

Cotella told them about Bristol, about how she wanted to go to school there, and how she rode the train and worked in a hospital, and what a hospital was. Dusk was approaching, but she could see the wonder in their eyes that this woman they knew, who gave them baths and cooked their meals, had done all that.

"Why didn't you stay?" said Pansy as they unlatched the gate to their yard.

"That's another story for another time. We're home now, and we're tired as can be. Let's eat and go to bed soon."

When all the children were asleep, she stretched herself on the bed. She had taken over Minnie's room, now thoroughly clean, the original mattress now a pile of ash. She burned it, hoping to destroy any infection. She used a folded quilt in its place, not the best, but she at least had a room to herself, away from the young-uns. Her feet felt raw, her back and arms ached and trembled from pushing Arthur in the wheelbarrow, but her eyes would not close readily. She stared at the ceiling, pondering, questioning, doubting, fearing.

All that walking, and nothing came of it except a few swigs of Coca-Cola and a conversation with Bailey's know-it-all great-grand-child. Well, and mailing a letter, maybe. Even the newspaper was no help. No one came out of hiding, except the moonshiner, on orders from the town doctor. Everybody seemed scared to death, scared *of* death. No, not "seems." They were. She had tried to find help too soon, maybe, but it might snow in the next week or so and then walking to town would be impossible for anybody but a strong, young man, and definitely not for her and four children. If she had to, she could leave Pansy in charge and make the trip herself, wearing Leroy's old boots she found in the barn. If she had to, she'd kill the pig herself. If she had to, she'd get these children through to spring, or to whenever someone remembered them and the world stopped dying long enough to be neighbors again.

Chapter Twenty-Four

Kaiser Wilhelm lived like a kaiser of pigs for four weeks. Cotella set the girls in charge of his water—fresh from the pump—and food, as much dried corn as he wanted. There were no scraps for the Kaiser because she and the young-uns ate everything she cooked. While Wilhelm lived his last days in imprisoned comfort, she surveyed the barn and tools to see how she would manage to bring him from the pen to the smokehouse to the table.

Living in the mountains on farms all her life, she had seen many a hog killing. In fact, she had missed one only a couple of years, one of those when she attended nursing school. For most, a hog killing was a party for inviting neighbors, who returned the favor so they too could fill up their smokehouse. A hog killing could be like a traveling dinner on the grounds. She loved them, especially after she went to live with the Elkins. She remembered little of life with Momma and Daddy, mostly only photographs in her head. But she did recall being six or seven and running away into the woods at the sights and smell. The blood, the pig's lifeless eyes, the guts pouring out of the large gash in his belly, and the men with the knives digging at the innards as they landed in a kettle for cooking.

Momma said all little girls went through that, and it was scary for them at first. Especially if they had seen the pig around the barn and thought of it like the dog or cat, which, Momma said, by golly it wasn't. A cat ran off four-legged varmints and a dog ran off human varmints and helped with hunting. But an old pig did nothing for nobody except provide breakfast, dinner, and supper. And they did that real good.

Having witnessed so many hog killings and having helped with the kitchen work, she knew the process. That wasn't the problem. The problem was doing a family-sized job almost all by herself, unless she could find something helpful for Pansy or Myrtle to do. Mary would probably run into the woods the way Cotella had at that age.

Cotella's first decision was about how to kill the pig. She'd seen men put a bullet through the animal's brain, and she'd seen other men swing a massive sledgehammer and pound the pig's head into the ground with one circular swing. In this case, she had a choice because she had found Leroy's rifle after a morning of searching. It was in the barn, under lock and key. Why he would store the gun there instead of having it handy, she didn't know.

She used an axe to break the lock since the key was probably on Leroy's body. When the lock and door to the cabinet were splintered, she pulled the gun out carefully and understood this was no ordinary gun. The .22 long rifle gleamed as if it had been freshly cleaned and oiled. If Leroy carried a pistol on him, he must have used the rifle for hunting and for shooting contests, for special times when a pistol would not do.

And to her surprise, in the same cupboard she found several mason jars of clear liquid, tightly sealed. So this was where Leroy kept his stash of corn whiskey, not the smokehouse, like Minnie said. Good to know, she thought. This was a temptation to avoid, but also a source of disinfectant.

Cotella found the cache of shells for the gun, experimented with loading the .22, and returned it to the cabinet. She didn't consider herself much of a shot, but she could get off rounds if she had to. Still, using a bullet seemed a less useful option for a pig the size of Wilhelm, so she chose the alternative. She would need to practice swinging the sledgehammer with the right aim so the Kaiser wouldn't know what hit him and would never have a chance to wonder. He had to be dead, dead, and more dead before she slit his throat.

Any chance of Wilhelm not being dead right off meant something might go wrong in the whole butchering, or the meat would not be good, or even edible. Then she would have to make sure the knife was so sharp there'd be no doubt of the blood spurting and the wound being straight and clean. And that meant finding the knife, whetting it to where it could almost split a hair, which meant finding the whetting tools.

Cotella sighed from contemplating all the actions, tools, and strength needed for a hog killing. Those steps challenged her enough, but her determined search of the barn implements yielded all of them. She cleaned two knives with six-inch blades and oak handles. She set up the whetstone and sharpened them to where she was afraid of them herself and put them up safe from the children. She set up a circle in the dirt as wide as her hand and practiced her aim. If she could hit that, she could kill the Kaiser really good and cold.

But the next part would take some carpentry, or more. The pig, after being stunned dead and bleeding out for a while, sometimes with the blood collected for pudding, would have to be attached to a pulley and lifted. Then she, and maybe Pansy if she didn't get sick to her stomach by then, could dump it in the washtub over a fire for the scalding and the scraping. She thought that was nastier than the actual gutting, at least to watch. The water couldn't be boiling—that would make the hair impossible to get off and ruin the meat, but it had to be hotter than a woman could normally take for washing dishes or laundry. On second thought, maybe Pansy couldn't do that, so she'd find her another job. Pansy was getting some sass about her and needed to get a taste of some real work.

Cotella searched in the barn for whatever Leroy and other men had used in the past to hang the hog over the water, let it down, and pull it out again for the gutting and cutting. She found two sets of two-by-fours that had been nailed to look like an A, with a foundation to keep them upright. A place for a cross piece of iron was attached to the top of both A's, and she found the chain, hooks, and the washtub near them. They had rusted and not been cleaned or oiled well over the years, but they would do. Tom Elkins had been particular of his farm tools, and they lasted longer that way.

When she wasn't tending to Arthur or cleaning or cooking in those weeks of Kaiser Wilhelm's imprisonment, she prepared the knife, chains, frames, and washtub. They were bulky and heavy and took all her strength. She was small but stout. Minnie's girls would be delicate, like Minnie, and fine-featured, probably not made for this kind of heavy farm work. Sometimes strength just had more value than pretty. Anyway, Cotella and pretty didn't get along.

A fire would have to be set up under the washtub, which she judged to be 50 gallons or more. That meant a metal platform for the tub to keep it above ground. She could turn some old buckets upside down for the tub to rest on. That was it--Pansy could stoke the fire and keep it high and hot. Cotella made a decision there and then—these long skirts were not going to work. They would catch fire too easily. She would wear Leroy's old dungarees or trousers, and tie a pair around Pansy. Some would call it a scandal, but nobody was there to criticize. If they were, they could slaughter the hog themselves.

Chapter Twenty-Five

She settled on December 2 for the hog killing. That was Mary's birthday, so they could celebrate with slices of fresh pork. Myrtle would have to be in charge of Mary and Arthur. The killing would take up all of Cotella's energy, and she had to keep an eye on Pansy and the fire. The day before, she arranged everything. She set up a wooden platform of any planks of wood she could find for laying the pig out. Finally she found work trousers for her and Pansy, rolling up the legs and tying a rope around their waists for belts. Pansy kept her views to herself, but seemed to like the freedom from a dress for the day.

From what she could tell, the days were plenty cold. For two weeks water froze solid in a basin she left outside to test the temperature, and it never melted much. Normally, that would mean regular wood chopping. Instead, she thanked Leroy silently for having the good sense to take care of that earlier in the fall and stack what looked like two cords of wood in the smokehouse. She always judged Leroy in her heart, she knew, and that was wrong, according to the Bible and to good sense. Leroy, most of the time, did the best he could and knew how, she figured.

The rooster woke them, and she made sure the children had a full breakfast of biscuits and cooked apples and oats. "Myrtle, you're the momma today. Treat Mary and Arthur good. Pansy and me are the men folk, doing men folk work."

"Can we watch?" Myrtle asked.

"You can watch out the window. It's too cold for you to be outside, and you don't need to be under foot. This is dangerous work. But if we do it right, we'll have something good to eat for supper tonight. I promise. Some meat, not just eggs." Even as she made the promise, she knew she was stepping too far ahead of herself. Kaiser Wilhelm needed to die fast. She needed to summon all her strength to pull him up by the chain, dunk him, and pull him back out. If she could do that, maybe, just maybe, the rest would go smoothly.

Pansy tended the fire between the downturned buckets and under the washtub and frame. Pansy, for all the times she had to be told twice to obey and do her chores, did herself proud; she kept the fire stoked and high with pieces of log brought from the smokehouse. The water warmed and warmed; no killing until the heat was right, and with ice-cold pump water, it would take a while. When Cotella couldn't bear to touch the water but it was short of boiling, she knew it was time.

"Pansy, you can stop with the stoking for a bit. Go get the pig out of the pen and bring him over here, with a handful of corn to tempt him."

Pansy brought him through the yard. The pig seemed more enthusiastic than he had a right to be. Cotella raised the sledgehammer. "See that circle in the dirt? Put that corn in there, and step right back, about ten feet." In a few seconds, the Kaiser lay on his belly, not just stunned but fully dead. Cotella didn't look at Pansy but winced herself at the short thought of killing a living being that had been free and happy a month before. "Help me!" Cotella said, turned him on his side, and in a swift move, slit the skin under the pig's head. She made another for good measure. Streams of blood landed on her face and neck and chest. While the blood poured onto the frozen dirt, she quickly thought there would be no pudding. She grabbed the hook and pulled it down to the ground, impaled the roof of the pig's mouth and pushed the hook into its brain.

"Now, Pansy, this is the hard part. We gotta get him in that water now. I'll pull on the chain and you guide him the best you can." Pansy did make a face and could barely keep her eyes open, but Cotella grimaced too, with the strain of all her weight on the chain. She'd donned Leroy's work gloves, but between the cold and the pressure, they burned with pain.

Somehow, they did it. The animal bobbed in the water. "Now, take this knife," said Cotella. "The best you can, scrape the hair off his skin. I know it's hard. I'll do the most, but if you can do any, it will help. Just scrape into the water, not up towards yourself. Keep your hands free, or you might cut yourself, and that can't be."

Pansy did the best she could, but the sight of blood and the skin of the pig got too much for her after a minute or so. She turned and vomited most of her breakfast. Cotella couldn't blame her and regretted that a ten-year-old girl had to help her with this bloody chore. "You go sit down on the porch step for a bit. I'll get this done. If you can throw on some wood, that will help."

Cotella felt the bile and acids in her throat too at the sight of the blood still oozing into the water and the smell of Pansy's vomit, but she kept her eyes on the skin she scraped. It was a good thing the smaller pig had come home with the girls, even if it didn't yield as much. This one was getting the best of her. The scraping took longer than she remembered because she was doing it alone. The skin below it was white, with a faint pinkness. She finished the back legs, and then the belly, then the front legs and part of the back. She didn't sing or talk but put all her force into it.

"Pansy, honey, all right, come here. We got to pull him out now. When he's up, we're going to turn over the water tub, that way, away from the house, and we'll let the fire burn out. While he's hanging, I'll do some cutting, and you don't have to watch that. But then I'll need you to help get him on the platform for the real cuttin' and butcherin'. Here, use this old jacket of your daddy's. The wash tub will be too hot for you to touch."

Pansy followed her directions and lead. Soon, the former Wilhelm lay on the platform, his head removed with two hard chops of an axe and his tail and each of his feet with one, all but a few tufts of hair scraped into the hot water that now flooded the yard, his skin exposed, his belly divided, and only a little blood still pooling.

"I need a rest," she said, falling onto the ground. Pansy followed suit. The child was soaked, bloodstained, and dirty. "You'll get a good soak tonight yourself, girl," Cotella said, smiling.

"I don't know if I want to eat any of that butchered pig meat, now," said Pansy. "It made me sick."

"You'll get over it, when it's cooked. Raw meat can do that to people. Especially pig meat." Cotella wanted nothing more but a big cup of coffee. How she missed it. But no call for thinking on that. "Whewee!" she stood up. "Go on in the house and check on your kin. Then bring me all the kettles and pans I sat out on the porch. We've got to get this fella cut into pieces, with the big knives and the saw, into the barrels and salted down today and tomorrow, but I'll save out some good chop meat and ribs for us."

The worst part was done, but not all the work. She'd already seen to the barrels for salting the meat for most of the winter and curing some of it in the smokehouse. She breathed thanks to Tom and Fanny, now both in glory, for teaching her butchering and insisting she help. Her mouth watered with the hope of a pork chop for dinner.

Chapter Twenty-Six

Snow fell two days after Kaiser Wilhelm gave his life, without his say in the matter, for their table. At first the snow was just ankle deep, and paused for a day, but then returned. Cotella dug paths through the snow to the smokehouse and the barn and the privy. She kept the fireplace going. The ribs and chops held out for a while, but most of the meat was preserving in the barrels, immersed in and rubbed with salt, sitting out in the smokehouse. Flour was failing them, and she wanted to make a cake for Christmas. Eggs held up. And still no sign of people beyond this holler. Survival and the children's needs took all her strength. Loneliness for a grown-up to talk to was settling around her heart.

At night she read to them, or had them read, from the Bible. By then she was usually so tired it was hard not to nod off. She had never known tired like this before, not in nursing school, not with all her mommas, not back on the farm with Fanny and Tom. She was doing everything she could for the children, but they needed more than cooking and cleaning. The children needed love. She held Arthur when he tired of running around. She let Mary sit on her lap when she wished, and she touched Myrtle's face gently at times. Only Pansy seemed to shudder at her touch. It wasn't the first time Cotella had felt that tremor from others when she came close.

Cotella had not encouraged them to talk about their momma and daddy. She knew that was wrong, but she didn't know what else to do. Not now. Not with more than a foot of snow surrounding them and no news, no visitors. She just didn't have the words to console them. She recognized, guiltily, that at least Pansy and Myrtle needed to talk and remember, and she heard them whispering at times, keeping secrets. She feared they would fall into a vale of tears at the mention of their parents and never come out of it, so Cotella tried not to give them a reason.

***

Around the fire one night, Myrtle said, "You didn't finish your story."

"What story?"

"The one about being in Bristol, in the city, going to that hospital school."

Cotella paused before answering. She swallowed, holding back tears. "Oh, that's right. I had to leave."

"Why?"

"I got sick. I started having—I mean, I couldn't go to school any more. I couldn't learn to be a nurse."

"Why?"

"My teachers and the doctors said me being sick would get in the way of being a nurse."

"Oh."

No questions. It was a disappointing end to Cotella's adventure story.

"So what did you do?" asked Pansy.

"I came home, and lived with the people who raised me after my—well, the people who raised me from thirteen, Mr. and Mrs. Elkins."

"Why didn't you get married?" said Mary.

"Mary! Hush!" said Pansy to her little sister.

"Don't all grown ladies get married?"

"She don't have no husband, Mary. She wouldn't be here with us if she had a husband."

"No, Mary, some ladies don't get a husband. In fact, a lot don't. They are called old maids."

"Are they all old?"

"No. But even if they are twenty, or twenty-five, and don't have a husband, they are called old maids."

"Why?"

Cotella shrugged. "I think to be mean. Some ladies can't find husbands, and some ladies don't want husbands."

"Did you want a husband?"

"Mary! You are bein' nosy. That's Mizz Telly's business."

"Momma has a husband. Daddy."

They fell quiet. Pansy hid her face but not her sobs, and seeing her sister cry brought tears to Myrtle. Cotella couldn't help it. She wept, not so much for Minnie and Leroy, because that was beyond her understanding. She wept for the four young-uns, left orphaned as she was and with even less chance of someone to save them from it. She had been lucky, or blessed, or whatever word fit. Tom and Fanny had rescued her that night, a lost child with the stench of house fire on her. These children had only her, an outcast from how people lived normal-like, trying to keep them fed and safe with no man, no money, and no way to change that.

Mary frowned, unsure what was happening. "Why are you all crying? Momma and Daddy are gonna come back soon."

Pansy wailed at this, and Myrtle looked horrified. "Mary, what are you saying, child?" Cotella said. "We talked about this. We had a funeral for your momma. Your momma and daddy, they died. They are in heaven with Jesus. Why do you think they are comin' back?"

Mary turned red, and started to weep herself, not from grief but from the humiliation and the example of her sisters and Miss Telly. "They went to see Jesus, but he'll send them back. Won't he? Why won't he let them come back? I've been waiting and I prayed for it, when we stood under the tree and Myrtle read the Bible and I sang for Momma."

Cotella shifted Arthur off her lap and pulled Mary to her. She smoothed Mary's corn silk hair. "Mary, that is real good that you prayed. But your momma won't come back. Daddy neither. I'm sorry. I'm sorry you didn't understand that."

Mary trembled and rested her head on Cotella's shoulders. Why didn't I see that she didn't understand? She never asked questions. She must have thought they were away on a trip, since Leroy traveled to find work most of her short life anyway. She never saw her momma's corpse, like she would have at a regular funeral. Something that was said must have confused Mary. Pansy and Myrtle tended to push her out of their play and ignore her. How lonely she must be. And now, how much sadder she'll be with no hope for what she prayed for and believed true.

Soon, Mary's body went limp and Cotella could feel the child's rhythmic but shallow breath. "Let's get to bed, girls. Look, Arthur's just laid down and gone asleep of himself on the rug. Poor child. How is that boy going to put up with you three silly sisters?"

Pansy and Myrtle found no humor in her words, but obeyed. She carried Mary to their room, where they all slept in one big bed, removed her little dress and slipped a nightgown over her. As she closed the door, she heard Pansy and Myrtle whispering, breathily, as if making secret plans.

After changing Arthur's diaper and laying him in his cradle, which she had since placed in the room where she slept to give the girls some space, she sat by the fire. Right now she wanted several gulps of Leroy's moonshine. She knew where it was and only needed to retrieve it from its hiding place. She was so unused to liquor that a few sips of that strong whiskey would make her forget, or at least think of something else than the snow, the children, the cold, the exhaustion, the dwindling food, and her grief.

Mary's questions about her being married were innocent enough. It meant that Mary, with her child's eyes, didn't look at Cotella's face and see knots upon larger knots so much that her original features were almost impossible to discern. Cotella herself, when she rarely looked in a mirror, had to peer deeply to see the face beneath. She had one photo of herself from before nursing school. Fanny had taken her to Clintwood when she was sixteen and paid a man with a camera to point it at her. Cotella sat still in her best dress and tried to look somewhat appealing to a man, or her idea of it. "You can give it to your sweetheart when he comes along," said Fanny, who liked the idea of courting, wooing, and romance.

That girl in the photo, which she kept in a cover in her valise or coat pocket and never let anyone see, was plain, unsmiling, with high cheekbones, like someone part Indian. She wore her long dark hair coiled in a braid behind her head. She'd seen plainer woman married to a good man, so maybe a boy would have come along, eventually.

If. If she hadn't gone to Bristol and said, "I want more than what the women around here have." Or really, if her body had not betrayed her. Most unmarried men, except good old Harley Vanover, turned away. Not out of meanness, she knew, but out of shock or confusion. Many of the married men, her mommas' husbands, had come to accept her. Some, like Harlan Rose, seemed to respect her like they would respect a man making his own living.

Respect felt good. Love would have been better, maybe, but at least respect noticed her. She got neither from Farley Stamper in 1911, even though she did get a marriage proposal, of sorts.

Chapter Twenty-Seven

June 1911

When Fanny moved to St. Paul, Virginia, with her sister and sold the farm to the coal company, Cotella had no home. Fanny's generous "legacy" to her of one hundred dollars was designed to take care of Cotella until she would find permanent work or marry, and Cotella had no hopes for the latter. Over the years, Cotella had spent most of the dollar bills in those months when she was without a momma to take care of and had to pay for her room at Lulu's. It went to buy her meager sets of clothes and hardy shoes, which she had to replace every two years with all the walking between mommas.

Cotella began her lying-in work at two months shy of her twentieth birthday, or what she knew as that. Because she had no home, she carried her clothing in her valise or on her back in a flour sack she had fashioned for that purpose, with straps attached to carry on her back. She kept five dresses—two for summer, two for winter, and one for church or parties, if those came her way. She carried some pairs of panties and stockings, two petticoats, two pairs of shoes, and her heavy jacket she usually wore except in summer. In the jacket she had sown hidden pockets for the photograph from her girlhood, her bills and coins, and her certificate of completion from eighth grade to prove to people who she was, if they asked or doubted.

She carried some writing paper, a pencil for writing, some soap, and her toothbrush. Some people in the mountains thought the toothbrush was foolishness, but the nurses at Watkins Hospital preached its use as part of overall hygiene. If she had brought anything from Bristol with her to these mountains, it was those early lectures on hygiene. She was known to insist on more cleanliness than most of her mommas saw fit.

It was not an easy life, but no one's life in the mountains was. Almost everybody, at least those she knew, was scratch poor, some a little better, a few, a very few, able to say they had more than enough. She had no home, few belongings, no children, no man, no horse. She had her two feet and two hands, as blemished and knobby as they were, and she had a little bit of what few women had: freedom to move on to something else.

She had been traveling from homestead to homestead, farm to farm, cabin to cabin, for five years when she received a letter from a new momma. Her name was Thelma Stamper, and she lived a mile outside of Clintwood to the north. That was farther than she usually traveled, but Mrs. Stamper said she would send a wagon for her wherever she was. In two weeks, Mrs. Stamper was to have her eleventh child. Her own momma had recently died, and her sister was unable to come help.

She asked around if anybody knew the Stampers. She received some uncomfortable, evasive looks and comments like, "Yes, I done heard the name one or twice." People didn't seem to want to talk about them. But, Cotella figured, beggars couldn't be too choosy, and in a way, she was a beggar for work. She wrote back, agreeing to come, and directing when and where for the wagon to come fetch her.

When she arrived, thankful for a ride for a change, she saw the Stamper's land was large and enviable. For one, it was flat and rolling for the most part. Farley Stamper, Thelma's man, owned fifty acres of farmland, which he used for corn, tobacco, orchards, cattle, and, of course, hogs. When she arrived, Thelma had already taken to her bed, and it was a chore to keep track of ten young-uns, the oldest being fourteen and the youngest, eighteen months. The woman spent all her time carrying a baby, thought Cotella.

Fortunately, Farley Stamper kept them in food and shoes and with a roof over their heads. There was enough money for the children to go to school, so the older boys weren't working the farm yet. Farley Stamper had several farmhands for that. The house even had three bedrooms, along with the kitchen and sitting room. The four girls slept in one room and the six boys in another. Cotella slept with the girls, as usual.

From birthing all those young-uns, Thelma knew what to expect, but this time, she said, was different. She was bleeding already, with some time to go. Every day her clothes and sheets were soaked. That alarmed Cotella. "You stay in the bed, Miss Thelma," she said. When the labor pains started a few days later, and still too early, Cotella sent the oldest child, Farley, Jr., to collect Granny Foster, the midwife in those parts. The midwife examined her and insisted a doctor was needed, and Farley, Jr., drove to Clintwood to fetch him.

By the time Doc Franklin came, Thelma was dead and the baby, a little girl, stillborn. She had hemorrhaged, he said, probably from having too many babies one after another. Cotella grieved for the woman whom she'd only just met. She had a decent home and filled it with children, but she'd left it too early.

Mr. Stamper, though, was nowhere to be found. The children didn't know where he was. "Pa goes off for a week or two," Farley, Jr., shrugged. "Kind of regular."

"Is he working?"

"I reckon. He don't say much about it, but he brings the little ones candy. He says he's gonna bring me home a gun soon. It's about time. Most boys have one by twelve. They make fun of me at school for not havin' a gun yet."

Cotella saw only one possibility—he was a moonshiner or doing something else he wanted to hide from his children. Maybe he was good at 'shine, prosperous from selling it over a broad area. Maybe Farley Stamper had the Sheriff in his pocket, and that was why they could live so well.

Still, someone had to get word to him that his wife and baby had died and needed a burial, so the doctor sent word to the Sheriff. Two days after Thelma's death, Farley Stamper showed up. Not drunk, not disheveled, not looking like he had slept out in the wild. In fact, he was not a bad-looking man. Tall, with light hair and green eyes. He came home wearing clothes that looked like a woman had cared for them. He was not what Cotella expected.

He showed up with the undertaker in tow, which meant Thelma would be embalmed and have a real casket and be buried proper. Farley Stamper immediately took charge, handed out sugar sticks to the younger children, and introduced himself to Cotella. After a pause to take in her marred and shocking face, he spoke to her in an even and friendly voice and shook her hand.

"Miss Barlow," he began.

"Nobody calls me that, Mr. Stamper. I'm Cotella. My mommas and their children call me 'Telly,' most of the time."

"Oh—your mommas and—oh yes, you take care of women when they are lying in. And my wife hired you. Things as they are, I hope you will stay until we, uh, can bury my wife and hire someone for the children. I know of a colored woman who does that kind of work."

"Yes, Mr. Stamper, sir, I can stay. I don't have another momma to take care of right now."

"I'm glad to hear it. I can see you've been working. It's been hard on Thelma. She was a good momma to these children." He swung his arm around slowly in their direction as if he was showing them off.

"Yes, sir." He left to talk to the undertaker, and she returned to her work. The bedroom where Thelma and the baby lay for two days waiting for the undertaker, had to be opened, aired, and cleaned. Laundry needed done and young-uns fed. And this man pondered about.

He was the strangest man she'd ever met. His hands, though calloused, looked and felt nothing like the scarred and leather-tough hands of other men. He talked like the men she knew, but then again, he didn't. More proper, like a preacher. He was dressed proper, too, not like a farmer. Well, he had hired hands to do all that, which she knew all too well because she had to cook for them. He didn't make a face when he talked to her. But he didn't seem a bit flustered or sad or anything about his wife's passing. "She was a good momma to these children," he'd said, as if they weren't his and he was talking about another man's wife. And the children definitely were his; the boys especially had his hair, eyes, and tallness. He also didn't seem sorry or embarrassed he was two days late, and he sure didn't seem to be grieving.

Yes, he was strange. And she hoped he came back and talked to her some more.

Chapter Twenty-Eight

Thelma Stamper was buried the next day in a Baptist church graveyard outside of Clintwood. A crowd of people came to the funeral, but of course, ten of them were the children. She held the youngest, Russell, and she kept three-year-old Hazel and four-year-old Una by her side. At least, she thought those were the names; she was still learning.

She stayed for a month, her usual time. She heard that a momma she'd helped two years before needed her again soon. She needed to settle matters with Mr. Stamper. He had remained at home the whole time, but always occupied with his farm and some other business she didn't understand. If he was a moonshiner, he was the cleverest one she'd ever heard of. At dinner, she asked if they could talk once the children were in bed.

"I've been here a month, Mr. Stamper," she started. "I usually stay with my families for six weeks, unless there's some other reason. Like if a momma has twins, now that's a sight. So I need to be moving on. Are you going to hire that colored woman you talked about?"

"Has it been a month already?" he said, as if he wasn't really hearing her words.

"Yes, sir. Your wife died on the twentieth of June. It's now July 22."

"I been real preoccupied," he said. "What if I paid you twice what you are making now?"

She didn't expect this. It tempted her, except that she was working three times as hard as she usually did, chasing ten children, feeding those farm hands, and cleaning a bigger house.

"That makes me think about it, some, but it's not what I usually do. I'm not like a hired woman or housekeeper. I don't stay somewhere permanent."

"What if I gave you your own room, so you could be away from the girls at night?"

"I don't see how that's possible."

"You would sleep in my wife's room."

She was shocked. "Mr. Stamper, isn't that your room? I can't do that." What in the world was he asking her?

"Pardon me, I didn't mean to be scandalous."

"Mr. Stamper, I don't think it would be proper, me staying here for a long time, and sleeping in your—your wife's room. Do you have some kin that could help?"

"Not that I trust," he said bluntly. "Let me think about this. Can you stay another week? I'll make some plans and decisions. You don't have to leave yet, do you? And I will pay you double."

"Yes, sir, I can do that. But for now, I'll stay with the girls. I sleep hard, so they don't bother me."

She decided she needed to solve some mysteries about Mr. Stamper. She would start to gossip with the farmhands. She had to cook big meals for them, so they might as well return the favor.

The next day they arrived for dinner at noon, all five of them. They seated themselves around the table outside the kitchen door. They ate in the yard, on stools and benches rather than proper chairs, during the hot weather. After she loaded the table with slabs of ham, cornbread, and white beans, she watched them eat.

"I won't be around much longer," she said. "I'll be moving on to my next job. So eat up."

"That's too bad, your cookin' is pretty good," said one of them. "Better than Mizz Stamper's." Like the ten children, she couldn't keep all their names straight. Anyway, it seemed sinful to talk of the dead that way, her not in the ground but a month or so.

"Hey, could you tell me what's wrong with you, I mean, your skin?"

These hands' mommas hadn't taught them manners. "It's got a long name you can't pronounce. It's not my skin; it's my nervous system. And you shouldn't ask sassy, rude questions of a woman who's plenty older than you, who you barely know and who ain't your kin."

"Oh." That silenced him.

"Sorry, Miss Telly, he don't have no sense," said one of his companions.

"Humph."

"Mr. Stamper's a pretty good boss. He stays out of our business. We stay outa his."

"And what exactly is his business?" Cotella said.

"Oh, Mr. Stamper, he does a little bitta this, a lotta bit of that, and a *whole* lot of something else." He nudged the hand that sat beside him, and they enjoyed a hearty laugh.

"What you mean?"

"Oh, we's just joshin'. Mr. Stamper, he's good with a dollar. He knows people. He's friends with the Sheriff, and with bankers in three counties. He does okay. But his daddy, now there was the smart man.

He bought up a lot of land in these parts, acres and acres, back thirty years ago, from poor farmers who couldn't make a living and moved their families to Louisville and Cincinnati. Now Mr. Stamper's gonna sell it to the coal and lumber companies. But we're not supposed to know that."

Cotella didn't know what to think of this. Making money was a good thing, she figured, if you could, but sometimes she wondered about this selling out to the coal companies, the railroads, or the lumbermen. She just wondered. Maybe it helped bring in better things from the outside world. Maybe it just pushed good people off their land.

"Tell me the truth. Is he a moonshiner?"

The fourth one laughed. "What made you think such a thing as that?"

"I don't know." She shrugged. "There's always money in liquor."

"If he is, he's smart enough to give the Sheriff his cut and keep it quiet," said the fourth one; she thought his name was Jefferson. That was an awful fancy name for a hired hand. He said it in a way that the "if" didn't belong in the sentence.

"Well, he sure has a passel of young-uns," she said. "They're pretty good ones, but I don't know how he's going to raise 'em with no momma."

"Yeah, he sure does have a passel." Jefferson seemed to be making fun of her. "All kinds of 'em, too." That set the five of them to laughing again.

"What foolishness," she said, and walked back into the kitchen. She watched them through the window as they kept laughing about something, probably saying things they wouldn't want their mommas to hear. They seemed to be making fun of her for something they thought she didn't understand. So what was it she still didn't know about Farley Stamper?

Chapter Twenty-Nine

A week after she told Mr. Stamper she would like to move on, he asked her to take a walk with him around the farm at 4:00. This was nonsense; she had ten children to chase and her feet hurt already after a day of cooking and laundry, which seemed to be the most of what she did. This family needed one of those big laundry machines like the hospital had, and she'd heard stories that some women in cities had smaller ones in their homes. Those required electricity and running water, two things even Farley Stamper didn't have out here so far from a city.

"Miss Telly, I'm taking you on this walk to see the farm and ask a favor, sort of."

"You got a real fine place, Mr. Stamper. It's kept up nice. It's big. The hands say you get a lot of crops and your livestock does well at market."

"I can't act like I built this all myself. My father came here from upstate New York in 1880 or so. He had money from his family. They owned a big, successful glove factory. He bought up a lot of land in this part of the county. He died young, and I was his only son. Now land is wanted for other things than farmin'. But I guess you know that."

"Yes, sir. I guess one of these days these mountains will start changing, will have paved roads and automobiles and more railroads. Electricity would be nice."

"Yes, it would. That might not happen while we're living."

She hoped he was wrong about that, especially about the electricity.

"Mr. Stamper, sir, I appreciate you talking to me, but I got a heap of work to do. Can you tell me why we're takin' this walk?"

"Miss Telly, I thought a lot about the children, and what you said, and all that. It would not be proper for you to be living in my house and caring for my children permanent-like. People would talk, and it would matter to Thelma what people were saying about her children's and her home. I know you would care, too. So, the best solution I can think of is, will you marry me?"

She laughed at him. It was the craziest thing she'd ever heard. He must be out of his head with missing his wife, she thought. "He must," she thought, "think I'm as crazy as he is."

"Mr. Stamper, I don't think you should make fun of me. That's not right. I thought you were a better man than that."

"Oh, I'm serious, Miss Telly. Wouldn't that make it easier for you to stay?" She stared at him; the laughter gone. Her legs trembled, but she wasn't sure why.

"Sometimes when girls get proposed, there's love in the middle of it somewhere."

"That's true. But some things are better than love, like a solid roof over your head." He looked her up and down. "And some new clothes and not having to travel home to home for the rest of your life."

And not slaving away all day with another woman's ten children, she thought. What did she expect? Well, not this proposal, but she didn't expect that from any man, ever.

"You surprise me, Mr. Stamper. That's all I can say. If you're serious—"

"I am, of course."

"I would have to think about it. Can you give me a few days? I don't have to be at my next momma's house for two weeks, so I can stay and work, too."

"Yes, a few days." But he said it like his mind was far away. "Can you find your way back to the house? I'm going to ride into town this evening to discuss a land deal, and I'll be back the day after tomorrow, maybe."

"Yes, sir."

"Goodbye, Miss Telly," he said, and left abruptly. Yes, a strange, odd man.

***

In the first hours after his proposal, such as it was, she didn't have time to consider it. Not until she lay in bed, exhausted, feet throbbing from not having sat down for hours, even eating standing up. Then she rolled it over in her mind. It was foolishness, she concluded. He didn't love her. She didn't respect him, well, she didn't know enough about him to respect him. For all his properness, at least compared to all the men around her, he seemed to be unreal, like a person in a story.

Yet, he did have some money to spare. She would have a house of her own. The children would grow up and she could train them not to wear her out so bad. The older ones would leave and the numbers would dwindle over the years. Not that there would be more young-uns. She was pretty sure, especially considering he didn't even reach out to shake her hand when he left, that he wasn't thinking of her that way. What man would? And Lord knew he had enough mouths already to feed. It was a business proposition to him, a way to deal with his problems.

And what if he decided he did want to marry again, for love? What would happen? No, it was nonsense, tomfoolery. Marriage was supposed to be more than an agreement to take care of orphaned young-uns in exchange for a decent life, free from daily want.

And yet.

And yet. Something . . .

She decided that the hired hands, in all their joking, were holding something back about her employer who offered her his name, if just for practical purposes.

She also decided to bake them a pie to get on their good side. She'd even whip some cream—usually too much work in this heat—for it. The children had picked blackberries, managing not to get snake-bit but also getting blood from the stickers and berry juice all over their clothes. All those children picking meant there were plenty of berries to spare.

"I got somethin' special for you all." She presented them with the pie, cut five pieces, and dropped a hefty spoonful of cream on each of them. "Eat up. This is some sweet, juicy berry pie."

"Oh, thank you, Miss Telly!" they said in tandem, finishing their pieces in a few hurried bites.

"Oh, boy. That's a real pie," said Jefferson, and the others chimed in.

"Why you being so nice to us today?" one of them said, with a sly smile.

"I need some answers. Mr. Stamper, he, uh, wants me to stay around longer, for more, well, money. I just want to know more about what kind of man he is. I like my job of taking care of mommas who have a new baby and need help. Most of 'em don't have this many young-uns."

"We already told you, he's a good boss."

"Sure. But he left last night. Where did he go?" she said.

They looked at each other. "How would we know?" one of them said.

"'Cause you all were laughin' and jokin' and it made me think you were holding back a secret."

They looked at their empty plates, any sign of pie completely gone, devoured, even the juice and cream licked clean.

"Mr. Stamper, he has him, uh, a lot of things to take care of," said the oldest, a curly-haired boy called Rodney.

"Yeah, that's it," the one named Jefferson added.

"Um humph. Where?"

"Like we said, he's a busy man, makin' money. Doin' deals," Russell insisted.

"Where?"

"Around. Clintwood. Pound, even Abingdon, I'll bet."

"You 'bet'?"

"Dern it, Miss Telly, we can't tell you."

"But how do you know this big secret you can't tell me?"

They all returned to their silence. One of them stood up, the one they called Lucky. "We gotta get back in the fields." And they left.

Now she was suspicious. Now she knew her answer for Mr. Farley Stamper, even if she didn't know why.

***

A letter came that day from the next momma she was supposed to help. The baby might come sooner than she expected. She needed to send a reply. Farley Stamper returned, riding into the yard on his strong, shiny black horse. He looked like something out of a picture book. Yes, that was him; somebody out of a book, not a war hero, but a dashing lover in a story. All he needed was a sword at his side and a broad hat with a feather.

After supper he approached her. "Have you thought about it?"

"I'll give you my answer after you give me one. Where did you go the last two nights?"

"To do some business, uh, in Pound."

"Pound? What kind?"

"That's not your affair, Miss Telly."

"If I'm going to marry you, it is. I should know where my husband sneaks off to."

"I didn't sneak away. I told you I was going."

"You haven't given me an answer. Are you a moonshiner?"

"Not in the sense you think of it. That's not what kind of business I was doing."

"I don't want to be married to a man who might get in trouble with the law."

"That won't happen. I see to that."

"Oh? Then where were you?"

He looked at her straight on. She almost faltered. Here was a man, a man with land, a man with hired hands and a good house, who wasn't afraid to look at her, who didn't turn away. This was a man that, for his strangeness, she could love in an equally strange way.

"Very well. If you must know, I was visiting Rebecca."

"Rebecca? Who is that?"

"The mother of my other children."

She took a step back, because it felt as if he had slapped her with all his force, like a direct punch. She couldn't speak.

"So, I answered your question. Will you get married to me or not?"

She turned and ran. She slammed the door behind her and ran out into the apple orchard and fell to the ground. She didn't cry, she just breathed hard, numb.

Soon she knew what to do. The sun set and fireflies sparked as she made her plan.

She threw herself into the work left to do. She would be leaving as soon as possible. Without a word. Without the extra pay he owed her. She got the children to bed, packed her valise, and left before sunrise. He could get that colored woman he mentioned to take care of these children. He could get his mistress, this Rebecca, this harlot, to run his house. His real wife was gone, buried—why not marry Rebecca, and make her an honest woman?

What he didn't tell her she learned later when she mentioned, off-handedly to folks, that she had worked for Thelma Stamper when she died. "Oh, her husband was that man with the colored family and the white family," she heard from more than one gossipy woman. Beyond that, she didn't ask questions.

In Virginia, of course, he couldn't have a colored wife. Cotella didn't believe a colored and a white could marry anywhere. Maybe in time he brought Rebecca into his home as a servant for no other reason than to keep sanity with all those young-uns. Maybe he hired that colored woman he talked about; maybe that woman was Rebecca after all. Maybe some kinfolk came. She didn't know, and didn't care, not about anything that concerned or inconvenienced Farley Stamper. She mourned for those children losing their momma, but Thelma Stamper knew. She knew she was second to her husband, despite birthing babies until she went to an early grave. She had to know, and maybe the hemorrhage was what killed her but she died of a broken, humiliated heart.

Cotella never told a soul about her one marriage proposal. No grown-up would ever ask; who would want to marry, and lie with, such an ugly woman? But children, really young ones, and Mary wasn't the first, sometimes asked, because they saw her kindness and hard work first, not her face and hands. They loved her and didn't see the ravages and disfigurements of her skin.

Chapter Thirty

December 24, 1918

The calendar told her it was Christmas Eve. Cotella was in a befuddlement.

Of course, the children knew. Pansy and Myrtle could read a calendar well enough. And they were grown enough to know this year there would be no gifts, not that they ever got many anyway. A new pair of shoes was a coveted gift for mountain children. Parents scrimped on some other necessity to buy a bag of juicy oranges from down south and a bag of hard candy. The Sears Roebuck catalog Bailey kept in his store made it all possible, that and the U.S mail service.

Bailey's Store was probably still closed. She couldn't reach it anyway in the piled, crusted snow on the uncleared roads. She hadn't seen the postman in months, which might mean there was no mail for them or that the service had been stopped. Maybe the postman had died. If there were people living and trading, coming and going in Dickenson County and beyond, she knew nothing of it.

Food was low. She was down to what looked like five good double handfuls of flour, less cornmeal, and a pound of sugar. The potatoes had sunk to the bottom of the barrel, there were some dried beans and a shelf-full of Mason jars with string beans, sweet corn, and squash. Salt meat, milk, and eggs were becoming their staples: not bad eating, and healthy for children, but monotonous. She did not worry about tomorrow's meals. It was thoughts of January and beyond, if no one came to their door soon, that made her anxious.

Yet, it was Christmas, and these young-uns had been through enough. There would be no presents, no momma and daddy to give them, no visiting neighbors, no church service. But they could have one good meal before they had to cut their meals to two a day and live on what the Kaiser, the cow, and the chickens provided.

One of the chickens had stopped laying. She had other plans for that hen. A quick wrench of the neck and a flurry of feathers, and she would be a good roast with sweet potatoes and some onions pulled before the frost and set up to dry. No biscuits or cornbread this time; the flour and sugar would be sacrificed for a cake with the last of the apples, flavored with cinnamon. Canned string beans, hard-boiled eggs, buttermilk. It would be a kind of feast for Christmas, the best she could do for these girls and their sweet little brother.

But she had an idea.

She'd heard some people in cities went out into the woods and cut down a small tree and brought it into the house. Folks wrapped pretty cut paper or popped corn on a string around the tree. The nurses had put up a small one in the lobby of the hospital, and she'd seen pictures in a magazine. One of those trees had electric lights and colored metal balls and looked like a full-grown fir in the rich person's parlor. Maybe, just maybe, they could do that, or pretend some way, even though there were no gaily wrapped presents to place under it, like the photos showed.

"Myrtle, I want you to put on your warmest clothes and your momma's boots—we'll put some rags in so they fit—and walk around the farm. See if you can find a tree about as tall as me, not much bigger. Not a tree that would have leaves that fall off in winter. Like a pine tree."

"Why?"

"Never you mind. You'll see."

Myrtle dressed and left to wander the property. She came back in an hour. "I think I found one. It's covered with snow."

"That's good. You're going to show it to me. I have to go to the barn first." They met outside, Cotella carrying a hand saw.

"Do we need wood? Why you got that saw?"

"No, we're gonna do what city folks do, or gonna try."

Myrtle shrugged and led the way to a slope of deep snow. A pine sapling poked three feet out of the encrusted white. "Yes, I think that will work. Help me scrape this snow away from around the roots."

Soon they pulled the small cut pine through the snow. Cotella stamped and shook it on the porch to clear the snow. Satisfied that it would not drip all through the house, she opened the door.

"What! You gonna bring a tree in the house?" Myrtle's voice went to a screech. She'd never seen such a thing.

Pansy stood to the side; her arms crossed. "How you gonna make it stand up?"

Cotella hadn't thought that one through. "I don't know." She studied the situation. "What do you all think?"

Myrtle became the expert on Christmas trees. "We can put it in one of those old buckets, just not the ones we use for milk or food."

"But it won't stand up, silly. It'll fall over," countered Pansy.

"Don't call your sister names, Pansy."

"We can put something around it to make it stand up. Rocks, or dirt or... "

"Where you gonna get rocks when everything is covered up with snow?" Pansy said, competing to be the Christmas tree expert. "Use pieces of wood that go in the kitchen stove. Put them standing up,"

That worked, after some wiggling and pulling and turning. A real pine tree, still glistening with drops of water and fresh with that forest smell, stood in the house now by the fireplace.

Pansy's resistance melted, and she got into the spirit. "What do we put on it? Ribbons? I know where there are some." She scurried to their room.

"I have some writing paper, pretty colors. We can cut them into shapes of things and hang them with strings," said Cotella, before she realized it. That was her special paper, for letters to those who mattered the most to her. There would be very little of it left if she let the girls use it, just like there would be a few ounces of flour if she baked a spice cake with the apples.

"Oh, we can make little stars and angels and animal shapes, like in the Bible," said Myrtle.

"I think people make popped corn and put thread through them for a tree," said Cotella, "some popped corn sounds like a treat." After that, the girls busied themselves with their Christmas present from the hills. Cotella found dried corn to heat in a pot until it exploded, and she baked the best cake she ever remembered.

Chapter Thirty-One

Christmas Day dawned, clear, with a pristine sky. The sun, big and golden, rose in the sky and warmed the snow, melting it and letting tips of dead grass appear. Chores never took a rest; collecting eggs, milking the cow, stoking the fires. Dinner was the feast she'd hoped. The girls filled their bellies and nodded off afterward, hypnotized by their creation, a tree in the house with paper figures, hair ribbons, their mother's lone beaded necklace, and threaded popped corn. Cotella reminded herself to have them read the Bible tonight. Minnie had always been a momma concerned that her children knew about God, and Cotella wanted to honor that.

In the late afternoon, with the girls drowsing and Arthur napping in his cradle, she settled into the rocker herself and stretched her legs before the fireplace. Mary crawled over from her pallet by the tree and pulled herself onto Cotella's lap. "Momma, I'm sleepy."

Cotella wrapped Mary with her arms. She didn't correct her. Minnie was dead for more than two months. Could Mary be forgetting her momma, or was it just the sleep? "I know, Mary honey. It's okay to take a nap. Babies aren't the only ones who need a nap sometime. It's Christmas Day, and that *is* special."

The name "Momma" sounded nice, Cotella thought. But she had stolen it. It wasn't proper for Mary to say it to her. Or Arthur, and he already made those sounds that grownups mistook for words. She sank into sadness. What would become of these young-uns? Did that postmaster find Minnie's sister, Viola? Did he even receive the letter or bother to read it?

She had so many questions, and no one to answer them. She was so tired. Taking care of mommas with new babies was hard work, but no harder than how all the married women with young-uns lived. By now, she would have gone on to the next family, or be living in that boarding house room, alone, waiting for the next momma to write or get word to her some other way. Or she might have caught the enfluinzah and suffered like Minnie. Who would have buried her if she died?

Her sadness fell into a darkness. Mary sighed in her sleep, and something about that sigh, something about Mary's soft hair on her cheek, her light pressure—pulled all the hope from Cotella's soul. She dropped her face into her hand, and for one of the few times she had allowed herself to weep since walking through the Goins' gate. This was a deep, mournful mood, and she really cried, not just leaking tears for a few seconds, shaking them off, and rushing to the next chore.

Then, she heard something outside; it was Master, howling. Fool dog. He never barked, just howled, usually at a coon or possum that intruded his circle of smell. The dog was lazy but did his job when the men wanted to hunt. Leroy

Goins was known by his dog and companion, Master. Maybe Master just missed his owner and felt as blue and lonely as she did, confused and confounded.

His howl subsided. Silence followed, and then—steps on the porch. It couldn't be! The sounds of pounding on the door told her it was true.

"Hello! Hello! Anybody here? We saw smoke from the chimney and the dog and--" came a voice through the door. Cotella settled Mary into her chair and ran to pull open the door. There stood a man and woman. A real man and woman, warmly and nicely dressed, as if they had just walked out of a church service.

"Come in, come in!" she said, pulling the woman by her coat sleeve. "I am here with the Goins' young-uns. We been alone for a long time."

The woman, however, resisted entering and stayed firmly planted outside the door. The man, a head taller and wearing a bowler hat, looked like he wanted to come in from the cold to the warm fire, but his eyes also searched the face of this strange person he did not expect to see at this isolated cabin. The woman beside him craned her head to look around the room. "Is anybody sick here?"

"Oh, no. No. The children are fine, eating up a storm today for Christmas. We have a Christmas tree. Please come in. Can I get you something to eat?"

"We are, um, from Caney Creek Methodist Church. That's the church Mrs. Goins went to, uh, sometimes."

"Are you the preacher and his wife?"

"No, I'm a deacon. Name's Saunders. She's my wife, Kolita. We been looking for people . . . that might need help."

"Oh, thank the Lord, thank the Lord. Oh, believe me, we are well. No sickness here. Not now. There was. We have so much to tell you. Please come in."

Myrtle, Mary, and Pansy had roused from before the fire and stood behind them. "Howdy, Mizz Saunders. I was in a Sunday School class with you when I was littler."

"Hello, child." Mrs. Saunders looked at the children carefully to convince herself there was no sign of illness. She looked at her husband. "I think we can go in."

The couple entered. "Where are these young-uns' momma and daddy?" the deacon asked.

"Um, I wish I could offer you some coffee. It's so cold. Coffee would warm us all up. We just don't have any. I miss it so. Would you like warm milk? Some cake? It's awful good. It does look like the sun is melting some of the snow, though. Is that why you were able to get here, the road is clearing?" Cotella heard herself jabbering in the presence of these adults. She sounded like Mary or Myrtle excited over a new chick.

"We are really fine. No need for food," said Deacon Saunders. "So, what about their parents?"

"Girls, can you go in your rooms while I talk to the deacon and his wife? We have grown-up talkin' to do."

"Our momma is dead," said Pansy. "She got real sick from the flunza. The baby died, too."

"Go on, Pansy, Mary, Myrtle. Look in on Arthur, and change his diaper. Play with him and make sure he is warm."

Myrtle stamped her foot when she turned, Pansy sighed in resignation, and Mary looked disappointed, but they turned toward their bedroom. Cotella watched. She wanted to tell this couple so much. She wanted to pour out her heart to these church people and hope they understood and had an answer. The words tumbled out as fast as her tongue could make them.

"My job is helping new mommas. I come and stay and take care of the young-uns right before the baby comes, and sometimes help the midwife, and then leave when the momma is over her lyin'-in time.

I know, that's an old country expression. It's usually a month to six weeks or so, and then I go on to another home."

"Yes, Miss— "

"Oh, I'm sorry, my name is Cotella Barlow. People call me Telly."

"Yes, Telly. Mrs. Goins told us about you, when you helped her in the past."

"Yes, ma'am, this is the fifth time I been here. I was here last year when Arthur was born. But when I come in October, Minnie was real sick, close to dying, but I didn't know it. I mean, I knew she was real sick, but I didn't know anything, or not much, about this enfluinzah sickness running through people everywhere so fast. She turned dark blue, and I feared she was going to die. I had some nurses training in Bristol a long time ago."

"Minnie Goins is dead?" said Deacon Saunders, beginning to comprehend. Cotella started to wonder if he was hard of hearing, so she spoke more clearly.

"Yes, sir. On October 12, I wrote the day down in their Bible. I kept the children, even Arthur, who is fourteen months now, away from her from the time I got here. They never got even a fever. I am proud of that."

The Saunders looked at each other. "And her husband?" said Mrs. Saunders.

"I ain't never heard from her man, Leroy. He probably brought the sickness into the house and died of it himself when he traveled back to his work crew. That's what the Stanleys, the neighbors, told us, well, told Pansy when I sent her to them so they would fetch the doctor. But they wouldn't help." And they still haven't, Cotella thought.

"We stopped to visit Mrs. Stanley. She lost three of her children."

"Oh, my. I'm so sorry to hear that. How awful for her."

"And you been here all by yourself with the children since then?" said Mrs. Saunders, her face strained with concern.

"Yes, Mizz Saunders. I can't tell you the whole story now. It's long, and it's been hard. I can't tell you. But I'm so happy to see folks. The only folks I've talked to were two in McClure, I mean, I saw 'em when we walked there, and they wouldn't come near us, or help, and Bailey's store was closed."

The Saunders looked at each other. "You walked them young'uns to McClure? In the snow?"

"Oh, no, it was back before that, in November. We did get a ride for part of the way back from a man in a wagon. He wasn't friendly but he helped. Probably carryin' 'shine, but I wasn't about to ask. We was running out of food. We still are. Need flour and meal and sugar, and I sure would like a cup of coffee. We got milk, and chickens and I killed a hog."

"You killed a hog? By yourself?"

"Pansy had to help. It was about the hardest thing I ever did, and he was a small one, oh, no, not like a big old thing, a little fella, but he tastes pretty good and it was sure nice to have some meat after all those weeks of eggs."

The Saunders sat in silence. "We came to, uh, see if there was anybody needing a fruit basket," said Mrs. Saunders finally. She seemed embarrassed. "We got some oranges. And candy for the young-uns."

"They'll like that." Cotella hoped her disappointment wouldn't show, but she really couldn't expect these folks to be carrying sacks of flour and cornmeal in their wagon. They were just out visiting for the church on Christmas.

"We don't have any of those other things you talked about, I mean, not with us. But now that we know you are here, we can bring you some, soon."

"That would be real nice. I don't expect you to give it to me. I got some money."

"It would be out of the church's benevolence, honey," said Mrs. Saunders.

Cotella had already figured that the deacon, probably a kindly man, was pretty gruff and not a talker. But his next words surprised her. "What did you do with their momma? Her body, I mean."

"I buried her. I had to."

"You mean to tell me you have killed a hog, buried a woman, worked these farm animals, and taken care of these four young-uns all by yourself?"

Cotella stiffened her spine. "Yes, sir, I have. And I sure would like to get some help from here on out, 'cause it feels like it's about to wear me out most days."

***

The Saunders left with a promise. The sun was setting, and the snow melting on the roads would soon freeze again. Cotella was sad to see them go. They weren't the best people in the world for talking, but they were grown-ups. They gave her some news from outside the county. The war wasn't all over, but the Germans had made an armistice. That meant they stopped fighting America. A lot of people had died from the sickness, they said. Almost every holler had several dead, and some families had more than one. The young-uns didn't seem to die, though, not very much, but their parents did. That meant lots of orphaned children in the county, and in the whole country.

"Is the enfluinzah over? What I mean to say is, have people stopped getting so sick?" Cotella asked them. No, they said, people were still sick and dying, but it wasn't as bad as it was in October and November. What that meant, she didn't know. All Cotella knew was that someone had found them, and maybe the mail would come soon. Best of all, the Saunders had promised to bring the food they needed.

After they left, Cotella's spirits lightened. She had the children gather round, read them the Christmas story from the big Bible, sang "Away in a Manger" with them, and prayed with thanks for their visitors that Christmas Day. She let them fill up on oranges and candy for dinner. How often would they get to do that? They could say God gave them an extra special Christmas present. She put them to bed and sat by the fire, her mind full of the conversation. She had never thought just talking could be such a gift.

The more she thought about the Saunders and their talk, though, she wondered. Would they tell the Sheriff that she was taking care of the children, orphans, with no right to? She wasn't kin. She didn't have money, not really, not for taking care of children for months and years. She had to make her own living, and these young-uns didn't fit into that.

But would the law come and take them away? Where would they go?

For the first time, that thought panicked Cotella. How could she live without these young-uns? Before, she didn't question that some kinfolk would come and get them. She didn't know how these things worked. She didn't know who was dead or alive now, or the laws about children who lost both parents. If Minnie had not had the presence of mind to mention Viola before dying, what would have happened? She didn't know about Leroy's or Minnie's other kin.

Maybe it was holding Mary and hearing "momma." Maybe it was seeing them truly happy today, smiling at their pretty tree, attentive to the story of a baby, born poorer than they were, announced by angels.

Maybe it was just her own moods, her own loneliness that usually she could forget because there was so much to do. No matter who conceived and birthed the four young-uns, that man and woman were gone now. Pansy, Myrtle, Mary, and Arthur were like her own children now. When the time came, she had to make sure the Sheriff, the law, and everyone else listened to her and believed it.

Chapter Thirty-Two

Cotella expected the Saunders to return within a week, at the most. She had tried to explain what they needed, and she hoped the Deacon and his wife understood how much she wanted a friend, any other woman to talk to. They saw she was there by herself with no man to help or even another woman to share the work with. But New Year's Day came, and she heard no heavy boots on the porch or knock at the door.

The flour, sugar, and almost all the canned goods were gone. Eggs, a few potatoes, and ham remained, and she considered killing another hen that had stopped laying. As January 1 turned into January 10 and then January 20, they ate twice a day, late in the morning and after dark before bed. Thank heaven for the cow. It produced more milk than they needed. She debated with herself constantly about what to feed the children and how much to eat herself.

If a man were living with them, he could go out in the woods and trap or shoot animals. Rabbit, squirrel, even a possum would help put meat on the table. A deer would be the best of game, but even if she could leave the house, tramp through the snow, and manage to kill one, she would have a pile of trouble getting the carcass dressed and home. A deer weighed a lot more than Kaiser Wilhelm, and she didn't have a notion on how to cut one up. She didn't have the right clothes, either, or tools for hunting like that. Master knew the business of hunting, but she didn't know the business of following a dog or getting him to flush prey. Hunting was just not in the upbringing of a girl, even in these mountains. It should be, though, she decided.

If she had to, Cotella sighed, she would get out Leroy's rifle—she'd found it and kept it hidden in the barn—and wander into the woods and try to shoot a small animal. That kind of meat wasn't her favorite, but they couldn't be choosy when the ham ran out. And she'd have to leave the children alone for the time it took to find some animals and work up the nerve to shoot, assuming she could hit one.

But, as the old saying went, necessity was the mother of invention, and Myrtle had an idea. "Can't we trap one? What if we could get a rabbit or squirrel to go in a trap?" She set them to work on it. If nothing else, it would keep them busy.

The children gathered two old crates they found in the barn, sticks, some string, and anything they could possibly use for bait. For a while, they took turns hiding behind a tree ready to pull a string if any animal wandered under the crate. That method had one drawback: sitting in the cold. It also didn't work because the animals could see them and stayed away. They tried to think of a way that the trap would work without them. That took some figuring to get the crate to fall on the animal just right, and fast, when it started to eat the bait.

Eventually, and Cotella didn't believe it would happen, a squirrel made it into the trap and couldn't get out. But it wasn't dead. This led to a discussion of how to kill it, with Mary saying no, let it go back to its momma and daddy or babies, Pansy saying yes, and Myrtle unsure.

Cotella didn't relish the possibility of getting bit breaking its neck, but she protected herself with Leroy's work gloves. They had squirrel stew that night. After that, Cotella hoped in her heart that their trap left the squirrels alone and caught a rabbit.

No matter what, Mary's pet rabbit was not to be touched. It was her last memory of her daddy and secured in its chicken-wire cage in the barn, safe from Master if he got any ideas.

After the Saunders appeared—had it been a dream after all? No, the girls remembered it—her spirits lifted. As days turned into weeks, her dark mood returned. She never liked winter anyway; not just the cold but the short days, the sense of closeness, and the awareness of scarcity and want. She found herself short with the children, imprisoned in the house for all but a few minutes of outside air and walking during the frigid days.

Mary called her "momma" off and on now, when they were alone together. She wanted somebody to call momma, and Cotella, even if she didn't look like that lady who used to be her mother, was there and took care of her. Arthur jabbered. His sisters, with little else to do, talked and played with him more than they usually would. He mimicked their words and sounds and intonations. "He's gonna grow up acting and sounding like a girl," Cotella feared, which made her long for green grass and sun, long summer days and other people, any people. The unfulfilled longings only sent her deeper into sadness.

In December, she thought that the enfluinzah sickness would soon be over. When the Saunders came, she knew it must be. Now, she wondered if they lied, or if, like another blanket of snow, the sickness had returned and done its wicked work again.

After Christmas Day, Cotella set down some new rules, more to relieve her own weariness than to discipline the children. Myrtle had to milk the cow. Pansy would do dishes, mop the floors, and churn the butter. Mary was put in charge of the chickens and eggs. At the same time, she decided that the girls needed some schooling. Not that she fancied herself a school teacher, but she reckoned she knew more than they did about numbers, reading, and spelling.

Figuring out how to teach them was more difficult than knowing what to teach. Pansy and Myrtle could read. There was precious little to read outside the Bible, a few outdated newspapers, and an old copy of a book by Charles Dickens, *Little Dorrit*, Cotella found in a box of Minnie's belongings. Cotella had heard of that author, so he must be a good one, she concluded. The book was thick and contained line drawings of a small but grown girl who sewed and lived in a kind of prison. Every day she told Pansy to read a chapter out loud to Myrtle, and then Myrtle read the chapter back to her, for practice.

Mary wanted to play school like her big sisters. She barely knew her letters and their sounds, so that's where she could start. Pansy and Myrtle needed to study numbers and spelling, too. But a search of the house unearthed only one pad of white writing paper, half gone, and two pencils. A slate board and chalk would be nice. Chalky stones were easy to find in the mountains, but not with snow on the ground now. She considered a bucket of coal from the barn; coal made marks for writing, but on what? The walls of the barn, maybe, and she could send the girls out there for a while to practice their letters and doing sums. They could come in when the cold wore them down.

By late January, writing spelling words and doing sums on barn walls in the cold no longer engaged them. Cotella didn't fuss. How could she? Her own soul felt so heavy. She felt her prickliness and short temper with the children. She felt their discontent as well, in her own bones, in their faces, and in how they dragged their feet when they minded her.

"I'm sick of ham!" Pansy threw her fork down one evening. Breakfast had been ham and eggs. Dinner was ham and a few slices of fried Irish potatoes. The same as the day before, and the day before. "I want an orange!"

"You all ate every one of those oranges back three days after Christmas."

"I don't care. I hate this ham."

"Ham is what we got, Pansy. Be thankful for that."

"Why don't we have no biscuits?" said Myrtle.

"The flour's gone, Myrtle, you know that."

"Momma, I don't want no more ham, neither," said Mary.

"She ain't your momma, Mary! Stop callin' her that! She ain't none of ours momma!"

Mary started to cry at the sharp, loud words from her bigger sister, and Cotella felt her face warm with anger and with hurt for sweet Mary.

"You made your sister cry, Pansy. Comfort her, say you're sorry."

"No! And I don't have to do what you say. You ain't my mother. You just came to take care of us because of the baby that was comin', and then momma died. Her baby died. And we ain't seen daddy, and Mizz Stanley said he died, but we don't know if that's true. Why don't our kin come get us? Or somebody! You ain't our kin. You keep telling us what to do, like you was kin, but you ain't."

Cotella sat motionless, cold at this child's truthful, hateful words. No, she wasn't their kin. She'd done as much or more for them as kin would, as kin had. She could have walked away a long time ago and left them to fend for themselves and die. She knew it was best not to trade mean words with Pansy. It would upset the other girls and make her seem like a child herself. But she was bursting with fear, anger, and hopelessness.

She got up, found her coat, and walked outside. She closed the door quietly, and started walking. She walked out the gate, up the path, to the main road. It was slippery, and dark, so she took it step by step, not big strides. She was not mad, not vengeful. She just needed to walk. As long as it took. As cold as her feet got. She wished she'd had the sense to strap on that old, almost-in-pieces pair of work boots Leroy left. Or wrap her head with a scarf, or put on another pair of socks.

Yes, she was cold, but the night air, the jewels in the deep blue-black sky, the moonlessness, swept her up and she laid in the arms of her feelings, all of them. She'd felt rejected, an outsider to most people, since she was 19 or 20 and her features disappeared behind bumps and knots and bulges. For every unkind person who said with expressions or words that they couldn't bear to look at her, a kind person took their place, touched her, trusted her. Children were different, though. Children could be scared at first, but they overcame it. Children weren't allowed to reject adults, anyway. Not good, kind ones who took care of them. Children who did were deemed naughty and got whippings. At least, that was the way it mostly went, the way everybody said it had to be.

Pansy just broke all those rules. She was unthankful and rude, worse than sassy, complaining, and disrespectful. Yet Cotella, in one part of her, understood. Cotella wanted to break all the rules, too. She wanted to yell at the sky, where God was supposed to live, that she was scared. That she was hungry from going without for the children and mad that the Saunders didn't come back when they said they would. She wanted to shake her fist in defiance for her ugliness, loneliness, and lack of kinfolk. Pansy had plenty to be rude and mad about, too, and she had a third of Cotella's years. How must that child see the world that she would enter? What did it offer her but privation and want?

You can give them more, Cotella. Even though it doesn't seem like it now, you can. And will.

She looked around, her heart pounding at the sense that someone was there, in the dark, within feet of her, and putting words in her ears without really making sounds. She paused. She repeated what the voice said to her, or its essence: She could give Arthur, Mary, Myrtle, and even Pansy something even their parents couldn't. How could that be? Young-uns needed a momma and daddy, and God in his plan, whatever it was, had made that impossible. Right now, all they had was her.

She didn't believe in voices and God talking, but she heard something any way, plainer than her thoughts. What she could give them wasn't much, just a clean house and order and a presence. That was more than anyone else could or would give them. Their own momma didn't send them to school, and not having schooling was a punishment in itself, one of the worst.

She stopped walking, unsure how far she had come on the road to the holler or how long she had been walking. It had to be after 8:00. She could keep walking, but where would she go? If she was going to abandon the children tonight, she should have planned better, dressed in warmer clothes, packed her valise, and carried a pocketful of money. She laughed at her own foolishness.

"You can't leave those young-uns, Telly," she chided herself. "Get yourself back down there and put 'em to bed, then read to yourself out of that *Little Dorrit* book to see if that girl's daddy ever gets out of jail."

***

Cotella returned, feet numb and wet with cold, her face burning with the sharp wind, to two little girls and a toddling child wailing with fear. Their older sister paced the floor.

"Oh, Telly, I'm sorry! I'm sorry! I'm so mean! I talked so bad to you! I won't ever do it again!" Pansy wrapped her arms around Cotella as much in desperation as in love.

"I know, I know," she held Pansy, whose tears came now. The worry that the only adult in their lives had left started to ebb away, but the child trembled. "I know you're sorry, and we are all tired and hungry and keyed up. Let's sit by the fire; I'm a block of ice, darlin'."

Each wanted to sit in her lap, but she chose Arthur, breathless from his tears. They sat by her feet and helped her to warm. She comforted Arthur, who fell asleep, and she asked Myrtle to re-tell them the story of the *Little Dorrit* book so far, to distract their minds. Then she told them how her momma and daddy died in a fire and how neighbors took her into their home to care for her like their own.

Chapter Thirty-Three

Pansy never lost her temper and sassed Cotella again. Cotella never walked away again. February wore on, eggs and milk and a little ham sustained them twice a day. They were never satisfied when they left the table, and Cotella could tell her waist was thinning. The ham was dwindling, and even the firewood looked depleted.

One afternoon Cotella did bundle up, take the rifle out of its hiding place, and walk the woods for a couple of hours. The children heard three shots ring through the holler. She learned that day she was not a born hunter. Handling a gun to hit a target at close range or to scare off an intruder was not the same as picking a running squirrel off a branch at thirty yards. Rabbit's ears seemed to catch the crunch of leaves and snow far off. The trap in the yard fooled a couple of squirrels. The skinny carcasses were hardly worth the effort, but they did provide a little variety.

Cotella took hope that the sun's path through the sky moved further from the southern horizon, the days were longer, and the blanket of snow was beginning to look like the brown grass was tearing it apart. In moments when she wasn't running, cleaning, cooking, shooing children, or changing Arthur, who didn't yet like the idea of making his water in the chamber pot, she could sit for a few minutes. Then she had to fight the darkness that she knew came from hunger and isolation. She had to keep from surveying her life, the loneliness and rejection, the unachieved dream of nursing school, the Farley Stampers, the stretches in the boarding house in Clintwood, watching Minnie die . . . and the months in this holler after Minnie's death.

In those memories, Minnie was conscious for only a few minutes and talked so little that it was easy to remember every word, to play them over and over like one of those Victrolas Cotella saw in a department store in Bristol. How Minnie wanted whiskey. How little she asked about the children. How she cussed Cotella in her pain and fever. And how she talked out of her head about a treasure under the boards.

Maybe the part about treasure wasn't Minnie talking out of her head. One day before the snow Cotella had taken Minnie's words seriously and went looking for pieces of lumber in the barn and smokehouse. Maybe those were the boards she was talking about. Cotella found a few wooden scraps, nothing fresh or strong or worthy of building with. They were tossed in a corner of the barn and forgotten, with nothing under them but dirt and bug carcasses. Nobody would put a treasure, whatever Minnie thought of as treasure, under old boards out in the barn with the cow. Cotella decided Minnie probably dreamt it in a wild fever. Minnie had confused a childhood story about pirates and ships with her fears and despair over the poverty of marriage to the man she swore to love.

Cotella sighed, wishing sleep would come as easily as hunger. Even if she found a trunk full of dollar bills or gold coins, she couldn't spend them. Not until she could walk to town or someone would knock on the door.

***

Late one night after the children were in bed, as she stared into the fire, Cotella could not think of anything but her hunger and food. She wanted to eat, to fill her stomach, but that would mean the children would go without in the coming days. A mug of milk, at least, would do. She rose to warm it, to help her sleep, and heard a mournful sound. It was Master, howling, but not his usual hound-dog-bay-at-the-moon way. This was a warning howl, not near the house and barn where he usually stayed, but off, away somewhere. Well, he'll stop in a bit, she thought. But he didn't. Master was not a dog to raise a ruckus for no reason. She decided he deserved a look before the children woke up.

She put on Leroy's worn-out boots that she had lined with cloths to make them fit her smaller feet, wrapped herself in the warmest clothes she could find, and headed outside. There was only a half-moon tonight, and she returned for the oil lamp. Master's howls grew louder, and she detected their direction—on the other side of the barn, to where the fields began, but up a slope and into the woods.

She held the lamp up as she struggled through the crunching snow to the barn, where she found Leroy's .22 and loaded it, putting two other shells in her pockets. If something or someone was out there bothering Master, the gun would only be for warning shots into the air. She wouldn't dare to shoot at anything, not in the dark and not with her lack of skill. She might hit Master by mistake, and the children couldn't bear losing this reminder of their daddy. Anyway, worthless as the dog could be, he did guard them.

"Master! Come here, boy!" she called. Master stopped his howling, and she could hear his whimpering for a few seconds, and then his barking. "Come here, Master, leave that thing!"

Master ignored her. Whatever it was had touched his instincts to track and flush more than listen to her feeble calls.

"Who is it?" she yelled at the top of her lungs. She raised the gun straight above her head and let off a shot that rang and echoed against the hills. This would rouse the children, she knew. It was premature and out of fear, and she regretted it as soon as she did it. As the waves of sound dispersed, Master barked even more defiantly, and then took on a low growl. She still didn't know what it was, but suspected it was a fox, bobcat, or catamount. Probably not a wolf. They were rare in this part of the mountains. A bear was another matter, but bears slept in winter and left people alone until spring, if they bothered humans at all. Master wouldn't put up that fuss for a possum or ground squirrel or rabbit. If it was a wild cat, Master was doing his job. A cat would get into the chickens and deplete their main source of food. But it might mean a bloody confrontation.

The lamp was little help, but she kept walking to try to see what was happening and if Master would sense her and come back. She set down the lamp and loaded the gun again, then waited. Master continued his growling, somewhere ahead of her and to the left, secluded in the barren woods. The low eerie sound did little to comfort her. She began to chide herself for being out there in the cold and dark, worried about an old hound. Master's noises—and her nervous gunshot—might have waked up the children and they would find her gone. Gunshots and her absence would scare them to death. Fool dog. It needed to obey her and come in.

"Master, now! Come! Leave it alone!" No response but more growling.

She'd had enough and turned to go. The two animals would have to resolve their differences the way animals did. Twenty steps back toward the house, a cat's screeching roar turned her around and she made out Master running toward the barn, chased by some sort of wild cat, a sleek, swift beast gaining on the coon hound unused to being pursued, only to pursuing.

She dropped the lamp and it went out. The faint light from the half moon and even fainter light from the fire in the house was all she had. Before she could get the gun up and aimed somewhere in the direction of the speeding cat, the cat had overtaken Master. They had struggled with furious sounds. The cat felled Master, who was now on his side with the cat standing over him, nuzzling his side as if to begin a meal.

Foolishly and instinctively, she yelled "Git" and then chided herself again for such nonsense. She aimed at the cat and missed, but the report was enough. The animal, probably a bobcat, she decided, had let the hound know who was boss, taught him his lesson, and run off.

Chapter Thirty-Four

Master lay motionless. Cotella's heart stopped for a second, mostly out of concern for the children. They didn't deserve to have their pet taken from them. Not that Master was worth much as a pet; he was a hunting dog who, with his owner gone, had nothing to live for and was only trying to act true to his nature tonight. The little girls still loved him, though, trying to teach him tricks and reserving scraps of their food for him in case he couldn't find his own game in the woods.

She approached Master, reluctant, doubting there was much hope for him. She found him breathing, and he responded when she touched him by raising his head for a second or two without snapping at her. She could barely discern the gashes on both sides of his hindquarters. They showed that the cat had won this meeting. Master was losing blood, and she couldn't tell how much.

She sighed and sat on the snowy ground in a heap. Was it ever going to stop? Another crisis, another night without sleep. No, it wouldn't stop tonight. Either she would save this dog, somehow, or hide him in the woods where the young-uns wouldn't find him. She couldn't bear the thought of telling them about death and disappointment again. She would try to sew up those slashes, if he would let her, without morphine or anything else to stem the pain. Well, she had whiskey. Would a little of it kill a dog? No telling; she'd heard of dogs getting into corn liquor and dying of it. But he would die from those bleeding slices in his flesh anyway.

But how could she get the dog into the house, to some light, to sew him up? He had to weigh sixty or seventy pounds, so there was no carrying him from so far out in the field through the snow and ice by herself. She could get him into the wheelbarrow. That was the start. She would need light. The thought of taking a dog into the house made her cringe; dogs belonged outside, not where people lived. But she needed the heat and stronger light of the fireplace. She would be able to sew him up better and quicker that way. And she would have to wake Pansy for help, as much as she hated the thought. Pansy had helped kill a hog and now had to watch surgery on a dog. It didn't seem right to put a child through such bloodiness.

In fifteen minutes, she had Master by the fire and could examine him. Blood still seeped from the wounds. She hoped the cat wasn't diseased or rabid. All this trouble might be for naught, then, in the long run. But Master was inside now, so she might as well do what she could.

She said thanks under her breath that she'd found Leroy's liquor in the smokehouse. To this point, she had resisted the urge to slip out and retrieve the Mason jar for a big swig late at night. But now, if she was going to sow up a bloody dog, she needed one good swallow—that was all she could handle—to calm her nerves. Even more, poor Master needed just a bit. A couple of quick licks would do its business to sedate him. And alcohol was the best disinfectant. As soon as she stuck a needle and thread into his flesh, Master, drunk or not, would come alive and fight, ready to attack the human who added more pain, or run away, terrified.

Time for Pansy, as much as she regretted it.

"Pansy, I need you to wake up," she shook the girl.

"What?"

"I need your help. Master done got himself torn up by a bobcat. I got to sew him up, and I got nothing to put him to sleep for the pain of it. Just some moonshine. I need you to hold his head and comfort him."

"I'm sleepy." Pansy rolled over against Myrtle.

"I know, you can sleep all day tomorrow. Come on, Pansy, get up."

Pansy rolled out of bed. "Here, wipe your face with this cold rag, it will help."

Pansy's eyes opened at the sense of the cold water on the rough cloth, and she followed Cotella out of the bedroom. "What did you say about a bobcat?"

Cotella didn't repeat herself. Maybe it was good Pansy didn't hear it the first time.

"Oh, what happened to Master?" Pansy was shocked into wakefulness by the bloodied black and tan mound by the fire.

"Him and a bobcat had a fight. I'm gonna sew him up, but I don't have a way to get him anistitized."

"What's anistized?"

"Put to sleep. I'm gonna give him a just a taste, a little . . . corn whiskey, and—"

"Where'd you get whiskey? Daddy don't—he didn't—keep it around here. It's the devil's brew, he said."

Cotella decided a little lie right now was for the best. "He kept a little bit for medicine. Whiskey's got a lot of alcohol in it, and they use that in hospitals for cleaning wounds and such, and that's what I'm gonna do. So, you've got to hold him down so I can use thread and needle to sew him up."

"He'll bite me if you stick a needle in him!"

"Now, we're going to wrap strips of cloth around his snout, and his feet, real tight, so you just need to talk to him and comfort him. You don't even have to look at what I'm doing. Just keep him from wiggling the best you can.

"Here, you can use this pillow to sit on. I'm sorry to have to do this, but I can't do it alone, and the only other choice is to leave him in the woods to die."

Pansy kneeled at Master's head. "No, he can't die," Pansy whispered, tears pooling in her sleepy eyes.

Cotella tied his mouth and legs. She took a swallow from the Mason jar. Sewing the dog's wounds up sounded like a good idea out in the field. Now it sounded crazy. If she was hungry before, any desire for food was gone at the sight of the open flesh. On top of that, drinking whiskey on an empty stomach would send it straight to her head. But it was too late to change her mind.

***

She counted; thirty stitches on his right rump, twenty-two on the left. She only guessed at the width of them. She blotted the stitches with whiskey on an old rag. A real doctor or veterinarian might have put more or less of them, and they would have been in nice, neat rows. All she knew was Master still breathed and went to sleep by the warm fire, finally, as Pansy stroked his head and told him what a good dog he was. He would get some scrambled eggs in the morning as his reward.

"Pansy, I'm proud of you. You done a good job of keepin' him calm. At two in the morning, that's the best I can say. I know you're tired. You can go sleep in my bed so you don't wake the others. I'll sleep in here and watch the dog."

"I'm not tired, now," Pansy said, getting up from the floor and sitting in one of the few chairs by the fire.

"You want some milk?"

"No, I'm sick of milk. You know what I would like? A soda pop, like that one we had at Bailey's store, the one we stole." There was a slight smile on Pansy's lips to show she was teasing Cotella, who often didn't understand teasing at first.

"We didn't steal it, you sassy girl. I left him some money. If we ever get out of this holler again, I'll make sure he knows."

"And you can tell him his granddaughter needs to learn some manners," said Pansy, shifting in the chair.

"Like all you young-uns."

They sat for a while. Cotella added a log to the fire and settled back in her chair. Master sighed in his sleep.

"Do you think dogs have dreams?" Pansy asked.

"Humph."

"I think they do."

"How would you ever know? They can't tell you."

"He might be dreamin' right now, about that bobcat."

"No, he lost that fight. I think he'd been dreaming about huntin' a possum or squirrel and getting him some wild dinner. He's gonna think he can come in the house now. Fool dog."

"I was havin' a dream when you woke me up," said Pansy. "About Christmas, when those people, Deacon Saunders and his wife, came. And those oranges. I loved me those oranges."

"Yeah, they were good, juicy ones."

"I wish somebody would come."

"I know, honey, I know it's scary for you young-uns sometimes."

Pansy fell into a deep silence, staring into the fire, but her eyes did not flutter closed or her head nod.

"When will I stop being a young-un?"

"You're almost eleven, aren't you?"

"Yes, ma'am, in March."

"That's right. I remember when you were born. You were my first little girl baby I helped a momma with. You seemed so little. But all girls are little. Boy babies feel like rocks beside a girl baby."

"So, when I'm eleven, will I stop being a young-un?"

"No, I don't think so."

"Then when?"

"Did your momma ever talk to you about such things, like getting to where you could have babies and such?"

"She did once. She said if I ever started having blood on my panties, to not get scared and to come tell her and she'd tell me all about it."

Cotella pondered this. Minnie meant well, but a young girl needed more warning about her bodily changes than that. Some girls would already have started their monthlies by now. Her own momma gave Cotella a good talking-to when Cotella was eleven, maybe too much of one, more fear and heat about men's bad intentions than knowledge and light about how babies got made. But she figured out the scientific part from the anatomy books in nursing schools, thank goodness.

"I'm not your momma, but I guess I'm the closest thing you got right now. I need to explain that to you before it happens. It hasn't, has it?"

"What?"

"You didn't have blood on your panties?"

"No. Should I?"

"Not yet. Maybe when you're eleven, or twelve, or thirteen. It's different for every girl. It won't just happen that one time. It happens every month, pretty much."

"Every month? For forever?" Pansy looked terrified.

"Well, for about thirty years, maybe. Except when you are having a baby, and then you go through the change of life and stop when you're maybe forty-five or fifty."

"I don't want that to happen!" said Pansy. "Bleeding on my panties every month for years and years?"

"I know, honey, but that's just the way it is. But when you do start having your monthlies, that means you can have babies. You'll get taller, and you'll have breasts like a woman. If I could get you a book, I'd have you read about it. But like she said, if it happens, let me know. Not your sisters, though, not yet. They wouldn't understand."

"I don't want to have no baby." Pansy's expression was half unbelieving, half horrified at the prospect.

"You won't have one just because you start your monthlies. You have to be with a man or a boy and he has to do somethin' to you."

"What?"

Cotella was not ready to explain all of this late one night after sewing up a hound dog. "Never you mind right now. It's too late for me to tell you all about that. It's something you shouldn't ought to be doing unless you're good and married and have a house and are ready to take care of babies. Like your momma and daddy was. So, if any boy tries to tell you about it, you run as far away from him as you can. He's up to no good."

"I don't understand."

"I know. Have you ever heard two cats screaming out in the fields?"

"Like they's fightin'?"

"Well, they might be, but they are as likely to be doing the same thing, cat version. It's where kittens come from. The male cat puts them in the girl cat."

"Cotella, I don't believe what you're saying. That don't make no sense."

"Pansy, it's late. We just patched up this dog and we're tired. If you want to stay up and ponder that and watch the dog sleep and breathe, you can. I'm going to bed if you ain't."

"All right. I'm hungry. I'll drink some milk after all. And think about what you said."

"Don't think about it too much. I didn't tell it right. I'll figure it out and tell you about it the way I should. Just remember, stay away from boys and come tell me if you start your monthlies."

"These young-uns," she thought as she climbed into bed. Then she smiled. "They aren't 'these young-uns.' They're *my* young-uns."

Part Three

Chapter Thirty-Five

Until she died, March 1 would always be the favorite day of Cotella's life, more than Christmas or New Year or the day she considered her birthday. The mail came, after almost five months. She had a sense, like a visitation, that told her to look out the door and up at the mailbox on the main road. She saw the delivery wagon easing away just then. She ran out without her coat to see if it was really possible that mail had come.

There were letters for Minnie and Leroy. She opened them, not from nosiness but from desire to read anything that came through the post. The first was a bill for a farm implement Leroy had ordered from a business in Clintwood. That would have to wait. There was a check for $25.00 for Minnie Goins from the Higgins Building and Works Company, with a letter saying that Leroy had not picked up his pay and they were sending it as a check to the home address he'd given them. His employer didn't seem to know he had died, at least by the date of the check, November 1. Or maybe they did know he had died, like so many others, and this was a letter, cold and official, all the widows received.

That money would come in handy, if she could ever get somewhere to spend it and if she could talk the banker into giving it to her for the children's sake. She'd never really had any dealings with bankers. That would have to wait as well. There were some letters to Minnie that looked personal. She decided to open those later and answer them when the time came. For now, she wanted to deal with practical matters, like money, firewood, and food.

At the bottom of the pile were two letters addressed to her, Cotella. Her heart quickened. The first was from the postmaster of Buckley, West Virginia, a Mr. Harold Sykes. He said that he did know of a resident of Buckley named Viola Wilson, now married to a Mr. Otis Farrell. He wrote that he had called on her to ask if she had a sister named Minnie Goins, and Mrs. Wilson affirmed that she did. Mr. Sykes gave her Cotella's letter with the request that she contact Miss Barlow, who was taking care of Mrs. Goins' children.

It had worked! It took almost four months to work, but it did. The letter was postmarked January 3, 1919, so the postmaster had been faithful and prompt in his office even if the U.S. Postal Service in Dickenson County was not.

The last letter in the pile also bore her name. It was from Viola Farrell.

Cotella trembled as she carefully tore off the end of the envelope and unfolded the expensive paper. Mrs. Farrell wrote a good hand, and the letter was easy to read, especially through tears.

Dear Miss Barlow,

My name is Mrs. Otis Farrell, née Viola Joyce Wilson, of Buckley, West Virginia. Three days ago, on December 27, 1918, I received a visit from the postmaster of Buckley, Mr. Harold Sykes. He gave me your letter of October 20 to read.

I am indeed the sister of Mrs. Leroy Goins, née Minnie Wilson. Unfortunately, I have not spoken or corresponded with my sister, who is several years younger than I, in several years. We came to a disagreement and a parting when she married Mr. Goins.

My sister was a headstrong young woman who met Mr. Goins under unusual circumstances. He was working in our community as a laborer on a road crew, even though his original home is the area in which you reside. I believe he had left there for work and to "see the world" as my sister claimed, but he planned to return at some point. I really do not know because we only met on two occasions, neither of which were cordial.

Somehow my sister and Mr. Goins struck up an acquaintance and began to spend time together. She informed us she was going to marry him, but our parents and I disapproved heartily. I was already married at the time to Mr. Farrell. Mr. Farrell is a respected businessman in Buckley. Mr. Goins promised her that they would have a good-sized farm in your county when his father passed away.

They were married about thirteen years ago and we have exchanged letters very infrequently. I do know that Mr. Goins' father passed away, but the farm does not contain a great deal of arable land. He had not been successful at traditional farming enterprises and he continued labor with construction crews and any other legal or nefarious ways to make money. I am aware that my sister gave birth to three or four children.

I am of course grieved to hear of my sister's death and that of her husband, and of the sad situation of her children. My husband and I have not been blessed with children ourselves as a married couple. We plan to visit them sometime in the spring and see what arrangements can be made for them.

Viola (Wilson) Farrell

"Never in my life!" thought Cotella. What a proud woman. That must be what the Bible meant by "haughty." Family meant nothing to her, not a thing. Why was she waiting for an easy, convenient time to come see to her sister's young-uns—and she didn't even know how many children Minnie had birthed! That woman should have been on the road or rails as soon as she got the visit from Harold Sykes!

She reminded herself not to judge too fast—the enfluinzah, bad roads, and crusted snow had made travel to this part of the county almost impossible, and maybe Minnie had some fault in all of this. It didn't sound like Minnie considered her family's wishes when she courted and married Leroy. Maybe her family had money and planned another kind of life for her, a city life, not struggling and laboring in the mountains, far from them. Still, the way this woman wrote a letter, nice hand or not, made Cotella want to either snatch her hair off or never meet her. She certainly didn't want the children—her children—being taken off by this proud, self-loving woman.

When she was calmer, Cotella decided she would write back to Mrs. Wilson The thought that a letter could actually go in the mailbox, to the mail wagon, and off to another place again, filled her with hope. Spring was almost here.

Chapter Thirty-Six

On March 3, the Sheriff of Dickenson County drove an actual automobile onto the Goins' land. They heard the odd, rhythmic sound of a rumbling engine and ran to the door.

"What is that? It's a machine, like a wagon with no horse! What is that, Miss Telly?"

"Don't you know? Ain't you never seen one of them? It's an automobile!"

"Oh! I done heard of them! Let me see, let me see!" Pansy was out the door before Cotella could tell her to dress warm. Myrtle, more practical, grabbed her coat and followed. Mary, not as sure about this new object, hung back. "We have to go see who has come to visit us. This is our salvation, Mary. Get bundled up; it's still too cold."

The driver had brought the automobile down the path and parked it outside the leaning, ramshackle gate. Myrtle and Pansy jumped up and down around the late model Packard. A tall, broad-shouldered man in a Stetson hat emerged from it.

"Where is your momma?" he said to the girls.

"Can we look inside? How does it work? It looks like magic!" they said, ignoring his question.

"I'm takin' care of the young-uns," Cotella called as she made it up the path, carrying Arthur on one hip and holding Mary's hand. "Are you real? This ain't a dream, is it? I haven't spoken to another soul since Christmas."

The imposing man took in this disfigured woman, the toddler in arms, and the fair-haired little girls. She sensed he was not a man to answer fast or heedlessly.

"No, I'm real, ma'am. And I'm glad to find you here, and a little ashamed, to tell you the truth. What's been happening here?"

"Do you have an hour or two to spare? I'd give you a cup of coffee and a piece of pie, sir, but we don't have either. We've been living on short rations of salted ham, milk, and eggs for goin' on two months, with a few squirrels and rabbits thrown in. But first, who are you?"

He pointed to a seal on the automobile's door. "I'm Ben Watson, Sheriff of Dickenson County. We are tryin' to find out who is, I mean, if people are needin' help, now that the sickness has died down. Countin' the dead and the livin'. Seein' about families needin' burials and such like."

"I got so many questions, and I got a lot to tell you. You don't have any flour or coffee, do you?"

"No, but if you make me a list of what you need, I promise, I'll bring it tomorrow or the next day, soon as I can. It looks like you got your hands full with four young-uns. Is this all of them?"

"Yes, yes, although sometimes it seems like more than four. I can offer you a glass of milk and a fried egg if you can sit a spell. I really need a grown person to talk to."

***

Ben Watson stayed and listened. He didn't have to ask any questions. Cotella handed him his milk and started talking. About when and how she got there, about Minnie, about her death, and the grave, Leroy, the work, the fruitless walk to town, the hog, the Saunders, the snow, the long stretch of time, Master and the bobcat, the letters from West Virginia. Words spilled out of her, sentences with detours for her own questions.

"The Saunders—I thought I was dreamin', but the children saw 'em too, like they were angel visitors or haints or somethin'. Except they didn't do what they said. Do you know them? Was I crazy?"

"No, Deacon and Mrs. Saunders were, I mean, are real. But... well, around Christmas, the influenza got bad again. It was like it started all over a second time. Deacon Saunders came down with it, and he died. The next day Mrs. Saunders caught it, too, and was sick for a long time. She lived, but ended up bedridden for a long while. She's still weak and just heartbroken over her husband, and she hasn't really gotten back to her normal self. But she sent word through the church that you were here with the children. The road's not been clear enough until the last few days."

"Yes, the mail wagon came two days ago. That gave me hope. I got another question. Right at the beginning, that was before everyone got scared and wouldn't leave their houses, our neighbors the Stanleys told Pansy their daddy, Leroy Goins, died. He came home and gave the sickness to Minnie, and went back to work, probably gettin' close to dying himself the more he walked. What do you know about him?"

"He was found, his body, I mean, at the train platform at the foot of Dante Mountain one morning. He didn't have no papers on him to say who he was, but another man who worked with him identified his body. By then, so many people were dying, the undertaker couldn't keep up. He finally got buried, by somebody, a preacher, I guess. He's in a grave at the cemetery behind Dante Baptist Church, but there's no headstone."

"Oh, my, Sheriff. Then it's true. I began to wonder if the Stanleys were mistaken, had heard wrong. The mail wagon brought a paycheck for him, written out to Minnie."

The Sheriff paused and looked out the window for a long time. "Miss Barlow," he began.

"Oh, it's just Telly. Cotella, but I'm Telly to most everybody."

"Yes, ma'am. I guess you've been isolated and kept from some of the worst of it. I know that sounds like foolishness, as hard as you and the children have had it, being here by yourselves like this. But hundreds of people, maybe over a thousand, have died from this. I mean, between this county and Scott and Wise, and no telling how many into Lee and Washington Counties. And then thousands more in the state, and so many more in the whole country.

"A lot of soldiers, too—they never made it to France or Germany, they died in their tents and barracks in the camps. That means things don't run. Stores don't open. Supplies don't get delivered. Doctors can't help the sick and undertakers can't bury. The newspapers in the big cities are saying that millions and millions of people are dead from it all over the world, hundreds of thousands in this country since October. It's the worst thing anyone has seen in, well, centuries."

It was her turn to be quiet. She looked out the window, to the yard, to the field, to the ridges beyond. The mountains sometimes were a prison, sometimes guardians. She hated them sometimes. Yet they were all she knew any more.

They didn't guard this time. They only made her ignorant. But maybe she was wrong, and they did protect her and the children. Maybe being here, so cut off and separated, had been a blessing, for once.

"I need to be on my way, ma'am," he said. "If you can write me a list of what you need, I can bring it in a couple of days. Bailey's store in McClure is open now, or we'll get it from Clintwood or Pound."

She made a list that would hold them for a couple of months or so: fifty pounds of flour; twenty pounds of cornmeal and ten of sugar, and a can of coffee, the biggest Bailey sold. A large sack of dried beans. If there were potatoes, some of those. And forty cents worth of candy. "I promised the young-uns."

The Sheriff let the girls sit in the back seat of the Packard. They hinted around how much they would like to take a ride in an automobile like it, but they knew instinctively it was too much to ask this stranger. Pansy asked what the big round thing was for and Myrtle wanted to know how it started and stopped. Mary's eyes stayed round, unbelieving, and amazed that a man in some kind of magic carriage without a horse or mule had come. Cotella had a feeling that in the long run, Arthur would be the one to love the automobile and its kind the most.

After Ben Watson left, she shooed the children back into the house for their chores and meager dinner. Hope renewed, but not as strong as at Christmas. It had a blizzard of disappointment to overcome. Could he possibly forget them now? If spring was on its way and the road could be traveled, and if he didn't keep his promise, she would venture out again. But something assured her she wouldn't have to. Ben Watson would keep his word.

Chapter Thirty-Seven

Ben Watson proved to be a man of his word. Two days later, right after sunrise, as she finished the day's washing, she heard the chug-chugging of the Packard automobile and the crunch of tires on the rocks and patches of remaining ice. Hope rewarded, she waved from the porch, offering her big, half-hidden smile.

He was not alone. "This is my deputy, Ralph Sims," the Sheriff called after stepping out of the car.

"Howdy," said Sims, a slender, much younger man. He opened the back door of the Packard and unloaded a fifty-pound sack of flour, hoisting it over his shoulder. "Show me the way."

Cotella met the men in the yard and escorted them into the kitchen. The Sheriff carried the sack of cornmeal. "There's some more in the car."

"How much do I owe you, Sheriff?"

"Nothin'." He let out a big breath from the effort and landed the sack in the place she pointed out.

"I don't want the children thinking we take charity," said Cotella. "I don't like it, and I know their momma and daddy wouldn't neither. They were poor but proud and would go without before letting people think they wouldn't work for what they got. Leroy told me so, more than once."

"It's not charity, it's what the governor told us to do, to get people back on their feet. So, I'd be insubordinate to the governor, ma'am, if I didn't bring you these things. It's my job."

The deputy made another trip to the car for the rest of the food. Cotella let out a whoop at the sight of a five-pound can of Hills Brothers. "Coffee! Let me make you a pot right now, fellas! Mary, Myrtle, Pansy—get up! I'll make hotcakes and sorghum this morning!"

The girls wandered in, wiping sleep out of their eyes, and fully woke up when they saw two men in the kitchen. "Go get Arthur, too, even if he's still asleep. We're all going to say thank you to the Sheriff and Deputy—and the Lord."

Cotella made breakfast, and the men stayed to eat. The girls jabbered, forgetting they were in their bedclothes, waiting for their first taste in months of something made with flour. They told their stories, sang songs, and acted silly. Cotella let them. It was the first time they had seemed happy in a long while. When the girls had their fill of hotcakes, she told them to leave the table and get to their chores so she could talk to the men visiting them.

The Sheriff and Deputy ate heartily, and the smell and taste of coffee, with extra sugar, was her favorite part. She asked if the war was still going on. It wasn't, at least not for America. "I heard there was an armistice—that's what poor Deacon Saunders told me. Bless his soul, him and his wife wanted to help so bad. But I don't rightly know what an armistice is."

"Germany gave up fightin' us, 'cause they were losin', partly because of this plague, but they're all still fussin' and fumin' over there. I hear the president is trying to make everybody get along, peace treaties, that kind of thing. We should have left them alone to fight it out."

"Yeah," said the deputy. Ralph Sims had been mostly satisfied to eat and be entertained by the children and the conversation. "We Americans—I mean, our people back then—came here to get away from those kings and queens and wars and nonsense. I still don't know why they were fightin'. They's always at war over there."

"If our boys weren't going over there, they wouldn't have been in the camps and wouldn't have gotten sick and died, so many of 'em," said Ben Watson. "Ah, politics. I get enough of that bullshit—I mean, kind of thing here, excuse me, ma'am." He turned his eyes back to his plate to hide his embarrassment. It was so nice to see adults that Cotella wouldn't have minded to hear some impolite words at the table.

"I better keep quiet anyway. The president of the country don't like nobody talking against the war, and me, a sheriff, I should know better. I hear people get thrown in jail in the cities for talking against the war. Or President Wilson, for that matter. And him, a Virginian!"

"Huh!" said Sims. "I guess that's one good reason to stay here in the mountains. People are less likely to turn you in for speakin' your mind!"

Eventually, the Sheriff and deputy made motions that they needed to leave and excused themselves. Cotella walked out to the Packard with them, out of the children's hearing.

"We got a few more deliveries," said Ben Watson. "To tell the truth, you were about the farthest out and had the most need."

"We got nobody close around us," said Cotella. "I never bothered to notice how much land the Goins have, or how far away the neighbors were, until this visit. Not really any of my business, you know. The land's not all good for farmin' though, from what I can tell. A lot of it straight up."

"What kind of a man was their daddy?"

"Not one to get to know easy. He was known to get into some meanness and laziness, but he tried to keep body and soul together, I suppose. Made and ran 'shine, like so many have to, or choose to. He brought that—how you say it, *in*fluenza— home from town, not knowing what it would do to him or his wife. What a sad story."

Soon the two men said their goodbyes and were gone. A day of work lay ahead of her, as always, and today she was thankful for it.

***

Cotella finally found time to sit down and write a long letter to Viola Farrell. She wasn't sure what the "nee" was about. Could the woman not spell "knee," and why was she talking about her knee when she was saying her name? She put on airs, for sure, in that letter. Cotella wanted to write as good a letter, but she didn't know all those words and knew that some of her grammar would probably be wrong. She wrote slowly in big, neat, cursive letters, but she got to the point. The knots in her hand now made holding a pencil and creating neat, even strokes hard. At least she now knew how to spell and say the word for the sickness.

March 17, 1919

Dear Mrs. Farrell,

I was proud to get your letter. We have had it very bad here with the influenza, and I did not get your letter until March 1, even though you wrote it on January 3. We were here by ourselves for more than four months, except for one man and wife from the Methodist Church who came on Christmas, but I learned the man died soon after that and his wife is still real sick. The Sheriff of the county came on March 3 and then came back with the food we needed so bad since December. I'm making sure the young-uns eat real good now.

Anyway, the real reason I am writing you is that someone who is kin needs to take care of these children. They are not my kin and I can't just stay here like I am, even though I have gotten real fond of them and they are good young-uns.

There are four of them, living. Minnie lost her first one, Mathis, right after birth. Minnie was about to birth the sixth one, but it died in her before she died from the influenza. Pansy is almost eleven now. Myrtle is nine and Mary is seven. Arthur is the baby, and he is a year and half or thereabouts. They are all sweet but he is the sweetest, I guess because he can't talk back or complain yet. I have tried real hard to take good care of them. They need parents and someone to send them to school and make something of theirselves. I think they would have a better life if they were allowed to live with you and in a bigger town and get schooling. I think they are clever.

You said in your letter that you would come in the spring, and that's soon, so I hope to get a letter from you about when you are coming to get them.

Yours truly,
Cotella Barlow

Chapter Thirty-Eight

Cotella read her letter to "Viola Farrell, nee Wilson" over five times to be sure it was what she wanted to say. Now that the postman came—once a week! —she could hand it to him with some pennies and know Mrs. Farrell would get it soon.

The next day, with the sun rising over the holler, warmer weather coming and the snow all melted, she needed a diversion. By ten o'clock she put Pansy in charge of her sisters, placed Arthur in the wheelbarrow, and set out for the Stanley's farm. For the first time in her memory, she took in the mountains and stopped on a crest to view the land around her from that height on all sides. A constant but comforting breeze blew. The mountain air awakened her to how much she had been surrounded by smells of wet hippens, cows and chickens, children needing baths, and a smoky fireplace in need of a sweeping out.

She knew, though, that her feelings of lightness did not all come from the weather. The presence of Ben Watson, a tall, strong man of few words but important and useful ones, had not left her when he and Ralph Sims said goodbye a few days before. She couldn't help it. She was feeling something new, despite her hopelessness, despite knowing how much ugliness people saw in her face and body. Ben and his deputy had not been two of those people. Thought of that breakfast on the morning of their food delivery remained in her mind. Cotella felt delivered from danger. The memory pulled her to itself like a magnet of happiness after a long period of near despair. And as much as Cotella wanted to see both men as their rescuers, Ben Watson prevailed in her heart and mind.

Arthur made an impatient little boy noise in the wheelbarrow. She shook her head and chided herself. "Back to walking, Telly." She took one last look back at the way she had come. How much of it was truly Leroy's, and now, maybe, the children's? And how did she miss how pretty it all was? Along the road and in clumps throughout the slopes below, pink and lavender wildflowers bloomed. Yellow flowers, jonquils, yes, that was what people called them, swayed, ready to open. Clusters of sprouting grass surrounded them, making a contrast between the deep spring green and the sunny golden flowers. She would pick the jonquils on her way back, filling the wheelbarrow.

Right now, in spite of flowers and breezes and stirrings in her heart, she had to visit the Stanleys. From what the Saunders and the deputy had said, the influenza had treated them badly. When she reached their yard, Cotella lifted Arthur from the wheelbarrow and entered their gate. She let him walk, holding his hand tightly to keep him from running off, but not to support him. Since he had learned to walk, he was rarely off his feet and never fell anymore.

The Stanley's place seemed deserted, but that couldn't be. She pounded on the door.

"Mizz Stanley! Beryl! Anybody home?"

She could see a shadow behind the window curtain, a slowly moving, huddled-over form. Cotella had always thought Beryl a handsome woman, with thick, coal black hair to be envied for its shine. Beryl had stopped her baby years before Cotella started her own lying-in work, so Cotella had never helped her with births or afterward. Beryl would visit the Goins to be neighborly and bring a kettle of something after Minnie's births. She had visited last when Arthur was born.

After a long pause, Beryl Stanley opened the door. No longer was she the handsome, active woman. In less than the time Arthur had been in the world, she turned gray and lined. Her tall frame, now hunched, looked twenty pounds thinner, and her eyes, the saddest Cotella could ever remember.

"Yes? Who are you?"

"It's Telly Barlow, Mizz Stanley. You know, I come and helped Minnie Goins when she had Arthur and her girls before that."

"Oh, yes," said Mrs. Stanley, absently. "Come in. Is that Arthur?"

"Yes, ma'am."

Beryl Stanley turned and wandered back to her rocking chair, which was still in motion. "I had a baby. I had four, like Minnie. I only have one now," she said, as if to no one.

Cotella let herself and Arthur in, closed the door, and found a seat in an overstuffed chair. The house smelled of something. Stillness, staleness, or forgotten death.

"Yes, ma'am. I know. I heard that from Deacon and Mrs. Saunders. He's passed away now, too."

"Ellis and James and Tommy," Beryl said. "All the boys."

"So, your girl, Franny, is still with you." Franny was, Cotella thought, about seventeen now.

"Yes. But she's a girl. She'll get married and leave me. I wish one of my boys was alive instead."

Cotella's heart felt like a hand had reached into her chest and squeezed it hard. "No, Mizz Stanley, you don't mean it, not that way."

Beryl Stanley fell into tears at that moment. Cotella wanted to comfort her, but she remembered a time she shook Mizz Stanley's hand. Beryl Stanley had stiffened so much at the feel of the tumors and bumps, and hid her hand behind her afterward, as if trying to wipe off whatever was wrong with Cotella's skin. Cotella was used to people acting like that, but the memory convinced her in that moment that Beryl Stanley was in no state to accept the solace of touch from her.

"I am so sorry for your loss, Mizz Stanley. They were the most special, good-looking, sweet, and hard-working boys in these parts. Can I get you something? Let me make some hot tea or coffee for you?"

"I want some whiskey," said Beryl Stanley.

"Are you sure, ma'am? I'm not sure that's a good idea."

"That's not for you to say. If you won't give me any whiskey, I'll get it myself and you can get yourself outta here."

The hand squeezed her heart again, this time even worse. "I don't take with hard liquor, ma'am. I will bring you something cooked, a meal, I mean, as soon as I can. I'll bring the girls over if you like."

"No, no children. But you can bring some food. Franny ain't much of a cook."

"Yes, ma'am." She stood and arranged herself and Arthur. "Arthur can say good-bye now. Go ahead, Arthur, say 'bye'."

Arthur waved his hand and said something like "g-bah." Beryl Stanley smiled faintly, and she waved her hand in a small motion at Arthur. "You take care, ma'am, I'll see you soon."

Cotella breathed deeply of the cool mountain air outside, almost gulping it in. The Stanley house smelled of loss and sickness, but it was more of a sense in her skin and bones. Poor Beryl Stanley. When

Cotella reached the main road again, pushing Arthur, who loved the ride, she stopped and turned a full circle. She could see for miles and miles, other farms, other homes.

How many houses with how many Beryl Stanleys did she see?

Chapter Thirty-Nine

On April 15, the Tuesday before Easter, Cotella received a letter from Viola Farrell.

Dear Miss Barlow,

My husband and I will visit Clintwood on April 30. We will be arriving by car sometime during the day. Clintwood is the closest town with a hotel, and we have made arrangements for accommodations there. We will drive to Minnie's home on May 1.

I plan to engage a lawyer in Clintwood to help us with the legal matters involved in my sister's estate.

Yours very truly,

Viola Wilson Farrell

Well, that's short and sweet, and just as uppity as before, thought Cotella. What in the world is she talking about, getting a lawyer? Well, Telly, that makes sense. There's probably some laws they have to follow about the children going to live with her.

After she pushed her opinion of Viola Farrell's letter out of her mind, she realized what this meant. Her children would not be hers anymore. If and when the Farrells came and took the children home with them, Cotella would never see them again. She had written the letter, and had gotten her answer, and now she would lose what mattered the most to her.

What had she done?

And what choice did she have if the law said the young-uns had to go with their aunt? And Cotella without the money to raise them anyway.

She decided not to tell the children their Aunt and Uncle Farrell were coming, at least not until the morning of May 1. She'd make sure they were clean, wearing fresh clothes and looking their best. They would get to ride in a car, and go to town, then go on a long trip, and live in what had to be a bigger house than this little one, not much more than a cabin or shack. They could go to school every day. The Farrells had money, that had to be true. How happy the girls would be!

And how miserable she herself would be.

The coming of the Farrells meant that she would move on soon. She would have to get the word out that her mommas could call on her now. If there *were* any mommas having babies after the influenza time. Some of them may have died like Minnie and Leroy and the Stanley boys. She didn't want to have to board at Lulu's in Clintwood for any length of time. It cost money when none was coming in.

Thoughts of boarding, and where she would go next, and when, and how, sent her to her purse that she kept in the bottom of Minnie's dresser. She counted out thirty-five dollars and forty-seven cents. Her life savings. And of course, the gold piece from Harlan. She held it in her palm. It was heavy, and warmed with her skin. It bore the image of a woman, a beauty with hair and dress flowing, as if in a breeze, and something like sun rays behind her. Cotella gazed at its glory.

Harlan Rose gave her the gold piece as a kind of insurance, she thought. Something to hold on to until she really needed it. Harlan meant well. He meant to say, "Thank you, you've been here and helped us many times with our young-uns. In these mountains, life is short and hard and you don't know when you won't be able to work anymore. When that happens, this gold piece will help you."

She began to tremble, and then to leak tears. Of course, that's not what Harlan said or meant. He just wanted to be generous because he'd made some money from selling the land and because he had six healthy young-uns. Maybe he wanted to show her he had that kind of money to give her. He couldn't fully know what her life was really like.

She wept because of her life, her face and body and how people tried but couldn't hide what they felt. She cried that her dream was smothered, and she cried because without her, the children could have starved to death and no one would have known it. When she settled down and stopped crying, she remembered that Pansy, Myrtle, Mary, and little Arthur would be taken away from her, and she fell back into weeping. It started to feel good to cry, to feel lighter, to sense that something was coming off her soul and shoulders, even if it meant the children she loved were being removed, too.

The cry didn't lift everything. Since March 3, the day that Ben Watson showed up in that big shiny Packard automobile with the seal on the door, something else had happened. The Sheriff had come back, once with the deputy to bring the food, and again to bring the children some candy, and twice again to "check on them." He let Mary and Arthur sit on his lap. He did not talk about himself, or about his wife or family, and not much about his job as Sheriff. He only mentioned that he grew up in Kentucky and came to Virginia five years before.

He listened to her talk about the time she and the children were alone and the world was dying around them. How she lived before she started helping mommas, how she learned nursing in Bristol and before that lived with Fanny and Tom. He drank coffee while she worked in the kitchen. The children showed out for him, and he laughed in his quiet way. She couldn't remember hearing a man laugh in so long.

She knew that he came to sit, talk, and listen because his job was sad and he met grieving people all day long. He tried to help people in the county and sometimes had to enforce the law and take someone to jail. She knew he liked to drink coffee and to see the children and he felt sorry for them because they were orphans. She knew all that and that he probably was married. Almost all men his age were, though he never spoke of a wife.

And she knew she loved him. She couldn't help it, even though she knew, nothing could ever, would ever, come of it.

Chapter Forty

May 1 arrived. And so did Mr. and Mrs. Otis Farrell, in a touring car, shiny black, no less, with a leather front seat and one in the back. They followed the Sheriff onto the Goins' land. An outsider to this part of the county could never find the Goins place without help. What Cotella called the main road to McClure was unpaved, part crushed rock, part packed dirt and now in early spring, still part mud. Ben Watson, who told her later he felt no obligation to help the Farrells on their mean errand, pulled up to the gate but left the visitors a flatter and less muddy space.

Cotella stood on the porch with Arthur by the hand on one side and the three girls on the other, well-scrubbed, in neat-pressed cotton dresses with hair combed and in ribbons. Mrs. Viola Farrell climbed down out of the car after her husband opened the door for her. He was not what Cotella expected. Next to Ben Watson, who she figured reached six feet and two or three inches, Mr. Farrell was, well, a shrimp of a man, not much taller than Cotella herself. He was dapper, though, in the sharpest creased gray suit and blackest fedora hat she'd ever seen.

Mrs. Farrell matched her husband for style, and beat him for size. Maybe it was her shoes, but she seemed inches taller than Otis Farrell. Anyway, those fancy heels were not the shoes of a woman who walked to town or had done farm work. Cotella knew her knobby feet probably couldn't balance in those shoes. The skirt of Mrs. Farrell's suit was full, but stopped at the top of her buttoned shoes. The suit of wool dyed green was set off by a green and blue plaid tam atop her piled-high brown hair—too brown for a woman with that many wrinkles.

Cotella swallowed, hard. She wasn't ready for this.

Mr. Farrell held his wife's arm as they approached through the gate and stepped carefully in the yard, trying to find places with patches of grass or stone and avoid the mud and Master's occasional piles of mess. Mr. Farrell, even for a small man, took charge, but he paused when his eyes laid on Cotella's face. Mrs. Farrell gasped, and there was no hiding it. Mr. Farrell had to gather himself, but he spoke in a friendly way to Cotella as they stepped onto the porch. "Good morning. You must be Miss Barlow. We are the Farrells, Miss Barlow. Could you introduce us to the children?"

"I'm pleased to meet you, Mr. Farrell, Mrs. Farrell," Cotella managed to say. Viola Farrell nodded, without a smile, but she did meet Cotella's eyes and hold them. "This is Pansy. She is the oldest, which I guess you figured 'cause she's the biggest. She's eleven now. She was ten when I got here in October, but that's been, oh my, goin' on seven months now. I done lost track of the months. Anyway, this is Myrtle, which I think is such a pretty name, she's nine now. And Mary, she's six."

"I'm seven!" said Mary, showing her fingers.

"Oh, I forgot, yes, she is. And this," she picked up Arthur, "is Mr. Arthur Goins, the sweetest baby boy I ever took care of all my years of takin' care of young-uns. He's more than a year and half and runs me ragged. When I got here, he was still crawlin' around and just startin' to stand up and take steps. That's the four of 'em. They're real good young-uns and I think they'd be at the top of their class when they start to school."

Otis Farrell smiled big, with all his teeth showing. Viola Farrell did not smile like him, just a slight upturn of her lips, but Cotella saw a light of recognition in her eyes. Mrs. Farrell seemed to see her sister's face in these children after all these years. Pansy, of the four, looked the most like Minnie, although she had her father's fair hair and green eyes with a hint of blue. "Hello, children. It is nice to meet you," said Otis.

Pansy stuck her hand out to her uncle, who showed his surprise, but he returned it. "Hello, sir," she said, quietly and shyly, but unashamed. Myrtle and Mary followed, and Otis offered his hand to Arthur, who laughed and let the strange man pump his hand. Viola did not greet the children and let her husband perform all the honors.

"Well, do you want to come in for cake and coffee, or I can offer you breakfast?" said Cotella. She looked at Ben Watson, who stood by the gate, watching it all, solemn.

"No, Miss Barlow." Viola finally spoke. "We do not wish to eat anything here. However, we would like to speak to you privately for a few minutes in the house, if the children can remain outside."

"Oh, well, yes, ma'am. Please come in." She moved to open the door. "Pansy, here, you take Arthur now," she said, setting him down. "And you all stay outside. Go up and talk to the Sheriff." She lowered her voice to a whisper, like a conspirator. "Maybe he'll let you sit in his car."

The three adults entered the home. Cotella grew conscious of the size and simplicity of the house, the few pieces of old furniture, the wood-burning stove—nothing like a house in a big town. "They'll probably think we are just dumb, poor mountain folks," she thought, and felt the warmth of humiliation in her face. "Please sit down—can I give you some coffee?"

"No, that will not be necessary," said Viola Farrell. "Miss Barlow, we are here to talk to a lawyer in this county about taking the children and moving them to the Presbyterian Orphanage in Bluefield, that's in West Virginia, about forty miles from our home in Buckley. The Orphanage has agreed to take the children. It is a very safe and--"

"Oh, no! What are you sayin'?"

"That the children will live in a very nice, orderly, clean, Christian home with other children like them. They will be together, at least for now."

"Now?"

"There might be a time when one of them—probably Arthur, the youngest, and maybe Mary, she's a pretty child and still young—would be adopted and taken into a good home."

"No, no, no! You can't do this."

"Why not? I understand that you have cared for the children since my sister's death and have become attached to them. But we are the only family they seem to have, and we are the ones you asked for help. If there are other family members that want to take them in, that want four children added to their home, especially now when there are so many orphans from the influenza, well, you should talk to them very soon. This is what my husband and I have agreed to."

Cotella's eyes jerked to Otis Farrell, whose smile was gone and replaced with a nod of agreement and furrowed brow.

"I really thought that, I mean, you all were coming here . . ."

"Oh, I see, you thought we were coming to fetch the children and take them home with us. I am afraid you misunderstood. I did not write anything of the kind in my letter. We are simply not in a position to take on four young children at this stage of our lives. My husband has children from his first marriage who are grown now. I am . . . somewhat older than my sister. We will give a large donation to the Orphanage, and we will see that the children receive birthday and Christmas presents and occasional visits. We believe this is the best choice for everyone."

"I don't see how you can say that."

"Say what?"

"That sending them to an orphanage is the best for them young-uns. it's just the best for you."

Viola Farrell took this like a firm slap, stiffened, and paused to collect herself.

"Miss Barlow, you wrote in your letter about how hard it was to survive this winter by yourself with the children, and the influenza, and no man to work the farm. You have done your part—well beyond it—and it's time for the children's family to take charge and see to their futures."

This woman talks like she writes in those letters, Cotella thought. So proper and educated and cold, with no heart.

"No."

"No? No what?" said Otis Farrell, finally speaking after his wife's confident declarations of how the future would work. At being contradicted, his toothy smile disappeared, and fiery eyes took over his face.

"No, I can't let you do such a thing to these young-uns!"

"Why?" said Viola Farrell. "And, Miss Barlow, it's none of your choice. You were hired to help their mother after her childbirth, and you have given more than you were asked to. We understand that, and we will pay you your wages. But we will have custody of the children, once we talk to the lawyer in Clintwood and go to court, and we will take the children to their new home in West Virginia."

Cotella couldn't speak. She didn't know that word, custody. This woman had fancy words. She had better clothes than a woman in a magazine. She had money, or acted like it. And pay, from her? Cotella didn't want her filthy money. This woman thought money could equal what she and the young-uns had been through. Cotella had been angry before in her life, but this was not anger. It was not just insulted. It was something deeper, and it reminded her of those stories in the Bible when the Lord God Almighty sent punishment on the disobedient, rebellious sinners. Wrath, that was the word the preacher used.

And wrath always meant something had to change.

She felt this way, when, yes, that doctor told her she had to leave the nursing school and go home. When Fanny said she was selling the farm and made her homeless. When Farley Stamper proposed marriage because he wanted a servant for the children and he had another woman and Black children, hidden away from the "nice" people he wanted to impress. When Minnie died and left her with four young-uns. And all those times she wanted to do something, to change the future, and she couldn't.

And now, it was like someone, in this case Viola Farrell, took a big branch of a tree and knocked her over the head from behind. She didn't know it was coming and couldn't stop it, couldn't turn around, and grab the weapon or defend herself.

How many times had she been struck over the head like that, and didn't know what to do? How many times more was somebody going to tell her how things would be and she had no say in it? Maybe lots more. But not this time. It was wrong, this woman was wicked, and her short little husband was false and deceitful.

"I won't let you. I won't let you take these children from their home and their mountains and, and from me. I will get the law on my side. It has to be, 'cause what you are gonna do is wrong and bad and, not Christian, not . . . not American. Not what neighbors or good people do, and sure not what kin do. I will fight you all I can."

Chapter Forty-One

The Farrells told her she was an ignorant mountain woman and didn't know what she was talking about, that if she gave them trouble, she'd go to jail, and that she should have the children's things packed in two days because that was when they would be leaving.

They left without a goodbye or politeness. She did not follow them out. She waited until she heard the car engine roar. She went to the porch, hoping they were gone.

"Do you need me to show you the way out?" she heard Ben Watson say at the top of his lungs, over the engine and from a distance. They appeared not to, because they pulled out in a hurry. If driving an automobile could show anger, Otis Farrell's did. She could see their mouths through the front window of the automobile, moving fast, like they were arguing. Good, thought Cotella. Argue yourselves into an early grave, for all I care.

Cotella looked at Ben Watson, who was, after all, letting the children pretend to ride in the car, with Pansy behind the wheel, jumping up and down in the seat.

She joined them. She loved to see the children happy.

"Who was that man and lady and what did they want?" said Mary.

"The lady is your aunt. Your momma's sister," said Ben.

Cotella was glad. Still seething, she didn't think she could talk like a sane person.

"Momma's sister?" said Pansy. "She wasn't like Momma."

"I don't like her," said Myrtle.

"Me neither," said Pansy. "She was mean-lookin'."

"What did she want, anyway?" said Myrtle

"Hush, young-uns," said Ben. "That's disrespectful to your kin and elders."

He was right, Cotella thought, but she felt grateful that the girls said what she wanted to say. Cotella turned and walked away. She could feel the tears coming, and she didn't want Ben Watson to see her upset. She looked up at Piney Ridge where oaks and elms were starting to reach their full yellow-greens, mixing with the deeper colors of the pines. Ben turned from the children and joined her. She felt his presence by her side and breathed deeply, trying to regulate her heartbeats.

"Do you know what they said to me, Sheriff?" Cotella finally said. "Do you know what they want to do with these young-uns?"

"Yeah. They done told me this morning when I met them. I tried to explain to them what you done for them young-uns and what you all been through, how hard it's been. That you were the only person to take them over and you kept them alive. How you buried their momma. They didn't much care what I thought about it, but I said so anyway. That's probably why that Mizz Farrell was so sour-mouthed."

"I ain't gonna let 'em."

"How you gonna stop it, Cotella?" He had never used her Christian name.

"I don't know. You're the law, don't I have some say in what happens to them?"

He took off his hat and rubbed his head. "Hard to say. Hard to say. Crazier things have happened."

∗∗∗

Those were big words I said there, Cotella thought. Too big for her and her situation. She didn't care. If there was anything she could do to keep the children from an orphanage in another state, and, in time, being split up and sent in all directions and never able to find each other, she would do it. She had no money, no authority, and only a few friends, but she had to do something. And fast. She figured, and Ben Watson agreed, that the Farrells weren't here for a long visit. Ben confided their words on the matter: that they wanted to see a lawyer and judge, if needed, within a few days, and move on, leaving the children in the Presbyterian Orphanage on their way back to Buckley.

Cotella kept her plans to herself, though, and tried to treat the children as if it was any other day. Anyway, spring had fully arrived. With the Farrells gone, they could change into their everyday clothes and spend the day outside. Myrtle was finally able to milk the cow all by herself—one less burden on Cotella. She put Mary in charge of the chickens, and Pansy in charge of Arthur. "See if you can't get him used to peein' in the chamber pot. He's young for that, but he's a smart little fella, and that means less washin' of those hippens."

She might not have much hope of keeping the children, and she didn't know anything about the law or judges or orphanages. She was going to keep training them to be polite and hardworking. It gave the girls something to keep their minds off the morning visitors who puzzled and frightened them. If she somehow got to keep the young-uns, they could start doing more of the chores, and if they had to leave . . . she didn't want to think about that.

The next morning, Ben Watson appeared with a big, sealed envelope. It reminded her of the official ones she received from the nursing school so long ago, but this one had the name of Josten S. Davis, Esquire, on it.

"What's this?" she said. "I don't want to open it. It's bad news. I can't take no more bad news."

"It's a legal letter from Davis—he's a lawyer in Clintwood."

"Yeah, I heard of him. Not good stuff, though. That's why I don't want to open it. If I don't, does that mean I can act like I didn't get it?"

Ben smiled briefly, but then shook his head. "No, you know you have to, because I delivered it, and I'm the law. You have to do what it says."

She sighed and opened it. The paper was crisp, the letters typed and dark against the white page. She read it slowly, not sure of all the words. "I think it says I have to get the young-uns ready for the Farrells to take them in seven days. I have to be in Clintwood at the lawyer's office then, with children, and if I don't, the law will come get them and take them away. Now, how do they expect me to get to Clintwood with four young-uns? It about killed us to walk to McClure."

"I can drive 'em, or send Ralph."

"Then you'd be helping the Farrells take 'em."

"No, Cotella," Ben said. "This is from a lawyer. It's not from a judge, so the lawyer can't really make you do nothin'. He can just threaten you and try to scare you. But this lawyer, Davis, is known to the judge, of course. You'd have to have your own lawyer if you want any say in this."

"How do I get a lawyer?"

"You gotta have some money first."

"Oh." Cotella thought for a moment. "Would a $20 gold piece do?"

"Where in the world did you get a $20 gold piece?" he laughed.

"Never you mind, I got one."

"Yeah, it might. Listen, I am the Sheriff, and I got other things to take care of, but there is another lawyer in the county, Thad Mullins. He and Davis hate each other. I think he would be interested in fightin' Davis before the judge if he can, just for the fun of it, and not even charge you full price. So let me talk to him today, and he can do the papers to see the circuit judge, who comes around next week."

"That is mighty kind, Sheriff. I don't know why you're helping us so."

"I got my reasons. I don't like them Farrells. I don't like people comin' into my county and taking our young-uns. I don't like the thought of young-uns who lost both their momma and daddy all of a sudden, especially in this plague, being put in an orphanage like nobody cares about 'em. And I'd love to see Mullins and Davis go after each other. It's a show, let me tell you. And you deserve better, yourself."

He paused. "But, I gotta tell you, even if Mullins takes your case, you got a problem."

"What's that?" Well, she knew she had problems. But she wanted to know his side of it.

"Cotella, this is gonna hurt you, but you got no man to be helping with the farmin' or bringin' in a paycheck. You don't really have much comin' in to live on."

She thought he might say the judge would take one look at her and decide the young-uns couldn't stay with a face like hers. He wasn't telling her anything she didn't know. Beside the gold piece and a few dollars in the bottom of Minnie's chest of drawers, she had nothing to keep them alive, and she didn't have the first thought on how to start the planting now in early May.

"No, I don't have any income, Ben. You're right. I know. But I'm gonna fight anyway. The Farrells will most likely win, but I couldn't live with myself if I let the four of Minnie's children get scooped up out of their home without a fight."

***

Ben was, as always, true to his word. He was the Sheriff of Dickenson County, after all. He visited Thad Mullins, who agreed to do the work for five dollars, considering what everyone had been through and in light of Ben's friendship. He drew up the documents and had them delivered to the court and the Farrells, and Ben brought a copy to Cotella the next morning. He drank coffee while she tried to read the complicated words on the papers.

"So what does this all mean? It's more than I can put in my head."

"It means you have to be in court before Judge Hopkins next Wednesday at ten o'clock. With the children, too. Mullins says the children don't have to come, really, but it would help his argument, your defense."

"Oh, my word. Defense? I didn't do anything wrong, did I? I didn't break the law. I didn't mean to."

"No, no, Cotella. That's just a lawyer's word for talking for you. He's a real word-spinner. He's gonna lay it on thick. He's gonna talk about how Mizz Farrell and her sister were estranged, I mean, not friendly, and didn't speak for years, and how Mizz Farrell don't have no interest in Minnie and Leroy's young-uns. He's gonna talk about how you all were up here on this farm almost starvin', workin' your fingers to the bone to keep the children alive, and how she and her husband never thought a bit about how it might be for Leroy and Minnie and the children, even after she got your letter."

"Oh, Lord, Sheriff. That's gonna embarrass me. It's not all true."

"Yes, it's all God's honest truth. And you need to know somethin' else, somethin' that probably won't sit well with Judge Hopkins."

"What's that?"

"Davis is trying to get the land turned over to the Farrells. Of course, they will sell it to a coal company for a little money. I don't think Leroy had much land, maybe ten acres, but money is money."

"They want the money, but not the children?"

Ben nodded.

"That's pure wickedness. I don't understand why they don't want their sister's sweet children anyway. They don't have none of their own. Except she did say her husband has grown children from his first wife."

"I looked into them and their reputations. I made some phone calls to Buckley. Sheriffs and police and such got connections. They put on a good front, but they ain't as rich as they wanna look. He's taken out loans, and things have gone south for his business. Anyway, everybody's business is sufferin' right now."

She pondered this. It was all as complicated as a storybook, as that *Little Dorrit* she and the young-uns finished reading. Little Dorrit got the love she deserved after all her suffering, even the trials made by her crazy daddy. Life wasn't really like that, and things didn't turn out happy all the time, but it was nice to read long stories where it did.

"My, my. I'm mighty thankful, Sheriff, even though I won't be able to sleep a wink or eat a bit before Wednesday. I'll be so keyed up about going to a courtroom. I've never done such a thing, and I never planned to. Courts are for thieves and murderers, not people like me."

"Nonsense. You got your rights, too. Just have the young-uns ready at 8:00 that morning, and Ralph'll come get you all. Just in case, though, bring their clothes in a valise or flour sack. If the judge decides against you, those children will have to leave right then with the Farrells. That's what Davis' papers say, remember?"

So Wednesday might be the end of her life. "Thank you. Any other words to keep my spirits up? I'm nervous as a cat."

"I hate to say this, but bring your valise and belongings, too. If Judge Hopkins decides for them, they'll take possession of this land and house, and you'll be without a home."

Chapter Forty-Two

Cotella tried to live the next six days as if nothing would ever change for the children. But they knew something was amiss. Meeting their aunt and uncle, who left mad, the Sheriff's many visits, and "Mizz Telly's nerviness," as Myrtle called it, told them something was up. Cotella wanted to keep their minds distracted from legal fights she herself didn't understand. She enforced new responsibilities on them. Myrtle's cow milking improved, except that she spilled most of a bucket one morning. Arthur had no interest in making water into the chamber pot, despite his sisters' fussing at him. Mary churned the butter, singing tuneless songs for herself, and Pansy's chores now included washing clothes.

Cotella had asked the Sheriff to bring some paper and pencils for the girls to work on their schooling in the kitchen rather than the barn. As Wednesday approached, she made them stay outside so she could begin to clean and pack their meager belongings into old flour sacks, one for each child. She neatly folded their mostly hand-me-down dresses, panties and petticoats; Arthur's nightshirts and diapers; a few childish gimcracks the girls had collected; and their favorite ribbons and bows.

If the judge decided the Farrells were right and got everything they wanted, she must be packed, too, and have the house right. Who would milk the cows or get the eggs, she didn't know. That would no longer be her concern after Wednesday morning. But out of a sense of pride, she wasn't going to leave the house the way she found it seven months before when she opened the door to a dying Minnie and four confused, disheveled young-uns. She was too nervous to rest much anyway, only when exhaustion at the end of the day sent her to bed. She might as well do one last cleaning. It would keep her mind off her troubles, at least.

She started in Minnie and Leroy's tiny room, where she slept now, behind a curtain. She had cleaned it like she would a hospital room when Minnie died, to protect them all from the little influenza germs like those in the nursing books' photographs. But she had not gone through the chifforobe or dresser thoroughly. There might be clothes in there Pansy could wear, or something of poor Leroy's that could go to the church bin.

"What you doin', Mizz Telly?" Myrtle found her at work.

"Spring cleanin'."

"What's that?"

"When the weather gets warm, you wanna open up the house and get all the dirt out. I'm startin' in this room."

"Can I help?"

Cotella turned and gave her an amused look. "You want to help clean? That's a surprise!"

"No, I just wanna see what's in here, and what you're doin'."

"I'm going through your momma and daddy's belongings, darlin'. I'm not sure you need to see those. If I find anything of theirs that's special, like a remembrance or locket, I'll let you know. I want you to always remember your poor momma and daddy. They were cut down too young by that sickness, like so many other people, like poor Mizz Stanley's boys."

"Oh. I would like a locket."

"We'll see. You go on. Help Pansy with Arthur. She has trouble keepin' up with him. He runs faster than she does now."

Myrtle left. Cotella methodically went through each drawer. No lockets, no watches. She found only aprons and petticoats. Hunting through Minnie's belongings like this, in such an intimate way, sent her mind back to those first few days there, the last of Minnie's life. She shivered, but not from the cold. In fact, a warm breeze, warmer than normal for May, came in through the open window. Yes, she slept in Minnie's bed, but usually after such a hard day of labor when sleep came immediately. And the cock always crowed too early.

There had been no time for her to lie in the bed and remember Minnie's last days of life. That lifeless bulge in her belly, her blue-black skin and bleeding legs, the racking, unending cough and raging fever, her mind going. And Cotella's own fears of the children catching the influenza, the almost relief when Minnie died, and a night digging a grave and filling it up.

Minnie's words at the end of her life were few and usually bitter. She had resigned herself, Cotella thought, to dying alone, the children kept far away for their protection, her husband who knew where. Did she know Leroy was the cause of her death? Not intended, of course, but he brought the illness into their home and put all of them at risk, only because he tried to make a living for them the only way he knew how. Cotella thanked the Lord that Leroy, for all his faults, was a hard worker and had cut enough wood for the winter early on. She didn't know how they would have eaten or been halfway warm without those cords of wood stacked up in the smokehouse.

What few words Minnie said, Cotella remembered them all, even the ones that made no sense. In the fever and pain, she rambled some and talked about the past and the children, getting their names and order wrong. And that thing about the treasure. Cotella hadn't figured that one out. "The treasure, under the boards." What boards? And what kind of treasure would people as poor as the Goins have? If they had it, why not use it rather than living so hard?

"Under the boards." Now Cotella wondered. She had already looked under and around and in between old pieces of lumber in the outbuildings and found nothing, as she expected. Why put a treasure in a barn or smokehouse where a thief could find it? Of course, what thief would come to this farm hoping to find money or belongings worth something? Well, Leroy was known to be acquainted with other moonshiners, who got themselves in trouble with the law on other accounts. Thieving wasn't above some of them.

Where else would boards be? Houses had boards. Roof boards, ceiling boards, wall boards. Floor boards. Maybe that's what she meant. Floor boards sometimes got loose over the years. Sometimes, they were just never made flush in the first place. That sounded about right in this drafty and creaky old construction.

Foolishness, Cotella, she thought. A body would have to go through every room with a knife or hammer and test every board to see if it was loose or uneven, and where would that get you? "I don't have time for that," she sighed.

But Mary, Pansy, and Myrtle did, and if there was something hidden under the house, it concerned them and their momma and daddy, not Cotella. It would be their treasure, not hers.

"Pansy, Mary, Myrtle! Come on in here. I got work for you."

***

She took over care of Arthur and put the girls to work to test every piece of lumber in the flooring. "Why are we doin' this?" Pansy said.

"Your sweet momma told me to do it, before she died."

The girls sighed as if they didn't believe her, and started in their own room. They found three loose boards, which they jiggled loose with a metal egg turner from the kitchen. They might ruin it, but no matter. The Farrells could buy another one, or not, Cotella thought, since they only cared for the money they could get out of selling the land to some outsiders. The girls found nothing under the boards in their own room but a long dead mouse and lots of dirt and dust. They had to move the big bed they slept in and their chest of drawers. She heard moans and complaints, but left them to it on their own.

"Now, I'll do the room where I sleep," Cotella said. "You all check the boards in the kitchen and by the fireplace.

After removing the makeshift mattress on Minnie's old bed, she scooted the bed as far from the wall as possible. She got down on her hands and knees and used a butter knife to manipulate the loose boards she could find. Under where the bed had sat, beneath a layer of dust and cobwebs, she dislodged a piece of lumber that then loosened the one next to it, and the one next to that. In the faint light she saw a metal box. This had to be it, in the most obvious place, under the bed where Minnie died.

***

The box was light, made of tarnished metal, about a foot by a foot, latched but not locked. She shook it. Despite its slight weight, it did contain something. She didn't call to the girls at first. There was no telling what was in the box, and there was no reason for them to see it before she could decipher its meaning. She sat on the bed, the strong box on her lap. She unhooked the latch and opened it, glad for this private moment.

She found, of course, paper documents: three sets of stiff paper, all folded in thirds as if to be stuffed in an envelope. She unfolded them. Clearly, one was a land deed. No surprise. The deed had to be somewhere, and the Farrells knew of the one on file in the county courthouse. Cotella did not understand the language, but she realized there had to be something about the deed that made it, in Minnie's fevered mind, a treasure. She read it carefully and then saw the answer.

This was not the deed to the land on which the house sat. It was for land elsewhere, but she wasn't sure where. She couldn't make sense of the surveyors' symbols and figures, but she could make sense of one number and three words: Two hundred acres. Wise County.

Leroy owned two hundred acres of land, but off this property? Yes, it was in his name. Two hundred? How much was that? And was it good, flat farmland, land where you could build a sturdy house and a productive farm, and where people would want to live, or just the side of a mountain, even more isolated than this? She felt her heart racing. Did the Farrells know about this deed?

Her hands trembled and her mind fogged. How did Leroy get this land? What did he use it for? Maybe his moonshining? Sure. It would be better, if he could, to keep his crimes away from the land he and his family lived on. She read on. From what she could tell, it was an inheritance. Yes, she remembered. Leroy's father had been a man of more means than most around here. This was Leroy's legacy, but why he held on to it and lived in near poverty, Cotella couldn't judge. She shook her head, befuddled, at the thought of all this unused and unknown land.

The box held more papers. The second folded collection was the deed to the land on which they were living. Ten acres, and the deed bore both his and Minnie's name. Cotella thought that strange. Some men in the mountains would not put their wives' names on a deed, even though it had been legal in Virginia for years. Minnie hadn't brought anything into the marriage, either, running off with Leroy like that. If her parents had money, she had shucked it all away marrying Leroy, someone they disapproved of.

The third paper was what she expected: Leroy Henry Goins' last will and testament. Again, more fancy words, more roundabout language. On the second page of typed letters, she found it. His heir: Arthur Wilson Goins.

Little Arthur, twenty months old, owned it all.

Chapter Forty-Three

Cotella's first fear was that the will was not real, not legal. She didn't know if Leroy had done everything right. On the will she found the signatures of Leroy and two witnesses, one of them John Stanley, their neighbor, dead over a year ago. Cotella remembered John Stanley worked on building crews with Leroy sometimes. That made sense, then, and the other witness's signature belonged to someone she didn't know. The typed name and signature of a lawyer in Wise County, where Leroy was probably working at the time, stood out at the bottom of the last page, followed by a big, fancy seal. Maybe he didn't trust the Clintwood lawyers. And if the deed for the 200 acres was legal and right, it would be on file in Wise County anyway, not here.

She checked the dates. Only the previous summer, although she remembered that Leroy's father had been dead a couple of years by then. Maybe there had been a problem with his daddy's will. She heard that kind of thing happened. Maybe Leroy was a lot smarter than she thought, even if he seemed to lack common sense. Maybe he was waiting for the best time to sell the land, when the coal or lumber companies were paying top dollar. Maybe he planned to do it soon, and died unexpectedly before he could bring his family out of their poverty. No one would ever know.

And Arthur, still sleeping in his momma's bed when she contracted the influenza, could have died. Or the girls. What then? What if Minnie had not murmured something about a treasure and boards? Cotella's head swam with the long trail of what-ifs and maybes and what-could-have-happeneds. And even more, with the what-would-happens when she showed these papers to Mullins and the Sheriff on Wednesday.

***

"Girls, come here, to the kitchen. You can stop diggin' up the floor."

They came running. "Did you find the treasures?" said Mary.

"Yes, I think so."

Pansy made a face. "That's just white papers in a box. I thought you meant it would be like green paper money, or gold coins, or necklaces and rings."

"They's all kinds of treasures. People can be treasures, too."

"I don't see how," said Myrtle.

Cotella had to smile at the child's honesty. Some folks were treasures, some not.

"What kind of treasure is this?" said Pansy.

"Your daddy was a richer man than people thought."

"He was?" Pansy's eyes widened, then narrowed with suspicion. She was old enough to know that living in their tiny four-room cabin at the end of a road in the mountains, a half-mile from the next family, was not a sign of wealth.

"He owned lots of land. Land I think other people want."

The girls gathered around her to look at the papers, but they were in small, close letters. "Is that what that says?" said Mary. "What are you gonna do with 'em?"

"Show 'em to the Sheriff next time he comes." And that lawyer, she thought.

"Oh." They seemed bewildered.

"Can we buy new dresses?" said Pansy.

"And hair ribbons?" said Myrtle. "And a locket?"

Mary, not to be outdone by her sisters, said, "I want a new dolly." Arthur now dragged the one dolly each girl handed down to her sister through the dirt in his daily play outside.

"There's plenty of time to worry about that. We found the treasure. Now, let's get back to the regular chores. I got to get dinner on."

The children didn't need to know any more. The girls were not rich. At best, little Arthur would have the money one day and be good enough to take care of his sisters until they found husbands or a way to make their way in the world themselves. Things might be different for girls in the future if they got the vote and schooling.

Then she remembered. It was not that easy. The children's fate was bound up in the Farrells and lawyers, decided by a judge and the law. Arthur was not even two, and two-year-olds didn't have rights like adults. The Farrells might get their hands on this land and keep the money from the children. Finding these papers meant something, but what, she wouldn't know without that lawyer's help. She hoped he was a good man who took her case to do the right thing and not just make Josten Davis, Esquire, look like a fool in a courtroom.

Chapter Forty-Four

By early Wednesday morning she had accomplished everything expected. The house was as spotless as it could practically be. The cow was milked, perhaps for the last time. The children's belongings were neatly folded and placed in four old flour sacks. She put the one china-faced doll, usually bedraggled but now freshly cleaned, in Mary's sack. Arthur had no business with a girl's plaything anyway. She wrapped biscuit and ham sandwiches for the girls and a butter biscuit for Arthur. She added those and a mason jar of fresh milk to each sack in case they grew hungry.

Finding the deeds and will had given her a temporary hope that had faded since Friday. She knew the Farrells, as Minnie's kin, had the claim on the children, whether they planned to leave them in an orphanage or take them home. She could only put her trust in the Sheriff and Mullins. Prayer to God might help, too.

Ralph Sims drove up at 8:05, as on time as one could practically be on the rutted and muddy roads. "The Deputy is here!" Myrtle cried and ran outside. Cotella had them dressed in their best, cleanest clothes—the ones they wore a week before when the Farrells invaded their world.

"Here, Pansy, take Arthur by the hand," Cotella said. "I have things to carry. The Deputy has come to take us for a ride."

"We're gonna ride in his car!" Mary began jumping up and down. The girls were out the door in a second. She gathered up their belongings and her valise, pulled on her coat, and closed the door. It had no lock or key. Leroy had never bothered to put one in, she guessed, on this isolated piece of land. Who would come here to do evil—other than the Farrells? She sighed, and felt the tears. Seven months she had stayed here, longer than any place since she left Fanny and Tom's house. It was her home—humble, drafty, small, and filled with young-uns, but home.

The children had climbed in the back seat of the Packard. They tried out the padded seats with jumps and squirms.

"You can sit up font, Mizz Telly," said Ralph.

"Why you carryin' your valise and those sacks, Mizz Telly?" said Mary between jumps.

"You all sit still. The Deputy didn't bring this automobile out here for you all to act like monkeys." Even scolding them tore at her heart. She always fought any temptation to fall in love with the children she took care of. She usually lost, though, saved only by the fact she had to get used to another set every six weeks or so. Not this time.

"Yes, ma'am," said Myrtle, managing to sit still for a few seconds. "What's in them sacks?"

"Never you mind. I'll show you later." Ralph shifted some lever on the automobile, and it started to go backwards. "Oh, my goodness! Oh, Lord!" she cried.

"It's okay, Mizz Telly. This is what it does. It's a new model, you move this metal rod here in the floor and it will go backward, just a little, so I can turn it around."

"It feels so funny."

"Wait till we get going thirty miles an hour," Ralph smiled. "But you've been on a train. The Sheriff told me you went to nursing school in Bristol."

"He did? What did he do that for?"

"Oh, we were just talkin'." Ralph looked back at the children and lowered his voice. It wouldn't have mattered if he spoke louder—the children were too excited to listen to grownups. She held Arthur on her lap, and he jabbered away competing with his sisters' chatter in the wide back seat. They had gone back to hopping on their rear ends. They smudged up the windows with their noses and chattered away about how it felt to move in a machine.

"I know why you all are goin' to town," the Deputy continued. "My wife and I prayed for the children. We don't want them sent to the, you know."

"Thank you, Deputy," she hoped the Sims' prayers were stronger in faith than hers. She felt plumb out of faith and hope, and only had love left. But none for the Farrells. Christian-like or not, she'd cursed them under her breath and in her heart many times since she'd met them.

The ride in this "car," as the deputy called it, rather than an "automobile," was not like one on a train. For one, it was bumpy and uneasy. Trains rode on smooth steel rails, not a mixture of mud, dirt, rock, and gravel. Trains went faster; going train speed in this car would have knocked her teeth together without mercy. Trains rocked side to side. The car rocked side to side, front to back, unevenly at least until they reached the main paved road from McClure to Clintwood.

Cotella felt sick to her stomach with all the rugged movement. When they finally reached a paved road, the ride improved and her nausea started to lift. The children didn't seem to care. They had so little fun that she was happy for them to get this treat, even though they would always think of their first automobile ride as part of this horrible day.

Sometime a little before 9:00—a church bell rang the hour, another treat for the girls—they reached Clintwood. They disembarked from the Packard in front of the courthouse, which was across the street from a small storefront building. Ben Watson stood out front.

"Cotella, come on in here. Bring the children. The lawyer wants to talk to you."

"I have something to tell him," she said. "I don't know if it will make any difference, but it's important."

She could not read Ben's look. He was a quiet, studied man, but his face sometimes showed vivid feelings. She wished she had more sense than to care for him so much. Nothing could or would come of it; she would just be heartbroken all her days. But that didn't matter now.

The six of them entered the office, and a prim, pretty woman said they could go on in to speak with Mr. Mullins. Cotella wondered which Mullinses he was kin to. It was a common name in the mountains and the county. She remembered her momma saying some of her family had married with Mullinses, and she'd taken care of at least two Mullins mommas over the years. They were almost all kin, some way or other, a century back, some of them said, but they didn't all claim it now. There were too many of them to keep track of, she figured.

"Good morning, Miss Barlow," said Thad Mullins, after the pause she always noticed and expected. His was shorter than normal. Ben had probably warned him about her looks and asked him not to show his surprise. "And these must be Miss Pansy, Miss Myrtle, Miss Mary, and little Mr. Arthur." Thad Mullins struck her as charming and a smooth talker. She figured Ben had told him all about the children, too.

"Yes, sir." She said, offering her hand, which he shook. "I guess considering everything that's going to happen today, the children might as well hear all this, even if they don't understand it. Girls, go sit over there on that settee. Mind your manners. This is an important place. No tomfoolery or talkin."

They obeyed, in awe and fear. "What I wanted to say, Mr. Mullins, is I know what Mr. and Mrs. Farrell want to do. It's just plain wrong. I know I'm not kin. I know I got no claim on these children, at all, except that I'm fond of 'em and know how they live, how they eat, their fears and faults and virtues and all of that. I know *them*. They need to be together, like family. They *are* family. I know, I know, I got no husband, I got no money, and I ain't kin. But I don't want the Farrells to do their meanness to these young-uns."

"Yes, I understand, Miss Barlow. And you are right. You don't have any claim, really. I don't know what Davis is going to say before the judge today. Now, this is not a trial. It's kind of what we call a hearing. The judge has to make a decision about custody of the children, only because I brought a suit for them. Do you understand?"

"Yes, sir, I do. Will I have to talk? I'm not so good at that, you know, because of, well. . ."

"It would be good if you could answer some questions from me. And the judge will ask you questions."

"What I want to say is, I found something in the house you need to know about. It concerns the young—I mean children."

"What is that?"

"These papers." She fished in her coat and pulled them out. "When the children's mother was, uh, dying, and she knew she wasn't long for the world, she said there was a 'treasure under the boards.' That's what she said. I thought it was just the fever, but I got to thinking about it last week, when I was cleaning and, um, packing up the house and such. So I set the girls and myself to lookin' up under the floor, and I found these papers."

She handed them over, and Mullins looked over them carefully through his spectacles. The room was so quiet she could hear his pocket watch tick. "These are the deeds to two pieces of land, one of them sizable. And Mr. Goins' will. It changes everything, Miss Barlow."

"Well, that's what I figured, they were deeds and his will. But I don't understand it all. What does it mean?"

"Mr. Goins used a clever lawyer. He wanted to make sure that the larger piece of land, which is right where the coal companies are starting to mine, stayed in his family and wouldn't go to his wife's. Her name is on the small farm deed, but not this one." He held up the papers from Wise County.

"If Arthur dies, the larger parcel of land goes to the remaining children, the three girls, to split. Mr. Goins must have known women would get the vote soon!" Mullins laughed. Cotella didn't think it was funny, but she was glad to know Leroy didn't forget about the girls.

"But if Otis and Viola Farrell get to have control of the children, won't they still get the land?" Ben said.

Mullins smiled. "That's why you hire a lawyer, Miss Barlow. The Farrells and Davis don't know about these papers. And they won't, until it's time and until we let them."

Chapter Forty-Five

At 10:00 Cotella and the children settled nervously into the courtroom's benches. It was as big as any church she ever sat in. Cotella told the children to act like it was a church, and they scooted into the seats behind the lawyers, who sat at big polished oak tables. A man, dressed in a uniform like Ben, told them all to stand up, and the judge came in. The girls gasped. She knew they were frightened, so she patted their hands but said nothing. There was no keeping Arthur from jabbering, but nobody seemed to notice. Ben sat on the bench behind her.

After some official words, the Farrells' lawyer started talking. Davis was a tall, skinny fellow, bald as a knob, wearing a suit that should have been sharp and stylish but looked baggy on his thin frame. Mullins, on the other hand, looked exactly like some of the Mullinses she knew, so they must be kin. He was full of movement and energy, as round as he was tall, with a full head of thick brown hair around his chubby face. David and Mullins were opposites. She didn't much take with either of them, from the first. But Ben said Mullins would do right by her and the young-uns.

Davis spoke. "I am representing Mr. and Mrs. Otis Farrell, the only known relatives of the orphaned children of Leroy and Minnie Goins of this county. Both died in the influenza epidemic, back in October. The Goins left three little girls and a baby boy, all minors. The Farrells wish to be granted custody of them so that they can take them out of the county. Mrs. Farrell is the children's aunt, the sister of their deceased mother."

"Then what's the problem?" said Judge Hopkins. "There are thousands of orphaned children in the state now. If family members want to take the Goins' children in and give them a good home, why shouldn't they?"

"Because the woman who has been taking care of them since October wants to stop them."

"Why? Mr. Mullins, you are representing this woman. Can you answer that question?"

Thad Mullins stood up, self-importantly. "Miss Barlow, my client, does not believe that would be the best future for the children. I think she should tell you why."

"Miss Barlow, your lawyer has said you can explain yourself. What call do you have to keep the children from going with the Farrells?" Judge Hopkins peered at her over his glasses.

"Stand up, Miss Barlow," said Davis. Cotella complied, swallowed hard. She didn't know if the words would come out.

"I—I—They don't want to raise the children. They want to put them in an orphanage. They told me so. They told the Sheriff that, too."

"Did they really, Sheriff?"

Ben stood. "Yes, your honor. On May the first, I met the Farrells in town to lead them to the Goins' property to meet the children and Miss Barlow. They told me their plans then."

"So, two people say it's true. What say you, Mr. Davis?"

"Uh, let me confer with my clients." Davis and Otis Farrell huddled in conversation, while Viola sat looking straight ahead, proud and unsmiling.

"My client, Mr. Farrell, says that is their plan. The Farrells believe that would be the best for the children. They are not willing or able to raise four young children themselves at this time."

"I could have had the children sent to the orphanage in Washington County myself without having two lawyers and people from West Virginia come in to help me," said the judge. "I assume there is a farm where the Goins lived. Do your clients expect to get the land?"

"Yes, your honor. The deed is in both Mr. and Mrs. Goins' names. Mrs. Farrell is the next of kin of Mrs. Goins."

"Not by my lights, Mr. Davis. That little girl over there looks to me to be the oldest." He pointed with his gavel at Pansy. "She's next of kin. I guess her parents would say the same, God rest their souls. You all must think I'm King Solomon here, deciding on the fates of children and how to divide 'em up. No, I am not inclined to give away the farm and land that belongs by rights to these children," pointing his gavel again at the four wide-eyed siblings, "to these people." He waved his hand at the Farrells like he wanted them to go away. "They admit that they want to hide the legal heirs away in an orphanage and take their inheritance.

"They only want the land to sell it, not to live on it and be part of our community. They don't want the children who are the reason for the land or why they are even here in the first place. Besides, these are

Virginia children, Dickenson County children. Why should they be carted off to an orphanage in another state?"

"But, your honor," said Davis. "Who will take care of them?" "Now is time for your client's side of it, Mr. Mullins. Does Miss Barlow have the means to take care of the children?"

"Not of herself, your honor. We concede that. However, some more information has come to light." He approached the judge and handed him the will and deeds.

The judge perused them. "Mr. Davis, did your clients know Mr. Goins had a will?"

"No, your honor. It isn't registered in this county courthouse."

"I see. It doesn't have to be, if it's witnessed and notarized. And it is, in Wise County. According to this will, Mr. Goins didn't seem to think the Farrells should be raising his children. No matter. Mr. Goins has left his land—and quite a bit of it—to that little boy there who can't even speak for himself. With going prices, and considering the extent of this land and its location near current mines, it's worth tens of thousands of dollars."

"What?" said Viola Farrell, jumping to her feet. "They just have that little farm, barely enough to keep them alive!"

"Mr. Davis, keep your client controlled in my courtroom." He paused until Viola sat and calmed herself. "Mr. and Mrs. Farrell, you would have been the guardians of a little boy with a lot of money. But I've already decided that he and his sisters are going to stay where they belong, where their parents clearly wished them to stay, and not in an orphanage in another state where they will eventually be separated from each other."

The judge now turned his full attention to Cotella. "Miss Barlow, why do you think you are qualified to be the children's caretaker? We have settled the matter of the money, which I will address in a minute, but you must give a defense of yourself. What are you to these children?"

"I—I—your honor, I'm an orphan myself, since I was thirteen, so I think I know what it's like for these four young-uns. I make my living helpin' mommas who have to lie in, you know, rest up after they birth their baby, and I take care of the house and the children while they do. I did it for Minnie Goins when all four of these young-uns was born. I was doin' it when . . . she died. Then everybody started dyin', and no one would come around, and we, we had to live somehow through the winter, until the Sheriff came and found us, in March. That's all I can say. I did my best. I did things I hope I never have to do again, Judge. But we're here. I'm fond of the children. They are sweet children, naughty sometimes, of course, but I think they like me and will listen to me. That's, uh, really all I can say."

"Judge, Your Honor, may I speak?" Ben Watson stood up.

"Yes, Sheriff."

"Miss Barlow is being too modest, Your Honor. She has worked like a field hand, a momma, and a nursemaid all in one to make sure these children live through the winter and this sickness. She buried their mother, dug the grave herself. She butchered a hog by herself. They ran out of flour and meal because they couldn't get to a store and no one thought to look for them. They lived on eggs, ham, and milk for months. She tried to have the girls do their schooling. If that's not being a momma, I don't know what is."

Cotella felt her eyes burn with tears, and her cheeks burn with embarrassment. Ben was saving her life, again. He didn't know it, but he was.

"Thank you, Sheriff." Judge Hopkins looked through the paperwork, then cradled his head in his folded hands. Mr. and Mrs. Farrell whispered, audibly to all, about the nonsense going on in this courtroom, not letting kin have orphaned children. "Mr. and Mrs. Farrell, I have already decided against you. Don't tempt me to put you in jail, too."

He sat for a few seconds longer. "Miss Barlow, I have something difficult to ask you. I believe you are a fine and generous person who has done everything you could for the children in a grievous time in our country. But and I hesitate to say this, I have to wonder if your—well, your disease, is something I should consider here. Are you well? Does it make you unwell? Could it lead to your death? I ask because it concerns me that the children will be ostracized because of how people I am sure react to your condition, and whether it might shorten your life to where you would not be able to care for them. I apologize for being so abrupt and seemingly unkind. But it does concern me."

Cotella didn't bother to hide or even wipe away her tears. There was no reason. Since the doctor and Sister Berta in Bristol so many years ago, no one had ever spoken to her so directly about her knots and bumps and tumors. Not even Fanny or Tom. None of the mommas, except Minnie. Well, some children had, and been told to hush. Everybody saw them, of course, and stared, winced, turned away, frowned, or squinted. No one asked her why, what was wrong, would she die from them, did they make her sick, or how did they affect her life. The judge made her felt seen, for once. She didn't know what that word ostrichized meant. They said ostriches put their heads in the sand, maybe that was it.

The judge had asked her a direct question, so she had to answer. "I, I don't know, Your Honor. I am strong. I work hard. I don't know how long I will live. I don't guess anybody does, do they? A lot of people died in the last year and I know they didn't expect it. A lot of them were young and healthy. I don't know why I didn't die from the influenza, too. I guess it's true about God's will for some people. Sometimes my knots and such hurt, but not too bad. Not so far.

"I don't know about the ostriches, but most people end up treating me pretty good. I got lots of mommas who are my friends, and their men—I mean their husbands—pay me my wages. I won't be doing that kind of work anymore if I take on the children. I won't be getting married, neither. If you're worried about me deciding I don't want to take these children on and raise 'em, I promise you with my whole heart that won't happen, no matter what. I'll swear to it on the Bible if I have to."

Judge Hopkins smiled. "I see why you have friends like the Sheriff, Miss Barlow. Mr. Mullins, I am going to appoint you the trustee of the Goins' estate. You understand the extent of what that means, so you can explain it to your client Miss Barlow and the children. Miss Barlow, you will have custody of the children. If you ever have any reason to suspect Mr. Mullins is not doing his duty as a trustee and agent of this court, you must let the Sheriff know. If he believes you are not fulfilling your duties, Miss Barlow, Mr. Mullins will call you into account.

"Mr. Mullins will help you with the legal and financial care of the children until they are eighteen. He will oversee the sale of the land in Wise County for the support of the children. Be sure they are well fed and housed, in school, in church, and well behaved. Those are my rulings. You are dismissed."

"Let's go, Miss Barlow," said Thad Mullins. "The judge has a full docket today, and we need to leave the courtroom." She gathered the children and herded them out the double doors.

She did not know what had happened. Her head spun, her knees wanted to buckle, her whole body trembled. Outside the court, she could barely walk. She wondered if this was what fainting was like. "I don't understand, Mr. Mullins. Am I takin' the children home? The judge was too wise and too good a talker for me to understand what happened."

"You will be the children's guardian, Miss Barlow. Let's go to my office so I can explain it. I'll ask my secretary to keep the children with her."

She followed, still shaky and dizzy. She had just told the judge she was strong and healthy enough to take care of the children, and now she wasn't sure.

"When you are done, have Jenny, Mullins' secretary, call my office," said Ben Watson. "Ralph will take you home when he's not busy." He tipped his hat. "Congratulations, Miss Cotella Barlow. You outfoxed the Farrells *and* Josten Davis. I like seein' that any day."

Chapter Forty-Six

Cotella spent half an hour in Thad Mullins' office. Jenny brought her coffee in a delicate teacup on a tray and then excused herself. Cotella fought to keep her mind on what Thad told her. He would be in charge of the sale of Leroy's land and making sure the money was put in a good bank, where it would earn interest. Every month she would get enough money to spend on the children's welfare and a small allowance for herself. He would keep account of it. She could get the money by coming to the bank, and the stores she used could send his office the bills.

"This doesn't seem right. You're doing all this work. Do you get paid?"

"Yes, I am allowed by law to take out my fees. I'm working for the court, not for you."

"Oh, I owe you money!" said Cotella. "I have it here in my purse."

"Don't bother. We will take it from this account. You shouldn't have to pay out of your savings for what's in the children's interests."

He explained to her what she could spend money for, and what she couldn't.

"I wouldn't even think about that!" she said when he mentioned jewelry or stocks for herself. "One of these days, though, it would be nice to have a horse to drive to town or visit. Walkin' that far is hard on the children."

"Miss Barlow, Arthur is by no means wealthy, but there will be enough money for the children to reach adulthood, go to high school, and perhaps go to college if they desire it."

"College!"

"Yes, keep in mind, they have enough to live decently in these mountains. You will still need to farm the land, put in crops, keep animals, and all that. You can hire a man to help. That also means yes, you can buy a horse and wagon. However, you might want to consider an automobile at some point in the future. Progress will come, the roads will be better, and the children will want to drive a car."

"They will have to learn that on their own! I'll never drive an automobile."

"You never know, Miss Barlow. Crazier things have happened."

That was what Ben Watson said. He was right, a crazy thing happened. She wondered what he was doing right then. If now he would stop his visits. If she would see him again, even today.

"Since you are in town, you might want to do some shopping. Have Steller's Store put it on a charge and send the bill here. Everyone in town is going to know what happened by this afternoon anyway."

"They will?"

"Yes. Did you see those people in the back of the courtroom? They are the town criers. Or the town gossips. They come and sit in court just to have something to tell other people. We have a newspaper, but I'm not sure why. Those fellas are the real newspaper. Word gets around fast here. This isn't exactly Richmond or Charlotte. So go on, get the children some new clothes. And treat yourselves to lunch at the diner on the corner there. The children deserve it, I think. They almost saw their lives taken away from them this morning."

She decided she liked Mullins after all. In court, he was a cocky bird, full of himself and not cowed by skinny Davis or even the judge. Now he was friendly and thoughtful.

"Thank you, Mr. Mullins. I'm mighty grateful."

"Think nothing of it, Miss Barlow. Let me escort you out." And he did, opening the door for her like she was a lady.

***

The children were strangely quiet when she collected them from Jenny, the secretary, and walked them to the diner on the corner. It bore the name "Grady's Restaurant," but it looked like a train car that got left on the street. The girls' eyes expanded as they mounted the steps to enter and sat at a table with a red-checked tablecloth. The waitress came and handed them menus, sheets of stiff paper with foods listed, sandwiches and dinners and such.

"You can pick out anything you want today," said Cotella. "Any other day, you eat what I fix. Today, that man over there will cook whatever you like."

"I don't know what this food is," said Pansy. "What is a ham-bur-ger?"

"It's ground meat, in a sandwich. And a hot dog is a long sausage in a sandwich."

"Can we have dessert?"

"Yes, some pie. Maybe they have ice cream."

"What's that?"

"You'll see."

The waitress returned and wrote down what they wanted. Cotella craved a full meal made by someone else: fried chicken, mashed potatoes covered in gravy, dinner rolls instead of biscuits, and English peas. She ordered soup and crackers for Arthur and the girls wanted hot dogs, beans, and fried potatoes, for some reason. And there was vanilla ice cream for dessert.

"Do people eat like this all the time?"

"Nobody I know. Nobody in the mountains," said Cotella. "In big cities, I think so. Like New York."

"I want to go to New York and eat a hot dog every day!" announced Mary. "And ice cream."

Cotella didn't correct her. She was seven. Seven-year-old little girls should get to say silly things sometimes. New York would scare little Mary to death. Even Bristol would put her in a faint. The excitement of one day in the small town of Clintwood would satisfy them for quite a while.

They said nothing about the courtroom. There would be many years, in God's will, for them to understand what had happened. Somehow, they could stop worrying about the next meal, every penny, every bite of food. Being poor could mold a person's mind and heart, Cotella thought, until that's all that matters, all they thought of. Maybe now she and the girls could begin to think of other things, like a future.

Chapter Forty-Seven

They did shop. She bought each girl three new dresses, a pair of sturdy shoes, and undergarments. They would need them for church and school in the fall. She bought the clothes a little large. Pansy was growing and would soon do what women did every month. Arthur got the most clothes; she couldn't resist a little sailor suit and several pairs of britches and shirts. The store had something she'd never seen; little rubber pants for the babies to wear over their diapers. What would they think of next? She bought some of those, and a pair of pretty white shoes for him, knowing he would outgrow them by the fall. She bought one cotton summer dress for herself. She felt like a foolish spendthrift, even more so when she said, "Please send the bill to Mr. Thaddeus Mullins' office." She then felt like a queen when the salesgirl said she would do just that.

She told herself she needed to leave the store and town before she did something she would regret. Ralph Sims drove them home in the big Packard that was now full of packages and children. The girls nodded off from the exciting day and Arthur slept against her shoulder. Ralph was quiet, but told her how glad he was about the way it worked out. "These children belong here, where they were born," he said, "and where their momma and daddy lived and died."

"I don't know where we would be without you and the Sheriff," Cotella said.

"Yes, ma'am, the Sheriff's a good man."

"You know, he's not much of a talker. He never says anything about his wife."

"He ain't got one. I mean, he's a widower, now. They had three boys, and they's grown and live back in Kentucky, where he came from."

"Oh. How did she die?"

"That I don't rightly know," said Ralph. "Like you said, he keeps his life and his thoughts to himself, mostly. But I do think he's sweet on somebody."

She then understood what people meant when they said a heart skipped a beat. "Why do you say that?"

"I don't know. He just likes to visit Thad Mullins' office more than is called for. He's been seen taking Jenny Thomas out for a stroll after church on Sundays."

***

The girls wanted to go to bed soon after a late supper. She suspected they wanted to whisper about the day's adventures, keeping the wonders to themselves in their room, outside of Cotella's hearing. She took Arthur for a walk in his new shoes, holding his hand as they strolled around Arthur's land, patted Arthur's cow, and gathered eggs from Arthur's hens. Arthur would never know another mother. He would call her "momma" even when Pansy and Myrtle called her "Telly." Mary would have to make up her own mind on that.

The sun set over the ridge, burning into the horizon clouds and creating colors she didn't have words for. Not orange, not red, but deeper and blazing, like fire burning the day away. She rocked Arthur and told him a Bible story about Moses as a baby being found by the Pharaoh's daughter. She always liked that one. The women in that story, Moses' momma and sister, the Hebrew midwives, and even Pharaoh's daughter seemed to be getting together to trick a bad man, Pharaoh. She guessed that meant he was a special kind of king. Pharaoh wanted to hurt them openly, so they fought him their way, secret-like.

"And Moses grew up in the king's house, and when he was an old man, he led

God's people out of Egypt and from being the king's slaves," she finished the story for Arthur. He jabbered, some of it words she understood. Some of the sounds just seemed to make him happy, because he laughed even when he made no sense.

The burning sunset reminded her of a fire in the hearth, warm and inviting as long as it stayed in its place. A fire had killed her momma and daddy. The preachers said there was a hell where sinners who hated God suffered and died forever. Yes, if it was true, it would be like dying over and over again to be in a fire like that. She didn't know how that could be. That meant a lot of people were probably there since a lot of people did wickedness and cursed God.

She didn't think she was wicked like a thief or murderer, but she wondered if there was a certain, small kind of wickedness in looking at all the good and bad of her thirty-some years and not seeing God's hand. In gazing at those beautiful colors and seeing God's judgment rather than his gifts.

She had held onto God lightly for so many years when she should have grabbed him with all she had. She prayed, but only because she was told to. She reminded the children to pray, for Minnie's sake, not their souls' sake or because God rightly deserved it. And now, on the other side of the trial of the last seven months, shouldn't she thank God for bringing them through it even though her prayers were weak as a trickle of stream water in August? Shouldn't she see God as good for bringing them together in happiness instead of cruel for making her ugly and lonely?

Happiness. Was it real? She hadn't had a call to be happy before this. Not much. She was happy at Watkins Hospital, for the first few months. Then that ended. Happiness couldn't last. It fled sooner than it came. She had been happy loving Ben Watson, in her way. She still did, but it would fade, and he would marry Jenny, and Cotella might see him in passing some time. She would then remember that he saved her life twice and she couldn't help loving his broad shoulders, quiet manner, and modest smile.

She sighed, and Arthur followed her example. She rocked him until he fell asleep in his new pair of rubber pants, new overalls, and new shoes. She looked out on the yard where she entered the gate in October, saw the disorder and gave the girls sugar sticks, where Minnie and her first baby laid under the maple trees, where she and Pansy had stunned and butchered Kaiser Wilhelm, where Ben Watson drove his Packard and found them, where the Farrells invaded their world and tried to destroy it.

The gate was closed now, and whenever she opened it again, it would not be to walk five or ten miles to the next new momma and passel of young-uns for six weeks. It would be to return shortly and sleep in the same bed every night and sit at the same table with the same children, her children, her Pansy, Myrtle, Mary, and Arthur.

If happiness only lasted for a moment, this was that moment.

Epilogue

June 15, 1939

Arthur Goins alighted from his 1934 Ford and jumped the gate of the Goins homestead rather than open it like a sane person. He wasn't sane today. He had just graduated from Virginia Agricultural and Mechanical College, class of '39; he had a job with a branch of the U.S. government waiting in Richmond, and he was home to see his mother, Telly.

His classmates and friends always asked why he called his mother "Telly." "Her name is Cotella Barlow," he said. "It's an old mountain name. Never met anybody else with that name." When they pressed him on why he didn't call her "Momma" or "Mother," he told the truth. "She's not my real mother. She raised me and my sisters. Our parents died from the Spanish flu." And after a pause he would always say, "And Telly saved our lives."

His buoyant personality kept him from sinking too deeply into considering where he might be now if Cotella Barlow had not shown up when she did, had not kept him from his infectious, dying mother, had not gone without food to keep them alive that winter. But now, as he walked to the porch of his childhood home, his wonders returned. Had the strain of it all taken its toll on Cotella? That stress of those months of privation and isolation and of keeping up a farm and raising four children. And most of all from living in her disfigured, rebellious body.

His visit was needed because she wanted to brag on him now that he was a college graduate. Cotella had made it clear in her last letter how much she wanted to boast about Arthur's accomplishments. Mary had beat him to a college degree, of course. She went to teachers' college and now taught high school in Abingdon. Pansy and Myrtle married good men, produced three babies each, and lived in Clintwood, visiting Telly twice a week and watching out for her as she had for them.

But he also needed to come home because Telly was not well. Doctors around here couldn't say what it was or prescribe any treatments. Her only hope was to go to a big city, perhaps Richmond, to get some form of modern medical help.

"She's in pain, Arthur. More than she admits," Pansy told him at their celebration lunch after his graduation. She had driven with Myrtle to see him receive his diploma. Pansy loved to drive. She earned a license as soon as she could after coaxing Telly to buy a Model T Ford in 1924. She drove them everywhere, and found every excuse to be behind the wheel. Her husband, a foreman in a coal mine, bought her a 1936 Buick that she kept shiny and in tip-top shape, like a man would.

"I tried to get her to come with us, but she made every excuse she could," Pansy continued. "'I don't think I can ride that far in a car, even your big fancy one.' she said. And 'You two will want to have fun, like schoolgirls away from your husbands. I'd just be in your way.'"

"I'm afraid she couldn't bear to be in a new place and have people staring at her," added Myrtle. "Anyway, she has trouble walking now. She has so many tumors and knots on her feet. It seems like they are turning inward, and pressing on her organs and bones."

Arthur observed how alike the two older of his sisters were, and yet how different. Both brunettes, while he and Mary had favored their father, Telly always said. Only two old photos existed of their parents. One at their wedding ceremony, distinguished only from a regular photo by the bouquet of flowers their mother carried. The other was of Minnie in a white, lacey dress, as if she were going to a party.

"Your momma's people had some money, I think," Telly told them. "Maybe this picture was taken at a cotillion or party."

"What in the world is a 'cotillion'?" Mary asked, ten at the time.

"I don't know. I just read that at the picture show," Telly answered, hearkening back to the silent movies.

But Myrtle and Pansy were both constant talkers, with strong but loving opinions, and both proud of it. He figured they passed for attractive, but they were his sisters. They were attractive enough to get good husbands in Dickenson County. Myrtle had probably made the better marriage from a financial standpoint. As close as the two were, competition seemed to run under the surface.

Mary had made excuses not to attend Arthur's graduation, despite Pansy's insistence. Mary was the reader, the studious one, the introspective one. It seemed Mary carried the scars of their early deprived childhoods the most, yet wanting to make her own way in the world as a single woman. She maintained a distance from her siblings the other three did not understand but accepted, sadly.

Pansy's words brought him back from his reverie to the conversation about Cotella. "I think she's always lived with pain, and never told us. Now, it's just unbearable for her," said Pansy.

"And the doctors can't do anything?" Arthur said.

"Doc Franklin gave her morphine for the pain. Not that morphine is the best solution. I've worried about her for years, living on the farm all by herself since you went off to college. Harley worked the farm for her, of course, like he did when we were growing up, so someone was there during the day. But he's dead now, from that heart attack last year, poor man."

"You know, I always thought he was sweet on Telly," said Arthur. "Like he would have married her, or wanted to ask."

"Really?" said Myrtle.

"Yeah," Arthur said. "He worked for us from the time the judge ran our aunt and uncle off, right? He was always around. It couldn't have just been for the pay. I don't think she could pay him that much."

"I agree they were fond of each other, in their way," said Myrtle.

"You know," Pansy said, "she had known him since she was a teenager. He worked the farm for the people who raised her. He knew her… before. Before she went to nursing school and got her… disease. Maybe her condition didn't bother him, like it did other people."

Myrtle thought for a moment. "They *were* like an old married couple sometimes. He drove out to the farm in that old truck three times a week, worked all day, ate breakfast, dinner, and supper with her, then drove to his room in McClure, and worked another farm the other three days. It's too bad she didn't just ask him to marry her. They could have been happy together."

"She was too old-fashioned to do something like that, even if she wanted to. Anyway, she loved that sheriff. Ben Watson—remember?" said Myrtle.

"Sheriff Watson? How do you know?" said Arthur.

"She told me once. I don't know why. Maybe she just wanted me to know that despite everything, she had normal feelings. She said he saved her life, twice. He showed up at our door when she didn't think she could go on much longer. And he spoke up for us in court to make Aunt Viola, the witch, go away."

"Telly should move into town," said Arthur, as if he had solved the problem. "We should just sell the farm. It's not much of one, anyway. She could live on the money in town. We could find her a nice place, and she could rest. She could go to church in town instead of depending on a ride to go miles away. She wouldn't have to keep working so hard."

His sisters looked at each other, then at him. He had seen that look before. Arthur, they said, thought he had the answer to everyone's problems and questions. It came from being the big shot scholarship kid in the university. And before that, from being the youngest. And the boy.

"She'll listen to you," Pansy said. "You're her favorite. Then Mary. I think because you all were the younger ones. You called her 'momma.' We never did. Not that she didn't love us like her own. I'll never think that. But you younger ones, she could love on and pet on you more, and she had you longer."

Arthur smiled. Of course. There would always be that difference between them. He had no memory of Minnie or Leroy Goins, of the shiftless but somehow savvy man who held on to all the land, for reasons they would never understand, until what became the right time, at least for them. The story of how Telly found the will and deed was their family legend. How Telly kept them alive, all of it. He knew nothing of his mother but her name and that her sister was a witch like in "Hansel and Gretel."

"Do you all ever think what our lives would have been like if . . .?" he said.

"Almost every day of my life," said Myrtle. "What I remember from childhood, or most of the time until I was nine, was being poor and hungry and isolated. And living in that drafty shack with no running water."

"And the outhouse. I saw a snake there once, and it scared me to death from then on!" said Pansy. "I have some distinct memories, but most are, well, dreary. I don't think our mother was happy. She made a bad choice and tried to make the best of it. If there was a best to be found in it."

"Same for me," said Arthur. "That is, before the Spanish flu and Telly coming. I don't know why our father had the possibility of all that money, but didn't spend it on us to live a little better. We'll never know, I guess."

"Oh, I know," said Pansy.

"You do?" said Arthur.

"Yes, I finally decided to look into it. You can go to the courthouse and learn a lot. I wanted to find out more about the Goins, who they were, why we never heard from them. I think I found some answers. Then Richard and I went to visit that same lawyer in Wise County who wrote up our daddy's will during the war. Richard wanted to talk to him about our wills, too," she said. Pansy liked to mention her husband's name as frequently as possible.

"This is news. Why haven't you told us?" said Myrtle.

"Because we only did it last month, and I'm still tryin' to figure it out. That old man, well, he's old now, said he remembered our daddy. There had been a lot of wrangling over his own daddy's will. He said Leroy planned to sell the land as soon as the price of coal got to a certain point, and then the companies would be willing to pay top dollar for his land. He waited too long, though."

They sat there, quiet. Yes, thought Arthur. Over the years, he had wondered if his father had tried, maybe out of male pride, to support his family himself without the inheritance. On the other hand, he often pondered if his father suffered from some sort of insanity, thinking he could make something of himself without help, even when it was clear the family needed more means. Or if he was just waiting for the time he thought he would make a killing in the coal business. Apparently, his father gambled on this venture, keeping his children in want, until it was too late. What a mystery one's ancestors could be!

After lunch with Pansy and Myrtle, he kissed them goodbye and prepared to drive four hours to their childhood home, leaving his older sisters to shop in the big city of Blacksburg.

So here he was, in the yard. He stopped to survey his homestead. He didn't remember the house Pansy and Myrtle spoke of, sometimes lovingly, sometimes with a shudder. The four rooms separated by curtains rather than doors, the fireplace, the draftiness. Over the years, Cotella had Harley make improvements to the structure. They added a large room on the side for the girls, each with their own bed, leaving him the tiny room the girls used to share. Walls and doorways were constructed, cracks around the windows sealed up to keep the precious heat in. And, of course, running water by way of a pump in the kitchen sink, even if they still had to use the outhouse for that business.

His adopted mother liked to plant flowers and pretty bushes. Normally, by now, there would be blooms encircling the house. Their absence made Arthur wonder if he had ignored the signs of Telly's condition for too long, and if his sisters were not even as aware of Telly's suffering as they thought.

Arthur leaped onto the porch and rushed through the door, first knocking loudly for warning but not permission. "Telly! I'm here! The college graduate. The engineer and not the train kind. Where are you?"

Silence. Arthur felt the sense of emptiness in the house. Maybe she was outside, he thought. He searched the barn, and the old smokehouse, which was no longer used. Electrification had come to the mountains, and with it her beloved Frigidaire, where meat, milk, and butter could stay cold. Where could she be? He hadn't looked in her bedroom, not wanting to think the worst. It didn't matter. One could not keep the worst back by thinking otherwise.

Arthur found her in bed. He shook her shoulder gently but knew it would not matter. Her olive-toned skin had already taken on the tinge of death. She was fully clothed in one of her best dresses, as if she were waiting for expected visitors, or to go somewhere. Actually, she looked as if she had prepared for his return home, and had laid down for a rest, face up.

He sat down in the wicker chair by the bed. Poor Telly. She was only fifty-three. She must have suffered a heart attack, he figured, her body worn out, from all the fighting. Since she was nineteen, her body had struggled against itself, making tumors on tumors that must have sapped her strength over the years. And for all those years, she had fought to endure the stares and gapes of others. Since he was a baby, she had fought to raise them, to be sure they had schooling, to make their lives better than they had been with Leroy and Minnie.

How strange that such a peaceful and modest woman would fight so much, would have to. She only went to court one time in her life. She didn't protest for any causes. He had never heard her say a curse word, or raise her voice much, and she didn't even whip them, just a swat on the rear sometimes.

Over the years of his childhood, Telly's visage had become commonplace for him. He saw her disfigurement, and yet he didn't. Now, having been away for so long, and viewing her lifeless form, he saw it afresh. Yes, it was frightening. Her eyes, especially. Tumors surrounded them, pushing the skin on her forehead down and her cheeks up. Could she see normally? How? Her nose also, where underneath bumps of skin blocked one nostril almost completely—could she smell like others did, or even breathe well?

He sat back, sighed, and let himself weep. He needed a handkerchief but had none even though Telly had taught him a gentleman carried one. He used his shirtsleeve, reminded of all the times Telly had warned him about spreading germs. He looked around. On the bedstand, a cheap piece of furniture from his mother's time, one never replaced by his humble second mother, lay three letters. One bore his name, and one his three sisters' names. The last was addressed to Ben Watson, now widowed again and retired from his position as Sheriff after twenty-five years.

Oh. Then he understood. He knew what this meant. Telly planned her death. Somehow, by her own hand or only by her will, she had chosen this, and perhaps written why.

He didn't want to read his or deliver the other two. He had no right to read them, of course, but he owed Telly this last request.

Telly had always insisted they have good penmanship. "People will judge you bad if you can't write neat and pretty," she said. Her message to Arthur looked like the work of a woman who wanted to create elegant cursive letters but whose hand was in a vise. He read it letter by letter, decoding and reconstructing.

Dear Arthur,

I know if you are reading this, you have found me at rest. I did not take my own life the way you think. That would be a sin against God, and you know that I made my peace with God when you all became my children that day in the courtroom. He loves me, even if I don't always understand how that works.

The doctor gave me morphine for the pain of my knots. I wanted to stop the pain, to not feel it for a little bit of time. If you find me dead, I probably took too much and it killed me. I didn't want to die, but I couldn't bear the pain any more. I just wanted the hurting to stop.

For a long time I haven't been able to breathe good. I can't sleep for the pain, it's everywhere. I don't want to eat. The doctor said my tumors are growing inside now.

Please forgive me. I love you and the girls. You don't need me anymore, not really, because you are grownups on your way in the world. I am proud to be the one who brought you all up.

If you can give Sheriff Ben and the girls the other letters, I will be obliged. Good-bye.

Your loving momma Telly

He debated with himself for ten seconds whether Pansy, Myrtle, and Mary should receive their letter. It wasn't his decision to make; of course they would, but not for a while. Not until Telly had her funeral and burial and time had passed. Ben would get his and know the truth, too, in time.

He found a blanket in the chifforobe and placed it over her body out of respect. He'd have to drive back to Clintwood to ask the mortuary to come take care of the body, then call the girls from a booth. Phone service hadn't reached this holler.

Arthur didn't want to do any of that yet. For now, he would sit by her bed, remember, and marvel.

Author's Notes

Although there is a common misconception that fiction is a work of pure creativity, that is only a partial truth. Most fiction, especially of the historical variety as this novel is, requires a substantial amount of research for realistic details, verisimilitude, accuracy, and credibility.

My first source was my upbringing. My mother was born and raised in Dickenson County, Virginia, in the 1930s and 1940s, ten to twenty years after this story. She did not have electricity until she was school age, nor did they have running water in the house. When we visited my grandmother and her people in the 1960s and 1970s, the area was modernized, but poverty was still widespread in that part of Appalachia. Environmental damage from coal mining and lumbering was only beginning to be understood and addressed.

Mom did not treat her upbringing like some type of history lesson for my two brothers and me, but we did see how different it was from our suburban Washington, D.C., life (Grandma had only one TV station!). However, her memories and comments about life then were a type of lens for seeing our own experience. Tales of hog killing, snakes in the outhouses, walking long distances, isolation. Christmas presents of oranges and candy rather than new-fangled toys or electronic devices. Yes, simpler, one might say, but far more hardscrabble. The center of the story of our Appalachian roots, for us, was Grandma, Josie Vanover Fraley Rose, who died in 2005 two months shy of her 98th birthday. She was a font of stories as well.

However, I am an academic by training, so that means published sources. The time period of the 1910s, especially 1918, was certainly newsworthy and full of historic events. The bloody war in Europe was coming to an end, at least of active warfare, with the armistice with Germany in November of 1918. I credit *The World Undone* by G. Meyer (Delacorte Press, 2006) for the background on World War I. It was also the time of the Russian Revolution and the beginning of communism that would lead to the Soviet Union. The novel also has sly references to women's suffrage, approved by Congress in May 1919 and ratified in August 1920, as well as to the stifling restrictions on free speech and protest during World War I.

Many websites contributed to my knowledge of what came to be known as the Spanish flu pandemic, especially in Southwestern Virginia and other parts of Appalachia. Again, my grandmother's memories not only added to my picture of life then, but were also a key part of what the pandemic was like. She said that the disease created even more isolation than the geography did, and neighbors were not willing to help neighbors, often because of the level of disease and death in their own homes. She herself had six siblings (one a sister named Cotella, whom I have chosen to honor here), and they all survived.

I wrote this book in 2021-22 and revised it in 2022-23, during the end (we hope) of the COVID-19 pandemic, when the Omicron variant was racing through the population, "more virulent but less deadly," as the phrase went. Comparisons between the (relatively) shorter but more deadly 1918 pandemic are inevitable. As the website https://www.healthaffairs.org/do/10.1377/forefront.20210329.51293/full/ states, the Spanish flu, by most recent data, killed .64% of the population in much less than a year. COVID-19 has killed less than .2%, over a longer period (almost two years); of course, we have better medical care and vaccines, so we will never know what the potential of the COVID-19 virus could have been without those interventions.

Whereas COVID-19 deaths have tended to cluster around those over 65 and with other significant illnesses, those 20-40 and generally healthy were the targets of the Spanish flu. This phenomenon was due to the virus' ability to create "cyanotic shock," which put the immune system of healthy individuals into overdrive, thus turning the victims' immune system against itself. Also, while some who have had the coronavirus report minimal symptoms, those who experienced the Spanish flu had more serious symptoms even if they survived.

According to the website https://vtuhr.org/articles/10.21061/vtuhr.v4i0.34/

"The particular strain of flu that infected the global population in 1918 was unusually severe. This is demonstrated not only by the mortality rates of those infected, but also in the symptoms displayed by the sick. For example, many ill individuals experienced violent epistaxis, or nosebleeds. One infected young woman spewed blood from her nose one foot across her bed linens. The destruction of infected patients' lungs was also terrifically severe. According to historian Tom Quinn, "some victims coughed up as much as six pints of pus a day."

I should clarify here that the commonly used name of the flu was in error. It did not start in Spain. Spain became the historical victim of the fact that their newspapers were not censored like other European papers since it was wartime for other European countries. The Spanish papers reported on the disease, while others did not, even though millions were dying across the world. The actual flu virus was later identified as H1N1 Influenza A).

Of course, I would have been remiss to write of this time without reading John M. Barry's work *The Great Influenza*, which was invaluable for understanding the pathology and spread of the viral infection and its impact on American history.

To answer one more pressing question, Cotella's condition in this novel is Neurofibromatosis. I encourage readers to search for it on the Internet and learn more about this disease of the nervous system. In regard to the work she does, my mother told me of women who would go from home to home in the mountains to take care of the older children when women gave birth. The thought of such a woman and such a life has incubated in my brain for a long time.

The core of my process was to write a story honoring women like Cotella, the humble, the outcast, the faithful, and the strong. I say this is a book about courage, love, and beauty, even though the main character is disfigured; there are different ways to see beauty and be beautiful. The 1918 crux of war, burgeoning women's suffrage, advancing technology, and influenza pandemic gave her a context to survive and conquer. I hope you are moved by this story, which is not "fiction" in the sense of "made up," but "quilted" in the sense of disparate yet real patches being sewn together for something more beautiful, useful, and unified.

Acknowledgements

This book is dedicated to Josephine Vanover Fraley Rose, my maternal grandmother, who lived all her life in Dickenson County, Virginia. She married young to James Otis Fraley, gave birth to four children, the first one of whom died in childbirth, and she was widowed by the age of 24 when my grandfather, 30, was killed in a train accident. He worked for a lumber company. This was 1930 and the depth of the Depression. She received a pension for about six years from his death, which allowed her enough to feed and house her three children, who were my mother and two uncles. When the pension ran out, she married again and gave birth to another son. Her children produced 18 grandchildren and far more great-grandchildren, who live all over the United States and even Europe.

    Thanks are due the members of the Northwest Georgia Writers Group that meets faithfully in Catoosa County. Amazing work comes from pens and keyboards of these folks, and it is made more amazing by their collaborative bi-weekly critiques. They read significant parts of this work.

I also thank my beta readers, who read the whole first draft in 2022. All of these people are avid readers and/or writers, hold at least one graduate degree, and know their stuff about good fiction. I will not name them here for their privacy, but they know who they are and they are fabulous.

Finally, thanks must go to Karli Donalson, who shepherded this story to publication. Thank you to Vickie McEntire of Colorful Crow Publishing for her support of the book and offering it to the wider world.

Milton Keynes UK
Ingram Content Group UK Ltd.
UKHW021942281024
450365UK00018B/1220

9 781964 271194